Sophia Duberly Delmard

Village Life in Switzerland

Sophia Duberly Delmard

Village Life in Switzerland

ISBN/EAN: 9783337152130

Printed in Europe, USA, Canada, Australia, Japan

Cover: Foto ©Andreas Hilbeck / pixelio.de

More available books at **www.hansebooks.com**

VILLAGE LIFE IN SWITZERLAND.

BY

SOPHIA DUBERLY DELMARD.

LONDON:

LONGMAN, GREEN, LONGMAN, ROBERTS, & GREEN.

1865.

PREFACE.

To publish a new work on Switzerland in the present day, would seem to argue primâ facie some degree of temerity on the part of the writer; since no country has found so many authors to write its praises, both in prose and verse. But having during a residence of nearly three years in a secluded Swiss village (where the principal inhabitant was the village apothecary) seen and heard much that, to me, was new and interesting in the habits and manners of the peasants among whom we lived; I have thought that a brief record of my impressions would prove equally novel to the public; since I am not aware' that any other writer has treated exclusively of the life as it exists in the villages and hamlets scattered among the Alps, where the peasants see and hear but little of the world without their mountains.

Bex: 1864.

CONTENTS.

CHAPTER IX.

CHAPTER X.

CHAPTER XI.

CHAPTER XII.

CHAPTER XIII.

a

CHAPTER XIV.

CHAPTER XV.

CHAPTER XVI.

VILLAGE LIFE IN SWITZERLAND.

CHAPTER I.

First Impressions of Bex—Hotel—Tempest—View of the
Alps — Dinner-hour — Motley Company—Anecdote —Table
d'Hôte—Maître-d'Hôtel—Return to Bex.

AFTER residing at Bex for more than two years,
and becoming every day more and more enamoured
of the place, I am almost inclined to believe my
memory must be playing me false, as I recall my
first impressions of it. We had come from Geneva
at the close of a stifling, hot, dusty day in June. For
some hours we had seen signs of an approaching
storm; the clouds that had hung about the sides of
the mountains since the morning gradually descended
lower and lower, everything and everybody seemed
to feel the depressing influence of the heavy atmosphere; and when a curve in the railway hid the clear,
cool-looking lake, that had been our companion for

B

so many hours, from our view, we felt we had left
behind the only thing that kept up our flagging
spirits. As the train whirled us on, the valley through
which it passed became narrower and narrower; the
ranges of mountains to our right and left appeared
as if closing upon us, rendering still more appalling
the increasing obscurity caused by the now quickly-
gathering storm; and I confess to the absurd fear
shivering through me—a combination of nervous
terrors produced by the intense heat and awful
gloom, and a floating remembrance of one of Edgar
Poe's horrid tales I had been reading the night before—that we had said farewell to daylight for so
long as we should remain shut up among those dark
mountains.

We knew nothing of the place to which we were
bound beyond its having been strongly recommended
to us by Baron S—— before leaving England, as one
of the most beautifully situated villages in Europe, or
perhaps in the world, where M——would find exhaustless subjects for his brush and pencil, and where we
might live as unconventional and pastoral a life as we
pleased; the place being little known to tourists, and
the peasants *en conséquence* more honest and simple
in their morals and habits than are to be found in
those parts where strangers most do congregate.

As we stopped at one of the most uninteresting stations possible, that looked as if it had tumbled from the clouds on to the midst of the houseless and, as it appeared to me in the dim light, naked plain, that here made a détour to the left and formed a sort of bay among the mountains, I felt so indescribably miserable at the prospect of spending, or rather wasting, our precious month's holiday in such a wretched-looking hole, that I pulled M——'s sleeve, and asked in as piteous a tone of voice as I could assume, 'Whether we could not take the train on to some pleasanter place?' Fortunately, he was too busy with the luggage and railway officials, or perhaps did not think the matter of sufficient consequence, to give heed to my vapours; and by the time I was seated in the little old omnibus that was to convey us to the hotel, I had made what I considered was the very stoical resolution, to remain for *one night* without grumbling, but at the same time had quite as resolutely determined to depart by the first train the next morning. I am afraid I was a little sulky at M——'s impoliteness, for I remember that when he joined me in the crazy vehicle there was a debate of some moments between my pride and curiosity, before I would condescend to ask, 'And pray where is this lovely village?' when he made me stretch out my

neck through the broken window, and about half a
mile distant I saw, thrown out in strong relief by the
dark heavy mountains behind, the whitish grey spire
of a church tapering above the trees, in which the
village seemed literally buried.

The exterior of the hotel—not an unsophisticated
auberge, as we had fondly imagined it would be; we
were bent upon finding everything primitive; but, as
it looked to our jaundiced eyes, a place of immense
pretensions to gentility and very little real comfort,
with its high square front that *had* been painted
white, but not this century, its dull formal windows
with green shutters baked nearly grey, and double
row of sad slaty-coloured steps meeting on a platform
at the top, as you see all through Switzerland—was not
calculated to give an encouraging turn to our opinions
respecting the place: and while we traversed the long
dark low passage leading to the stairs at the other
end of the house, we had abundant time for wishing
our friend S—— in no very creditable companionship,
for having been, poor man, the innocent means of
sending us there. However, our bedroom—which,
as every reader of *Bradshaw* knows, serves for your
sitting-room as well—was well furnished, very clean
and comfortable, and moreover boasted a fireplace,
which, though useless at that season, was pleasant to

see, and a luxury indicating that, after all, things were not so bad as they seemed: and when I pushed open the half-closed shutters to catch the last glimpses of daylight, the first lightning flash of the storm that had been driven to bay in that corner revealed to me for a moment something so white, so dazzling, that I felt as if I had had a transient glimpse of another world. M—— laughed at me, and declared I had got the railway fever, which sarcasm compelled me to hold my tongue and smoothe my indignation as best I could, waiting for morning to clear up the mystery.

And 'lang' the morning seemed 'a coming,' for the thunder, wind, and banging of one hundred out-side shutters, were enough to have roused the seven sleepers. After raging about four hours, the tempest suddenly ceased, as if the Great Master had said ' Peace,' and there was a calm—a phenomenon I have frequently noticed here; and with the quiet I slept, till the hot sun roused up the flies, when it was ' good-bye to slumber.'

As my feelings were still smarting under the recol-lection of M.'s stinging remarks of the preceding night, my first thought was to rush to the window; and never, never so long as life lasts, shall I forget my first look at the scene that lay before me; those only who behold, for the first time in their lives, those stupendous Alpine heights, can enter into the sensations that absolutely overcame me.

I looked, not on the valley, no longer appearing naked and bare in the glorious sunlight, but covered with crops of golden grain—nor on the village, with its quaintly roofed and chimneyed houses, lying among the orchards laden with rich promise for the autumn—nor the mount further on, crowned with the ruined château, where I have since spent so many happy hours—nor the low range of chestnut-wooded hills, dotted with picturesque farms and châlets, that stretches across the valley : my eyes were fixed on those sublime heights, peak after peak rising higher and higher, till the snowy range of Mont Blanc, eternally white, immeasurably grand—my vision of last night, but to-day a reality far surpassing any dream—closed up the view. As I write, I have the same scene from my window; and ever and anon, as I raise my eyes to gaze upon it, I feel that I experience the same pleasure as when I first beheld it : if I am weary, it revives me; in the overpowering heat of summer, I am refreshed by the sight of those cold white peaks ; and when careful and troubled, and inclined to despond, their pure serenity elevates my thoughts to a throne eternal with the heavens.

But I must descend from my sublimity to break-fast, at which, as every continental traveller knows by experience, one sees little or nothing of the rest of the company that may happen to be stopping in the house, everyone taking his cup of coffee, and roll of French bread, when and how he likes; but at dinner—the hour for which varies considerably in different localities, it being usually much earlier in those places that have great pretensions to fashion, than in out-of-the-way villages, such as Bex; as, for instance, at Stuttgart, the residence of the king and court, it was half-past eleven, and here it is two—one meets all the visitors save the great invalids, if there are any, and the indefatigable pedestrians, who are absent on some mountain excursion.

As we sat down, our place at table being indicated by the number of our bedroom, written on the back of a playing card, tied round the napkin by a piece of broad scarlet braid, I thought I had never seen such an uninteresting looking company assembled together for the purpose of feeding. At the head of the table sat a little German Swiss, who, I discovered, prided himself upon the correctness with which he spoke our language, and said to M——, by way, I suppose, of proving that his pretensions were not ill-founded, 'I parle Inglish ven I can.' Speaking of languages, reminds me of an anecdote I heard not many days ago, about an Englishman stopping at G——. It seems that like many, I had almost written *most*, of our country men and women, he was no great linguist, and his knowledge of French was so limited that, wishing to speak to a chambermaid who was passing, and being ignorant of the proper name by which to designate her, he hit upon the bright idea that, as a man waiter was called 'garçon,' a female domestic must be called 'feminine garçon,' which he actually shouted out, with a strong accent on the 'nine' to make it more French, to the no small amusement of everyone who heard him.

Next to me sat a fat German, who ate enormously of everything, and smacked his lips: a thin ditto was my *vis-à-vis*, who must certainly have been ill, as his appetite was no larger than a robust Englishman's, and who used his knife so awkwardly, cutting his meat with his left hand, that I expected every moment to see it inserted between the ribs of his neighbour, an exceedingly proper-looking, thin, light Englishwoman, whose husband, a fine old general with decorations, that showed he had shared in the dangers of many a hard-won battlefield, had yet such a fear of his prim wife, that he never hazarded an observation without turning towards her and saying,

'Am I right, my dear?' Then we had a French
gentleman, and his ugly but clever little wife, who
played and sang so divinely, and whose agreeable
society, in spite of our romantic yearning for solitude,
helped so much in rendering our stay more pleasant
and agreeable; two German ladies of middle age,
travelling with their *femme-de-chambre*, who always
ate at the same table with them, and was addressed
as 'Du;' and a Swiss family, consisting of papa,
mamma, two grown-up sons, who never went out,
even for a walk, without asking leave from their
parents, and one daughter, dressed in the highest
fashion for Swiss demoiselles, namely, low body, with
high net tucker, and short sleeves, with long limpy
white ones descending from them, and light hair,
plaited so tightly off her forehead that it seemed to
have also tightened the skin all over her face.

The dinner was good and abundant. There was no
ceremony, no restraint, no grand toilettes (save the
young lady's); everyone seemed to have come there to
escape awhile from the trammels of conventionalism,
and to enjoy himself each after his own fashion. We
had only one little waiter, who carved so expertly,
and had such a queer bit of a nose, that you were
irresistibly inclined to believe that one day in carving

too quickly, the knife had turned wrong way, and cut off a slice, leaving the nostrils all wide.

When we were about half-way through dinner, I saw two or three of the company rise and shake hands, with every demonstration of satisfaction, with a tall stout man who had just entered the room, and whose face was so smiling and good-tempered, you felt you would like to shake hands with him too. 'He is our landlord,' said my neighbour, the fat German, in answer to my inquiry, 'one of the best fellows in the world; he has been away for three days, and the house has been as dull as a hospital without him.' Praise well merited, as I found from pleasant experience afterwards; and who that has stayed in his house will not bear testimony to the untiring cheerful assistance, in all matters, his guests receive at his hands?

Here we spent one of the most delightful months of our lives; and I well remember that, as we were seated in the train on our return home, I said to M——, as I endeavoured to get one more look at the little village that had become so dear to me, 'I feel that we shall see this place again,' a presentiment fulfilled not long after, when, for reasons that need not be entered into, we removed with all our family to reside upon the Continent, and having found, after residing a year at S——, that it did not suit either our healths or our purse, we were casting about for some more eligible place to live at; I suddenly exclaimed one day, after a long discussion respecting the comparative merits of, I cannot tell, how many places, ' Why not go to Bex ? ' a suggestion that met with unanimous approval, and was acted upon as soon as we had received a letter from our good host of the Hôtel de l'Union, telling us that we should have no difficulty in procuring a house in Bex, as several had been built since we were there.

My children had heard so much of the place, that they were almost wild with delight when we made the announcement, that we had decided upon going there with as little delay as possible. They had never liked S——, therefore almost any change would have been agreeable ; but to go to Bex, from which they had received so many pleasant letters, the place that was a sort of El Dorado to their young imagination, was beyond all things delightful. What joy, what happiness! All the long two days' journey, they were incessantly asking ' how far they were from Bex;' and when at last we neared the little well-remembered station, we could hardly restrain them from jumping out before the train stopped. It was pleasant to be welcomed

so cordially by our host, M. Wagner, who had come
to meet us; and on reaching the hotel, we found that
his thoughtful care for our comfort had made him
give us rooms in the pretty vine-covered *pension*,
communicating with the main building by means of
a covered gallery, looking into a garden full of roses,
oleanders, pomegranates, and orange trees, about
which scores of the lovely humming-bird hawk-
moths were flitting, as graceful, and almost as beautiful, as their more brilliant namesakes, and rows of
acacias cast a pleasant shade upon the seats beneath.

CHAPTER II.

Our first care, after a night's rest, was to procure a
house; and as we had been subjected to all sorts of
disgusting annoyances at S——, thröugh so many
families living under the same roof, a nuisance you
may as well make up your mind to submit to on the
Continent, we were desirous of getting one to ourselves; preferring a small house and privacy, to a
large one with the espionage and interference of the
landlord and tenants. In our mind's eye we had
visions of a delicious châlet, embowered in chestnut
woods on a mountain side, with balconies *à la
Suisse*, trellised with vines, a fountain making
dulcet music to the ear, and a splendid view over
'all the country side.' But, alas for our châlets in

the air, we were soon told that *they* were only for
summer use, and that to take the whole of a house
was a thing unheard of, impossible, as they were
large enough for barracks.   So, with a sigh, at having to relinquish our cherished project of living in a
real Swiss châlet, we sallied forth to inspect the
rooms that were offered for our selection.

Our first visit was made to an *étage*—which, I must
explain, means all the rooms on the same floor—on
the second, in England we should call it the third,
story of a tall whitewashed building, decorated with
the invariable green shutters, to which we mounted
by means of a filthy flight of wooden steps, leading
on to a dilapidated balcony, hung with all sorts of
wearing apparel, dirty rags, &c. and garnished with
various articles of crockery that *we* think it decent to
keep in our bedrooms.   From the balcony, an inner
flight of stone stairs brought us to the *maison à
louer*, which consisted of four bedrooms and a
kitchen, all having brick floors, and not a shred of a
carpet.   The furniture, though clean, was of the
very poorest description.   There was no sitting-room,
or *salon*, as it is designated : the kitchen, not large
enough to swing a mouse in, had no cooking appa-
ratus, merely an ordinary stove about a foot square.
Every drop of water we should have required would

have had to be carried from a considerable distance, no small consideration to people who consider daily bathing as an absolute necessity; and I
soon discovered that it was a house suitable only for
a family who took their meals at an hotel, and did
not cook at home, and who, moreover, did not require it for the winter months, as the absence of
stoves, and other comforts, plainly showed that it was
intended only for a summer let.

Thence we proceeded to the residence of M.
Vantard, who had formerly been *maître-d'hôtel* here,
but, having failed, had retired from business with a
considerable fortune, and built himself an exceedingly pretty house on the outskirts of the village,
with large barns and outhouses, all in the true Swiss
style, for storing the produce of the farm and garden,
separated from the house by a court, which boasted
the rare luxury of a private fountain, shaded by a
large plane tree, the whole forming as charming a
picture of a complete Swiss domicile as one would
wish to see. We found these rooms, as regards
situation, arrangement, and furniture, very superior
to those we had just left, but as there were only two
bedrooms, and the proprietor would not hear of our
converting either the *salon* or *salle-à-manger* into
another *chambre-à-coucher,* and we could not very

well see how, by any system of cramming, we could squeeze five children into one little room, we were compelled to search further, not without casting many a wistful look at the bright clean-looking house, with its tasteful pinewood balconies encircling three sides of the building. The price, too, asked for these rooms was exorbitant, exactly four times the rent of the first we had looked at.

After these two experiments, I began to think that house-finding in Bex was not so easy an affair after all as M. Wagner had led us to expect, and that the troubles arising from such a need are pretty much of a muchness all over the world. However, have a house we must; for though the cost of living at the hotel is very reasonable, only four francs a day per head, it soon amounts to a large sum when you are eight in number.

I should fill a volume if I were to give an account of all the houses we visited in search of apartments; of the number of flights of stairs we mounted, some of the rooms being five, six, and even seven stories high; or of the wonderful treasures in the way of old furniture, to which it was impossible to affix any age, that were revealed to our admiring gaze. More than once, M—— sallied forth solus, determined to do or die, but with no better success, although he declared he had been into every house in the village; and he added, ' I have seen more ugly old hags in one hour in this place, than I ever thought of seeing in my life.'

At the end of a week we grew desponding, as we seemed no nearer the attainment of our desires; and were even beginning to impute selfish motives to our smiling host for having assured us we could so easily procure a house—when he verified the popular adage, by entering our apartment with the joyful announcement that he had met with exactly what we wanted, in a new large house, erected by a *notaire* in a charming situation, at the entrance to the village from the railway; so of course we started off instanter, and were not a little pleased to find that the accommodation was enough, though none to spare, the rooms lofty and of moderate size, the furniture sufficiently good to last our term out, which is all you must ever hope for, and the position of the building unexceptionable—with such a view, that, if the rooms had lacked all other *agrémens*, I think we should have been tempted to take them for that alone.

There was a *salon*, three bedrooms, a small bare room for M——'s studio, a large *empty* kitchen, and last, not least, a magnificent balcony, of which more

c

anon. A cellar, down three flights of stairs, was at
our disposal for storing our provisions, a wash-house
when finished (as an instance of the remarkable
despatch used in building in the Vaud, I may mention
that, at the expiration of two years, it is still in the
lath and plaster state), and a room for servants in the
roof. When I mounted to the top story to inspect
the latter, I found that all the rooms in that part
were only partitioned off by means of boards, laid so
carelessly and roughly one above the other, that in
some places you could thrust your hand between; and
I shivered as I pictured to myself how the wind
would blow through them in the winter. As I entered
the little low chamber (it would be much more ap-
propriately designated as a den), I knocked my head
against an immense beam that hung down a foot and
a half from the low roof, and in the only part of the
room where, but for that, it would have been possible
to stand upright, as the remainder of the roof sloped
down to the little window, about a foot square. There
was a small bed, a dilapidated wooden chair, a jug
and basin on a projection formed by another beam in
a corner, but of dimensions so tiny that I cannot
suppose they were placed there for use, and a wee
looking-glass nailed against the wall, in so low a
position, that to be available it must be approached

on the knees, a circumstance much more mortifying to Swiss female vanity, than the impossibility of washing the skin.

When I looked round the wretched little hole, so bare and cheerless-looking, even at that season, and contrasted it with the comfortable, almost luxurious apartments our servants have in England, I positively shuddered, and, turning to the Frau A——, who conducted us over the house, I asked if she did not think it would be difficult to induce any servant to sleep there? I am quite sure she thought I was out of my senses, for her astonishment was so great that it was some moments ere she replied, with considerable asperity, that '*Her* domestics slept on straw and were satisfied; that the bedroom I saw had been provided with extra comforts (jug and glass, I thought) to meet the requirements of any English family who might take the apartments; as, from having had them lodging with her before, she had found out that English servants were not content with such accommodations as were thought sufficient for their own domestics.' And no wonder! for I declare that in England I have seen pigs better lodged. However, as I certainly had not come to Switzerland as a reformer of existing abuses, and moreover had no intention of engaging any other 'helps' than those the country afforded, I thought it was no business of mine to enlighten those to whom 'ignorance was bliss;' so I said no more to the very unamiable looking Frau (she is a Bernese), whose appearance was so remarkably unprepossessing, that I did not much relish the idea of living in too close proximity with her. I was quite unable to determine whether the miserable discontented expression on her pinched features was attributable to disease, ill temper, or sorrow; but, as she said to me, in German, with a sigh, when I spoke of my children, 'You are happier than I; for I have never had but two, and one is dead,' I was charitable enough to lay it to the score of the latter; especially as M——, whose greater knowledge of French and German permitted him to converse more freely with her, thought she evinced signs of greater intelligence than he had yet discovered in Bex. This *spirituelle* lady and her lesser half, over whom she towers by at least a head, are such a curious ill-matched couple that the reader will very likely hear a little more about them, and their *ménage*.

The husband is a very little man, not more than five feet high, with short legs and very long arms, that could easily tie his garters standing—a large wooden face, that gives not the slightest index to the inner man, and a pate so bald, white, and shining, that when I look out of my window and see him sunning himself underneath, surveying the properties of which he is 'monarch,' I have the most mischievous intentions towards it, and cannot help thinking of a bald coot; especially as he has a habit of flirting out his coat tails, after the manner of that bird.

Une maison meublée à louer does not include pots and pans; therefore, as soon as we had concluded all necessary arrangements with the owner, we set about purchasing in the village all that was required; and I am sure that poking about in quest of these necessary articles gave me a much more elevated idea of the resources of the place than I could have believed possible. To tell the truth, I had no very definite idea respecting the size of the village. I had been told that it contained nearly 2,000 inhabitants, but believed it an exaggeration to enhance its dignity in the eyes of strangers, as I was quite sure the houses I had seen (though one is liable to be deceived, with so many families in one house) could not contain a third of that number. However, my eyes were opened (as they have been about other things since I came here) when I made acquaintance with the trading portion of the place, which boasts

of a market-place, adorned in the centre with the
never absent poplar tree of liberty, but here sadly
in danger of never attaining either a flourishing
appearance or great age, from the friction bestowed
upon its trunk by the cows passing to and from the
fountain, an Hôtel de Ville, where local justice is
administered, and drink retailed, the latter being by
far the most flourishing half of the business, and the
privilege of the Syndic, who is also purveyor for
suppers at balls held in the building, a large square
house, forming one side of the market-place, the
residence of the doctor and other dignitaries, and
some twenty or thirty shops, among which may be
found those of an apothecary or druggist, a modiste,
and a confectioner—professions not *always* to be met
with, even in much larger towns.

But what queer shops! no wonder I had scarcely
noticed them in passing, when most of them are half-
buried under-ground, and you have to descend
five or six steps before reaching the door, above which
hangs a small brass handle attached to a cord communicating with the story, usually the highest, verifying
the saying that 'extremes meet,' where the owner of
the shop has his home.   Very pleasant it is, in cold,
rainy, windy weather, to stand in the filthy badly-
paved streets, with the water pouring on you from

the roofs (for, though every drop of water has to be brought from the fountains, no one takes the trouble to catch any of the bountiful supply that so often falls from heaven, nor indeed do they appear to know its value for domestic purposes), ringing, ringing, until Monsieur or Madame, always full of polite apologies, chooses to descend and attend to your wants.

My first essay in shopping was not subjected to any of these *désagrémens*, it was simply amusing diving into those dingy caves, from one of which I managed to extract as many plates, cups, and saucers (for cups read basins) as sufficed for our moderate wants: but the price paid was exorbitant, and I puzzled myself to discover what my informant, who had told me that crockery was 'very cheap in Bex,' would call *dear*: as I certainly paid more for the very commonest ware I ever beheld, and from which the glazing peeled off after a time's washing, than I have given for good china in England.

The shop of the ironmonger must not be classed with those in cellars; and deserves especial mention on account of its elevation above the level of the street, and its windows glazed with panes, not less than a foot square! in which was displayed an assortment of moderator lamps, Sheffield ware and cutlery, quite bewildering to the eyes of the simple villagers,

and I confess that I was myself so overcome by the .
sight of a *real* metal teapot, that I went more than
once to look at it; from looking it got to longing;
and at last, in an alarming fit of extravagance, I
carried it home in triumph, having bought it for
about three times its value; but then—as all my
readers who like tea, and I hope they are many, will
confess—it is something to get a cup of bohea out of
the genuine article, and one expects to pay for
luxuries.

Our needs in the way of saucepans to suit our
potager, not forgetting a gridiron and a large iron
pan, perforated with holes as large as a two-franc
piece, for roasting chestnuts, were soon supplied, but
it was not quite so easy an affair to impress Monsieur
with the idea of a large shallow bath that we wished
him to make for us.   After giving him a sketch of
the thing we wanted, and writing down the exact
dimensions in length, breadth, and height, we felt
pretty secure against mistakes, as nothing had been
left to the imagination of the maker; but when, after
waiting full two months, it *did* arrive, we saw how
delusive had been our fond hopes.   In the first place,
it was so heavy that two men had difficulty in carrying
it up stairs; and secondly, the sides were so high that
it required a small ladder to scale them! but it was

Hobson's choice, and I rather think that the severe exercise of getting in and out had a beneficial effect upon the system.   We had all sorts of schemes to provide a place for it; as in our agreement with our landlord, it was especially forbidden to use any of the rooms for bathing purposes, lest we should injure the floors, which are really very nicely inlaid with different kinds of wood.   The only one with a plain floor was the little room appropriated to M——'s studio, and that of course was out of the question; the boys suggested the balcony, as there they could dry themselves in the hot weather without the bother of towels, and I was almost at my wit's end, having suggested all the places I could think of, when some one was bright enough to mention the corridor, and it ended in our having that portion of it leading to the balcony partitioned off by means of a door-screen —I don't know what else to call it, as it was neither one nor the other, which could be fastened back as soon as the bath was removed.

When we were making our first tour of the house, Frau A—— pointed out to me with visible pride, a small stone tank in one corner of the kitchen, for keeping a store of fresh water in the house.   By her manner I saw that it was no ordinary luxury, but a thing to be proud of, a step in advance of the times,

an innovation upon existing Swiss prejudices against
the *un*healthy use of water, that we had no right to
expect. So I tried to feel the thankfulness that she
evidently thought *ought* to be in my heart, and
suppressed the ungrateful remark that had risen to
my lips, when I saw that its dimensions were no
larger than an ordinary foot-bath. As we had always
the fear of goître before our eyes, it was some
consolation to be told that the stone of which it
was constructed had a beneficial effect· upon the
water, of which every drop had to be brought from
a fountain on the opposite side of the road, and
carried up two long flights of stairs on the back of
our servant, in a wooden thing called a *brante*, of
a shape and make so unlike anything I ever saw in
England that I can compare it to nothing but an
enormous bucket flattened at the sides.   When I saw
that the back was the ordinary beast of burden
among the Swiss, no one appearing to think that *it*
came within the limits of the laws for preventing
cruelty to animals, I ceased to feel any qualms of
conscience when I met my servant toiling up stairs
three times a day under what would be considered a
heavy load for a man. I used to wonder they were
not wet through long before they reached the kitchen,
but found that they knew exactly the height to

which to fill it with safety to themselves; and they walk with so slow and measured a step, that they rarely spill a drop. Once in passing through the village, I saw a girl who was evidently new to the work, walking at an ordinary pace across the market-place with one of these *brantes* on her back, and at every step she took, the water went flying into her neck, and out at her heels !

For a week after taking the *notaire's* house, we ate at the hotel and only slept in our new home, as the servant we had engaged was not able to come immediately, and we were then not quite so independent of their services as, afterwards, necessity compelled us to be. As soon as she arrived, we commenced housekeeping in good earnest, and then my troubles began. Long ago, I had forgotten all the French that had been dinned into me by a very indifferent English teacher, but as I never doubted that M——would accompany me to make my purchases, *at least*, until I had learned the names of those articles most in common use, I did not trouble myself or give a thought about the matter until, shawled and bonneted with my lists in hand, I presented myself at the door of his studio with the intimation that I was 'ready.' 'Ready for what?' he asked, looking up, with what seemed to me a most malicious smile of triumph. I

timidly explained; and then, seeing that he did not
offer to move, added 'that it was quite out of the
question for me to go alone, as I was sure no one
would understand my spasmodic attempts at French;'
to which he made answer, 'That to all things there
must be a beginning, and that the sooner I began
the sooner I should learn;' to which I gave my
humble assent, in the hope of softening his ob-
duracy by my amiability; but it failed in producing
the desired effect, and he left me standing in the
passage, feeling very much like a naughty child
that has been whipped and turned out of school.
There was no help for it, we must eat or die—and it
was better to live and be laughed at, than die and
make no sign; so I made out a list in French of the
principal articles I wanted, and thus fortified, but
with a feeling like a flat iron on my chest, I set out
upon my errands.

I was not afraid of being *openly* laughed at, for
nowhere out of England do you encounter that rude
ignorant laugh, with which a foreigner's ignorance of
our language is sure to be greeted; still I reflected
that there *were* people who, like the Irishman's
parrot, might be 'devils to think,' though I daresay
I was doing the Bex shopkeepers a great injustice
in imagining any such thing, for they were so polite

and good-natured when they saw my ignorance and
perplexity, that they assisted me as much as they
could, substituting the right words for the absurd
ones I made use of, and waiting so patiently and with
so much appearance of good feeling, till I could point
out what I wanted, that I felt quite grateful, and
could not help thinking, even in the midst of my
distress, that their manners might give a lesson to
the best society in England.   There is never that
shamefacedness or *mauvaise honte*, none of that
affectation of something unsuited to the wearer, that
makes the tone of our most friendly intercourse
unnatural and forced. Whether they address prince or
peasant, their manner is the same—easy, simple, and
obliging, without a touch of servility ; and I have no
hesitation in saying that the peasants in the French
cantons of Switzerland are some of the politest
people in the world.

But there I am, standing with my bit of paper in
hand; and what a mess I made, it makes me feverish
to think of it, floundering here and there, now
getting a little light as I stumbled by chance upon
the right name, now lost in darkness again, as I
learned from the puzzled look of my unwearied
auditors, growing frightfully red in the face when I
found that all hope of a rescue must be abandoned ;

I tried to laugh, but it was forced and sepulchral,
coming from the source whence tears were ready to
well forth ; and it ended in my returning home, without having the slightest idea whether I had succeeded
in conveying to any *one* person the least notion of
what I wished to purchase. I was not in the least astonished to find, when the meat made its appearance,
that a man and a boy were employed to carry the
immense quantity I had bought by signs ; that lard
came instead of bacon for our morning's meal, and
that a lot of tobacco-pipes were sent for soup, in lieu
of macaroni! However, all troubles produce some
good, at least people say so, and M——'s system of
taking the bull by the horns, though a forcing one,
proved effectual in my case.

   To housekeepers, it may be interesting to know the
prices of some of the most important articles of diet ;
and I am especially anxious to make them known,
as I have no doubt there are many others who, like
myself, believe, till rendered wiser by experience to
the contrary, that most things are to be bought in
Switzerland for ' an old song ;' and that living, which
includes everything in the way of expenditure, is to
be accomplished at one half its cost in England. We
shall see ; but before I proceed further, let me
premise, that if ever, dear ladies, you intend to

reside on the Continent, *pour faire des économies*, it would be well if you were to look into your geography (Cornwall's will do, as he seems to have an eye for domestic economy) and ascertain whether the country you have selected for your abode possesses colonies that supply it with 'sugar and spice, and all that's nice;' if not, choose another that *has*, that's all—for you will find to your cost, that what you save in meat and vegetables is more than swallowed up by the high price of those articles we are accustomed to class in a lump as groceries. They are less expensive in Switzerland than in Germany, where the duties are much higher—sugar, of which there is usually a larger consumption in a household than any other single item, being much cheaper, on account of the large manufactures of that article from beet-root at Berne, and other towns—but even here they make a material difference in household expenses, especially as, with the exception of coffee, all are of a very inferior quality, unless you go to the principal town of the canton to purchase them. Dried fruits are at a price quite beyond the reach of the greater portion of the inhabitants, and I suppose *that* is the reason why one never meets with them in any articles of confectionery. King Arthur, 'who ruled the land and ruled it like a king,' would have entailed upon his

subjects an immense national debt, to have made a
pudding in Switzerland like the one of which the
leavings were fried 'next morning.'

Coffee is always bought green, and roasted at home,
which gives it, to my thinking, a superior and much
fresher flavour to that we get ready roasted in
England. I used to regard coffee-roasting as a very
mysterious art, quite beyond the powers of any private
individual to achieve; but I have found it so simple,
that I certainly shall never return to my old custom of
buying it browned. You have merely to fill your
frying pan, or any ordinary iron saucepan, half full
of green coffee, setting it *over*, but not *too close upon*
a brisk fire, and stirring it constantly with an iron
spoon till it is done, which you can ascertain by biting
one of the berries—if it break crisply and is brown
through, it is burned enough, and may be used immediately.

Some one has remarked, that the progress of a
country in civilisation may be ascertained by the price
of soap; and if this be a true test, the Swiss must be
some centuries behind most other European nations,
as it is double the price I ever paid for it anywhere
else, and *very bad*. Meat is reasonable, and when you
first inquire its price, you congratulate yourself that
at last you *have* discovered *one* thing on which there

will be a considerable saving; and, after returning
home with your brain teeming with all sorts of pleasant schemes for disposing to advantage of the six or
seven francs that you are to save from your weekly
meat bills, you are wofully undeceived when you exa-
mine the basket the butcher's boy has brought, to find
that with the joint you have purchased, weighing seven
or eight pounds, there is laid three or four pounds of
pure bone, for which you must pay the same price
as for your joint; so that, after all, 5d. and 6d. a pound
is not so much cheaper than 7d. or 8d. in England,
where you can pick and choose for your money.

Milk is about 2d. a quart, and butter not dear,
varying, according to the season, from 10d. to 1s. a
pound, but then there *is often little or none to be had*;
which reminds me of an Irishman who was once
working for me in S——shire, and of whom I had one
day been inquiring, ' Whether he would not like some
books to read when his work was done?' ' Please,
Ma'am,' said he, ' I can't read; but Anthony ' (one of
his fellow-workmen living in the same cottage) ' is a
grate scholar and reads finely; ' upon which I renewed
my offer, observing that as the same Anthony was so
accomplished he could read aloud to the others;
when he replied, with an expression that no one but
an Irishman could throw into his face, ' Och, Ma'am,

sure an' he is a fine reader, *but thin he can't see!* '
The reason of this scarcity of butter is, that in summer
the cows are on the mountain pasturages, and most
of the butter then and there made is exported to
other countries or stored by the owners for winter use,
and that during the latter season the people say it is
not worth their while to make it, when selling the
milk pays them better. Bread, which is not good,
being raised from leaven instead of barm, is a trifle
dearer. I am speaking of the *pain bis*, the ordinary
bread of the peasants, for the white is one fourth
dearer.

There is an immense deal of exaggeration in all the
accounts I have ever read about living being so cheap
abroad; for my part, I believe all the world is becoming
dear, and it is time people should be disabused of the
idea that they cannot live as cheaply in England as
in any other country in Europe. I don't deny that
people (English, I mean) spend less money abroad, not
that things taken in the aggregate are cheaper, but
simply because they learn to do without many things
that they considered indispensable, indeed necessary
to health and life when at home, and make use of many
articles for food, at which in England we turn up our
noses in disgust and disdain. If we *will* do the same
there as here, we *can*, and find great advantage and

profit accruing to our health and purses. Where is
the need of eating fresh meat three or four times a
day, when you find that you have better health when
only taken as many times a week—replacing it, the
other days, by a nourishing soup that costs not one
quarter of the sum? And why need we raise and buy
such expensive salads, when our fields and pastures
produce abundance of the same plants, of which they
make such excellent and healthful salads all over the
Continent? I have seen scores of people searching for
dandelion roots in the country in England; and since
I have lived abroad and learned to think its leaves
the pleasantest of all herbs with oil and vinegar, I
have wished I could make known this far more
agreeable way of using it. The lamb's lettuce, a
plant once highly esteemed in our own country,
'when,' as an old botanist of Queen Elizabeth's time
says, 'it served for a salade herbe of which it is none
of the worst,' is eaten in great quantities in the
winter and early spring months, as it defies the frost
and snow, and the poor people make of it a soup by
no means bad. I prefer the blanched leaves of the
dandelion, found in the mounds of earth thrown up
by the moles, to any lettuce I ever ate; but I can
never forget the look of astonishment and disgust with
which a visitor of ours, from England, surveyed a dish

of this sort when placed before him—he evidently thought that we were in an alarming state of health, akin to that of a famous Jewish king; nothing could persuade him to touch it, and so he returned as prejudiced as he came.

I speak from experience, when I say that I believe English children would not suffer as they do from stomach complaints, if they had a simpler diet—less meat, gravies, pies, and puddings, and more bread, soup, vegetables, salads, and fruits. Since mine have altered their mode of living, they have not known a single day's illness, notwithstanding the difference of climate—the effects of which people in general so much dread upon the health of their children. We know how to make rich and expensive soups (which I may be pardoned for not thinking by any means the best) as well as any people in the world, but we are lamentably ignorant of the way to concoct a good nourishing family soup, at a cost which places it within the reach, not only of the middle classes, but of every labouring man in the kingdom. With a few potatoes boiled and mashed, two or three onions, a little parsley, and a bit of butter, or what is still better, a small slice of the flitch that hangs in most English cottages, you have a soup for a king; and a handful of rice with the indispensable onions, a little pepper, nutmeg, or a few cloves, and a piece of butter, make one equally palatable, while of half a pound of baked flour, a spoonful of dripping, pepper, and some thin slices of bread, you may make soup for three days.

When we come to the matter of dress, we find the advantage decidedly with us; and I am quite sure that I speak within bounds, when I say, I can dress better in England on half the sum I spend here. Calicoes, even before the American war, were one-third higher in price; all woollen goods are frightfully expensive; common flannel of the coarsest description costs three francs and a half the aune (there are four yards in three aunes), and I have bought fair silks in England for less money than I have paid here for alpacas. Mentioning silks, reminds me that they too are more expensive, which is to be wondered at, seeing that the duty is inconsiderable, and Lyons not far off.

The pay of mechanics and labourers is lower than those of the same class in England; a carpenter gets from two to three francs per day, while a farm labourer has never more than a franc and a half, and if he lives and eats in his master's house, he thinks 150, or at the most 200 francs, ample payment for a year. The wages of domestic servants are pretty much on a par with ours—more than we give in the country and less than is asked in the towns. A cook gets from ten to twelve pounds, a housemaid or *femme-de-chambre* seven, eight, or nine; and in all cases a substantial *cadeau* is given at Christmas. 'The greatest plague of life' is one of the greatest annoyances everywhere, until one learns, like us, to do without; and certainly here, under the blessings of a republic, I beg pardon, a *free* republic, you meet with it in perfection.

For a people to be capable of conceiving and executing the idea of forming themselves into a republic, argues that they have reached the highest point of civilisation, intelligence, and virtue of which humanity is judged to be capable—I am quoting the gist of a good deal of information, with which from time to time I have been favoured—*ergo*, it is rather presumptuous in a citizen of a benighted country like France or England, that is still bowing under the yoke of a despot, or what is worse—I am not joking when I say that this has been said to me by more than one educated Swiss—'the rule of a haughty and overbearing aristocracy—to expect or desire obedience from any member of a state so far in advance of the rest of Europe. I was foolish enough, when I first came, to imagine that I had a reasonable right to the services of my servants, in

return for good wages paid, especially as I had made
no contract *au contraire*; but I was not long in
learning to know my own ignorance, and most
assuredly could not class myself among those blessed
people 'who expect nothing and are never disappointed;' for though I have had since coming here
near upon thirty servants, I have never met with one
who had the slightest intention of doing anything
for her money, *if she could help it*. No doubt modern philanthropists, who believe that all mistresses
are bad and that all servants *would be good* if they
had better mistresses, will cry out that this is an
overstatement. Nevertheless, ' 'Tis true, if pity 'tis'—
I haven't a Shakespeare here, so may be forgiven if I
quote incorrectly—and a melancholy fact that, coupled
with some few others, goes far towards disabusing
one's mind of those Utopian notions we are so fond
of nursing respecting this happy land of liberty, by
our 'ain hearth-stanes.' Like all republicans, at
least like all I ever met with, and having been a
red-hot one in my youth, I speak *feelingly*—they
permit no one to be free in their country but themselves; and further, I doubt whether any but a Swiss
would call himself free, living under those laws of
which he is so fond of boasting, that 'he has imposed
them upon himself.'

I was not so unreasonable as to expect the work in
my house to be done according to *my* notions of
order, propriety, and despatch; I should have been
only too happy if my domestics would have done it
their own way, or indeed any way at all—but when I
found that *we* had to be the workers, while they lay
in bed (a curious fact, as all other classes are early
risers), positively refusing to get up until long after
the early morning's work was finished, and even till
breakfast was well-nigh over, I began to think that
keeping servants in Switzerland was an expensive
luxury and a doubtful comfort, and at last it ended
in our doing our own ' chores,' since which time we
have been much happier, and have gained so much
experience in common things as to render us quite
independent of any help from servants.

If ' cleanliness *be* nigh unto godliness,' then heaven
help the Swiss; for of cleanliness, as representing in
some sort moral decency, they have not the faintest
conception.   It is quite useless and absurd to attempt
to teach them that certain things are for certain uses,
and that to appropriate them to dirty purposes is an
offence against decency, for they no more comprehend
you than if you held forth upon Animal Magnetism.
As ' all's grist that comes to the mill,' so anything and
everything they can lay their hands on is fair game

for any available purpose whatever; I have found my
fine damask dinner napkins and table cloths degraded
to the most disgusting offices, quite unfit to mention.
Soapy dirty water, that had served for bathing the
children, elevated to the office of washing and even
boiling the vegetables. Pieces of soap laid on the
same plate as the butter; your omelettes and potatoes
being fried quite as often with one as with the other;
the cooking stove used for a toilette table, and you
had the pleasure of discovering that what stopped up
the spout of your coffee-pot, was a mass of hair combed
fresh from the head of your cook. When such dis-
comforts occur, it is superfluous to mention the minor
annoyances of plates and dishes coming to table, day
after day, *wiped* but not washed; of silver never
dried—not even in hotels do you ever see it polished;
or of knives uncleaned, and not often washed—these
are things one gets to look upon as unnecessary
luxuries, and not worthy of notice. Indeed, when you
have found, as I did, that the foul linen of your baby
and the breakfast service were washed in the same
water, you will prefer the remnants of the last meal
on the crockery to the impurities left by such a
doubtful cleansing.

Personal ablutions beyond washing the hands, and
the face on extra occasions, I never dreamt of; but

they did not extend even to that; and to hint, as I once did to a girl, that soap and water, or merely the latter, if only once a week, would improve her complexion, or that an outside garment that had done duty, I should be afraid to say how long, would be no worse for an acquaintance with a wash-tub, was tantamount to telling her 'to be off.' One excused herself by saying that 'washing her face wrinkled it,' and another declared 'she was afraid it would give her a moustache.' With one or two, from whom by their credentials I was led to expect better things, I took infinite pains, and even held out the most tempting bait possible to them, namely to take them with me to England, if they would try and accommodate themselves somewhat to our notions of cleanliness, &c.; but it was a thankless task, and I only gained the knowledge, as doubtless many another has done, that 'he that is filthy will be filthy still.'

I could not enumerate the number of articles stolen from us by these helps, to themselves; for it would be a list as long as the one sent out periodically by the 'lost luggage office,' shoes, boots (always new and in pairs), dresses, stockings (for which and flannel garments they had an especial weakness, on account of their being costly articles here), pocket-handker-chiefs, carpet bags, music; and one stylish young lady

who had lived some time in France, and intended to
have done us the kindness of adding another member
to our already numerous family, had we not been
cruel enough to discover the trick just in time to
frustrate her benevolent intentions, helped herself
liberally out of my baby's wardrobe, and was matter-
of-fact enough to cut off pieces from our new blankets,
as 'she thought she might want it.'   When I came
from England, I had supplied myself with two cases
of fine scissors of various sizes, that were always reserved for my especial use, but these too disappeared,
'and I was left lamenting.'   They have, however, one
virtue, and sometimes it is a most provoking one,
they rarely lose their temper or speak impolitely.

For all these misdemeanours you have no redress ;
or rather, the redress you *can* have is not worth
the getting.   First, you write a letter stating your
cause of complaint to the Juge de Paix, who, as it is
an office nobody likes to take, is usually selected from
the lower orders, and is sure to have a weakness for
culprits from his own class ; and after waiting ten
days or a fortnight, during which time the delinquent
has had time to escape to the Antipodes if she wished,
you receive a communication from that respectable
magistrate, stating that ' before proceeding further in
the matter he must receive from you a certificate, to

prove that the person against whom you have lodged
the complaint, is really and truly the individual named
in your letter *and nobody else*, which gives you the
interesting occupation of addressing a letter to the
curé of the town, or village, or parish in which she
told you she lived, in order to ascertain if Sarah
Jones *be* Sarah Jones; and if you receive a reply in
the affirmative, you are lucky; as ten to one she has
given you the wrong address; but supposing that you
have sent the required certificate to Monsieur le Juge,
you imagine that your troubles are over for that time
and that all will proceed smoothly,   No such a thing;
after the lapse of another fortnight you are honoured
with another billet from the Juge, in which he informs
you 'that as you had engaged the servant in question
without previously ascertaining whether she was under
age; and as he, the Juge de Paix, has the honour to
communicate to you that he has discovered her years
to be only eighteen, at which tender age she is not
responsible in the eye of the law (a blind eye in this
case, one would say), he cannot assist you any further
in the matter,' in other words, washes his hands, and
in very dirty water, of the whole business.   The
cunning functionary takes care not to give you any
information that might be useful in preventing any
future stumbling on the wrong side of the law, and

so you go on sinning and repenting until some good
Samaritan, who has been bitten often enough to open
his eyes, tells you that all servants, male and female,
under twenty-three years of age must be engaged
from their parents, who up to that time are legally
responsible for their children, and the parties
to be proceeded against if you wish to obtain any
satisfaction.

It would be an act of injustice to omit mention of
two accomplishments in which Swiss servants excel,
and those are, making black coffee and *gauffres*.   Do
you know, ladies, what the latter are? if not, I advise
you to learn, as they are especial favourites with the
gentlemen with their wine; and, as a preliminary to
the lesson, I will try to give you an idea of the machine used, for without one you can have no cakes of
this description.   These rather cumbrous-looking iron
articles, which give the name to the cakes, have two
handles from three to four feet long, by means of
which you open and shut the dampers; those
dampers being made of cast-iron plates, about six
inches broad and three wide, with a pattern on the
inner sides.   A paste made of flour, butter, sugar,
and lemon, is rolled into little round balls, about the
size of a pigeon's egg; two of these are placed in the
dampers, which are shut immediately, and inserted

in the fire. In a few moments they are done; and
when you open the irons, you find your little balls
spread out the size of the plates, and impressed with
the pattern. They are delicious, being crisp, light,
and as thin as a wafer, with a peculiar flavour,
caused by the way they are baked or toasted, or
whatever you like to call it, which is so quick an
operation, that several hundreds are made in an hour.
The usual time for this fun is in an evening, when
the young folk are assembled, and then everyone
takes his turn at the cooking, one of the company
being provided with a lump of butter, held in a
piece of paper, with which the inside of the *gauffres*
is well greased each time, before the paste is put in.
On New Year's Eve, everybody in Switzerland is
employed in making *gauffres*; and on New Year's
Day, everybody is eating them for breakfast. But
no one can tell me when and how the custom has
originated; and perhaps, it has no more reference to
the time, than our custom of making toffy has to the
'gunpowder plot that shall ne'er be forgot.'

This brings to my mind, that every fifth of November, since coming here, we have endeavoured to make
some of that sweetmeat; certainly, not out of respect
to 'King James of blessed memory,' whose name, with

the blasphemous dedication, ought long since to have
been expunged from our English Bibles—but, because
one likes to keep up a custom that has so many
cherished recollections of childhood's happy time, to
recommend itself to our safe keeping; but, alas! we
have never succeeded; the sugar being of so bad a
quality, that it always formed an uneatable compound
like hard sand.   Always the children have said, 'if
we could only get some treacle, we might manage,'
but no such a thing is ever seen here, and very few
persons have ever heard of it.   Nor have I, with all
the eloquence of which I am mistress, been able to
inspire any one person with sufficient respect for its
usefulness and manifold virtues, to induce him to
procure me a supply.

I have a theory, upon which, if I find it popular, I
may perhaps enlarge at some future period; that the
advance of a country in enlightenment and civilisation
depends upon the amount of treacle it consumes;
and to prove it, I will only cite that England, 'first
flower of the earth, first gem of the sea,' uses more
than any other country; France, if second at all,
second only to *us*, comes next in showing her
appreciation of the article; while Germany, always
speculating, dreaming, and talking of liberty and

fatherland, and never getting any *farther*, does not consume so much in the whole of her large empire as Lancashire; and Switzerland, which, take it all in all, is about where it was, I am afraid of saying how long ago, uses none at all.

CHAPTER III.

EVERYONE tells us—and we find it the happiest plan
to try and think the same—that we have been marvel-
lously fortunate in getting this home, which is built
in a most substantial manner, with walls that would
appear ridiculous in the eyes of the builders of our
mode n suburban villas, where one lives in constant
dread lest one's 'local habitation' should be levelled
with the ground by each succeeding gust of wind, and
in which the wood, through being but half seasoned,
shrinks so fearfully, that money once rolled on the
floor is never found again.   Assuredly, we can make
no such complaints here, for the walls, both inner and
outer, save those in the upper story, are three quarters of a yard in thickness ; and the ceilings and
floors have so great a space between them, that no
sound is heard through them ; while the windows

E

are closed with upright iron bolts, that require more strength than I possess to fasten: but you have no conveniences, no closets, no cupboards, no nice little corners and recesses so dear to every housekeeper, for storing preserves, pickles, cakes, &c.; all such things must be kept in your kitchen, whence they vanish like snow before the sun, or in your bed-room—which it is not pleasant to convert into a pantry—unless you choose to descend into the cellar every t'me you are hungry.

I find the large stove in my bedroom very useful for storing away a miscellaneous assortment of articles, and the little ovens lined with porcelain are delightful for airing and drying linen in the winter, and, when made very hot, can be used for cooking a variety of little dishes; but in placing things therein one must be careful to guard against accidents, such as happened to one of my friends, who had pur-chased several pairs of fine shoes in Paris, and wish-ing to season them before wearing, had placed them in the oven of her stove, intending to take them out before winter fires commenced, but long ere that time came she had forgotten all about them, until they were recalled to her recollection by the strong smell of burning leather pervading the apartments. Rushing to the stove, where a roaring wood fire had been burning for two days, she tore open the door of the oven, and beheld all her beautiful French shoes frizzled up like pieces of toasted bacon!

Many people object very strongly against the common practice of having all the rooms communicating, on account of the draughts caused by so many doors; but for my part, as I cannot own to that thoroughly English horror, I think the fashion very convenient, and indeed almost necessary, for in these huge houses, containing several families, with but one staircase, up and down which people are passing all the day long, it is almost the only method by which you can have any privacy.

There is one nuisance to which I never could get reconciled, a disgrace to all civilised countries in which it exists, about which many foreigners talk *sotto voce*, and all English grumble outright, but I am not aware of anyone having published his discontent, doubtless for the reason that the matter is not a very pleasant subject to write about. Still, as the public has no chance of obtaining a removal of the evil save by publishing it, and thus shaming the inhabitants into remedying a filthy mischief to which they appear insensible, I think it right to say a few words on the matter. I allude to the beastly state, and horrible odour, arising from their faulty construction,

of those places which in all the houses are met
with in lieu of water-closets, the latter a decent
luxury quite unheard of here.   As there is one to
every *étage*, leading from the stairs or close to your
room, you never enter a house without being nearly
suffocated by the horrible effluvia that not only pene-
trates the system, but clings to your clothes long
after you have left the house.   The only thing that
saves the occupants from decimation by pestilence is
the custom of leaving the large entrance doors, both
back and front, always open ; and that during the
spring, summer, and autumn, when the heat is greater
and the poison most deleterious, they spend nearly
the whole of their time out of doors.   To an English
man or woman, with their heads full of precautionary
sanitary measures, the prevention of epidemics, &c.
&c., the existence of such a foul corner, whence the
smell spreads into every part of the house, is like the
grim phantom pestilence stalking behind, and great
is the consumption of chloride of lime, and all other
disinfectants, in the hope of staving off the evil.

As briefly as possible I will endeavour to give an
account of one day's aggravated suffering from this
cause, which will give some idea of what we endured
about eight times a year, in addition to the every-day
bouquet. We had been here about a month, when one

morning in August, the hottest time of the year, every
soul in the house was awoke by a suffocating sensation
succeeded by vomiting; the rooms were filled with a
stench so disgusting and overpowering that it was
almost impossible to breathe, and, finding when we
opened the windows that it only made matters worse,
we endeavoured to fumigate the apartments by
means of fresh-roasted coffee, burnt vinegar and
sugar, tobacco, &c., but one might as well have tried
to illuminate the world with a farthing rushlight—
the stench overcame, annihilated all; and at last, as
we were all ill and could not touch a morsel of food,
we left the house and spent the day at the hotel. We
remonstrated with our landlord, and even ventured
to ask if such places could not be removed to a
distance from the house instead of in it, but he seemed
to think that the possibility of having to walk a few
steps in the open air during winter was a far worse
evil than any stench *could be*, and I left him more
and more convinced that a stink is a blessed savour
to the nostrils of every Swiss. That evening when we
returned home we discovered that the white paint on
all the doors and windows had turned brown, and our
plate was literally as black as ink. There is no law to
prevent this; anyone may empty his cesspools, which
are always under the house, when and where he likes;

and if he throw the filth under your drawing-room window, no one can prevent him.   The interior of these places, especially at hotels—in France they are far worse than here—is usually quite too beastly to be described ; but the floors ! oh shade of Hercules! it would require a power mightier than thine to cleanse them ! I have said enough, and hope that my example will lead others to protest against an evil fraught with such direful consequences.

To turn to a pleasanter subject; I do not think it possible to have a more splendid balcony than ours, extending the whole length of the house, and eight feet wide.   There we spend the greater portion of the day, screened from the fierce rays of the sun by a blue curtain, which is drawn back as soon as it becomes a little cooler; there we promenade in the evenings, and watch the crimson flush of the sun, already gone from our sight behind the mighty *Dent de Midi* to the west of us, lighting up grey peak after peak, each higher than the last, till, having reached the further point of the *Diablerets*, greatest giant among giants, it flashes it for a few moments, and then, fading slowly away, leaves all grey as before in the deepening twilight; but, strange to say, the flash comes again on the *Dent de Morcles* and the *Argentine* before daylight disappears, but this time not so rosy, but more flame-

coloured, giving them a strange unearthly look, as if
the demons of the Alps were holding high revel there.
In the whole world there can be no finer view than
we have from this balcony, for it embraces everything
that is beautiful in Nature, and in the most harmo-
nious proportions. What stupendous mountains, some
purely white, others only flecked with snow, their
immense glaciers looking to be no more than the
patches of snow left after a thaw in the hollows of a
ploughed field, while those of less elevation, bare and
grey, at the top meet sloping verdant pastures, where
the cattle spend their pleasant summers, and on the
nearer ranges, their steep sides clothed with firs and
pines, in places inaccessible to human foot, and
seemingly of no use to man, but in reality rendering
him a greater service in staying the progress of the
avalanche, or lessening the force of its apparently
resistless might. I can see the treeless places left bare
by their ravages last spring, and still wider spaces
that show plainly the desolation they have caused
after severer winters than any we have passed
through. There is no sound that I have ever heard
so penetrating, so transfixing, as the fall of an
avalanche, and none with which I can compare it.
The distant roll of thunder, the firing of artillery,
the blasting of mines, are comparisons often used,

but none of them give you the slightest idea of its fullness, solemnity, and grandeur. In its reverberations there is a deep music that affords me the intensest pleasure, and though I have witnessed scores, it was never without feeling strangely excited; and when I saw the peasants, whose sluggish natures seem incapable of responding to any touch of nature, and who all their lives have been familiarised to the sight, cease from their occupations and shout out frantically, ' *Une avalanche! une avalanche!* ' I was not surprised at the intensity of my own emotions.

Our balcony has to do duty as *salle-à-manger*, schoolroom, laundry, and I know not what; for though we endeavour to persuade ourselves that we have enough and to spare, we know very well, like Bob Cratchet's family with their Christmas goose, that we could do much better with more; it also serves as a capital drying-ground for our linen, which is literally roasted if hung out an hour (how different from the trouble one has in England!), so that there is no fear of my guidman saying, ' There 's nae luck about the house upon a washing day.' Labour is always sweeter in the open air; and such air! so warm and yet so fresh; so invigorating that, coupled with the lovely sights and sounds around us, it gives a marvellous buoyancy to the spirits. Some times our eyes and ears are regaled with other sights and sounds than those of nature; for our little land-lord and his thin wife, who treats him with immense disdain on account of her superior mental acquire-ments—an assumption founded upon the fact of her having once sent some lines of German poetry to a magazine or newspaper—generally choose their balcony.below as the arena of their domestic strifes. The despotic Frau has a handsomely-furnished room of her own, but into this the poor little man is never allowed to enter without special permission ; and, as it would be too lowering to her dignity to descend to his, which is a small box partitioned off from his office, they meet on the balcony as a sort of neutral ground

Like all Germans, and German-Swiss, they shout so very loudly when talking that it is impossible not to hear what they say, and I have learned a curious piece of domestic history from the quarrels to which I have been an involuntary listener. He is not a bad fellow, as the world goes, and has raised himself to his present position, as first *notaire* of the village, by his industry and good conduct, a circumstance that redounds to his credit in the eyes of everyone but his wife, who, better born, as she is the daughter

of a man, lord of his fifty acres, while *his* father rented
the ground he tilled—all the difference in the world
between aristocrat and plebeian—never ceases to taunt
him with his base extraction.   He was taken as a
dernier ressort after courting her for seven years,
and when her good looks were fading away from
mortification and disappointment at not meeting
with a more eligible *parti*; and it appears that, as
she had no love for her husband, she immediately
commenced looking out for some one upon whom
she could bestow her wasting affections, and accordingly selected the village Figaro, whose exterior
proves that the lady was not influenced in her choice
by the vulgar attractions of good looks.   *On dit*,
that the injured husband, who is very avaricious and
appears to take matters very philosophically, would
not be quite so cool about the aspect of affairs, and
would even sue for a divorce, if he were not afraid
of losing the property to which she will succeed on
the death of her parents; and in the meantime he
revenges himself by keeping her so short of cash
that she cannot even indulge in the female (?) vanity
of fine clothes.   Before the world she manages to
keep up appearances pretty well, and it is mon-
strously amusing to those who have been a little
behind the scenes to see the meltingly affectionate

manner with which she pets him, he having all the while very much the look of a tame bear.

This accommodating husband is captain in one of the Swiss regiments—a fact that surprised me, until I learned that any male citizen of this free republic may be an officer after attending one of the military schools for the whole term of six weeks, and, as I know a commandant who can neither read nor write, I do not suppose the course of study is very severe—and when we had resided here about two months he sent us a polite note inviting 'as many of us as his carriage would hold' to accompany him to a *tir cantonal* that was being held at a town about five miles hence, an invitation we were very glad to accept, seeing we had already been amused spectators of one in Bex, and were wishful to witness another of these national shooting parties on a larger and grander scale, as we were given to understand this one would be. These meetings are held annually, for the purpose of making the people expert in the use of the rifle, and also, I doubt not, to prevent a warlike spirit from dying out among them, of which, to judge from the number of shooting grounds, the authorities must have a well-grounded fear, every village, hamlet, or cluster of houses being provided with one, where the men are assembled two days out of the seven during the summer, in the winter not so often, Sunday being always one of the days set apart for this amusement, consuming large quantities of powder, and much larger quantities of wine. Sometimes these ordinary meetings are rendered extraordinary by being thrown open to all comers, when everyone who enters the lists pays after the rate of three francs for five shots, and the sum thus collected serves to purchase the prizes.

Though the Swiss as a nation are not much given to humour, it has always struck me that they must have some hidden meaning—doubtless very amusing, if one were but worthy to know it—in always selecting dead plucked fowls as the rewards at these local *tirs*. But it is of a more important affair that I have to speak, as was plainly to be seen by the getting up of the splendidly accoutred individual whom I passed in the lobby, on my way to the carriage (a vehicle about on a par with those one sees stored away as lumber under the cow-sheds of ancient farm-houses in England), whose stature was so immensely exalted by the high cocked-hat and plume he wore, that I had not the faintest notion it was our landlord, until I saw him mount the little high seat reserved for the driver; and certainly I had no reason to regret my apparent want of politeness, when I saw that the apology I made was infinitely more pleasing to his feelings than any recognition could have been.

We had a charming drive through the valley, the magnificent walnut-trees that lined both sides of the road shading us from the sun; and it struck me as a very convincing proof of the honesty of the inhabitants towards each other that the fields, looking far more like the market-gardens in the vicinity of our large towns, with their innumerable patches of vegetables, buck-wheat, hemp, maize, and here and there a strip of emerald green for the eye to refresh itself on, all lay open to the road and one another, without fence of any kind. As we entered the town we had some difficulty in steering our way through the crowded, narrow, crooked streets into which vehicles—mostly of the sort in common use here, a kind of long, low, narrow wagon, very light, but without springs, across which one or two seats are slung with ropes—were pouring by every inlet; thousands of peasants, in the costumes of their respective cantons, were pressing forward to the scene of action; the houses were crowded to the roofs; outside the windows and across the streets lamps and Chinese lanterns were hung in readiness for the

illuminations that were to wind up the festivities;
and on every face sat an expression of the greatest
good-humour and pleasure. I saw many persons
drunk, but none quarrelling, a remark that I am
confident could not be made of any assemblage of
equal size in England; for when only two of our
nation meet and get drunk there is sure to be a row,
and most likely bloodshed, before they are separated.
I am no advocate for drunkenness, but I must say,
that I have seen many Swiss who, when the worse
(or the better?) for liquor, talked fluently and sensibly
enough, and would have passed in society for intelligent, agreeable men, but who when sober were the
greatest dolts alive.

We left our carriage among scores of others in a
field at the side of the hotel where we alighted, and
proceeding onwards on foot followed the stream of
people for about twenty minutes, until we arrived at
the extremity of the town; where is a wide open
plain, then covered with shows, booths, stalls served
by splendid-looking Tyrolese in their most picturesque
dresses, lotteries, shooting pavilions of private specu-
lators, at five centimes a shot, swings, hobby horses,
and all the amusements one meets with at a Continental fair. Having threaded our way through the
motley crowd, we reached a wooden pavilion of

immense size, in the form of the Federal cross, set
out with tables and benches, capable of seating from
2,000 to 3,000 persons. Flags, banners, flowers,
evergreens decorated the walls; scores of young men
and women wearing white rosettes were preparing
the tables for dinner, workmen were hammering away
at the tribune in which the patriots, desirous of
distinguishing themselves, were to hold forth when
the eating was over, and millions of wasps, that
exceeded all I ever saw for size and impudence, were
everywhere; they covered the tables as thick as an
army of locusts, got into your hair, dozens were on
everyone's hat or bonnet, and it seemed to me the
chief business of the day would consist in waging war
against those marauders.

The tail of the cross was appropriated to the
culinary department, and there, having been allowed
to enter by favour of M. Wagner, who was purveyor
of all the good things that sent forth such a savoury
steam throughout the building, I had the pleasure
of witnessing the gigantic preparations making to
refresh the bodies of the brave defenders of their
'*patrie.*' I had to stand still some moments before
I could see anything through the cloud of steam
that filled the place; and the first object my eyes
lighted on was a tall gaunt woman, uglier than

Hecate, and having what I am sure Hecate never possessed, a tremendous goître that reached nearly to her waist, fishing hams out of a boiler (quite large enough to have held the Yorkshireman's big turnip) with a pitchfork; these she carried to a table where half a dozen men, with their shirt sleeves rolled to their elbows, were carving as if their lives depended upon finishing a certain amount in a given time; at another board more men, with a machine like a chaff-cutter, were chopping up bread, which they threw into baskets; immense joints of meat were stewing over fires in all directions, boilers of potatoes were bubbling and seething, and as I passed out I saw so many casks of wine and beer, that it struck me they would go far towards making a good-sized artificial lake.

In the front of the pavilion was an immense fat obelisk, completely covered with what I supposed was the stock of some enterprising ironmonger, who had taken that conspicuous method of displaying his goods. I thought M—— would never have done laughing, when I remarked 'what a capital idea it was,' and I laugh myself as I think of the contrast afforded by the face of our landlord, to whom I turned for an explanation of M——'s immoderate fit of laughter. It was so grave and severe that it would have awed the comic Muse herself, as he informed me that 'all the articles I saw before me to the number of 5,000 were prizes for the ·best marksmen.' After the unpardonable insult of which I had been guilty I dared not ask any more questions, though sorely tempted to know what *un pauvre célibataire* could possibly do with smoothing irons and lots of other articles I saw suspended, that are generally used by the female sex. As we walked towards the shooting ground we passed two carts laden with coals and a great millstone, which I was told were the three first prizes. The coals being a scarce commodity would, I could imagine, be very acceptable to anyone, but the latter article would prove literally a millstone round the winner's neck, unless he was so fortunate as to possess a mill to put it in.

The shooting was nearly over, but I saw enough, coupled with what I had before witnessed at Bex three weeks before, to convince me that the prowess of the Swiss in this respect has been immensely overrated. The ranges were from one to three hundred yards, and each man had five shots. The targets were circular, and from the bull's-eye five circles were drawn and numbered; and as soon as a shot was fired, the marker, who was seated in a *tranchée*,

F

pulled a string that elevated to the front of the
target a piece of cardboard on which was written a
number corresponding to the one in the circle the ball
had hit; if it missed, the marker made no sign. The
rifles were of the same make as those used in chamois-
hunting, very clumsy and heavy looking, but said to
be *juste*, and as proof of the latter quality I may
mention that M—— tried *his skill*, and the renowned
Mr. Tracy Tupman's astonishment at discovering he
had brought down a bird with his eyes shut, could
not have been greater than his, at finding he had
hit the bull's-eye twice, a piece of good fortune that
never befell him when in the rifle corps at ——.

Among 6,000 soldiers I did not see above two or
three that could be called fine-looking men; what
they would have been if they had had better tailors
and drill-masters I cannot pretend to say; but as
they were, there was not one with a soldierly mien
or carriage. All stooped and walked with the rolling
gait peculiar to the Swiss, and their clothes, of strong
and coarse material, were so loose and large, that you
imagined it would make no material difference in the
appearance of the army if they took it into their
heads to have a swapping of garments.

When the dinner, which consisted of excellent
soup, beef, ham, vegetables, including sauer kraut,

fruits, cakes, and wine *ad libitum,* for the moderate sum of one franc, was despatched, the firing
of two pieces of artillery, stationed about forty yards
in front of the building, announced that the speechi-
fying was about to commence; and as I turned my
regards towards the tribune, I saw the head of a
little man, 'with hair on end like fretful porcupine,'
emerge from the floor which he slammed-to with
great vehemence as soon as his foot touched the top
of the ladder, and then briskly stepping on to the
middle, began without more ado to gesticulate with
all his might. I supposed he was talking as he
opened his mouth very widely, but of what he said I
had no more idea than if he had been talking from
the moon. After he had worked away for about five
minutes and become very apoplectic-looking in the
face, he bolted down again through the trap-door,
reminding me exactly of a 'jack in a box.' Then the
two cannons boomed again, and another gentleman
with a splendid blue scarf tied round his arm came
into the little pulpit, whose appearance seemed to
give as much pleasure to the people, as their cheering
did to the gentleman. By this time the tables were
cleared, and I hoped with more quiet to have heard
at least some portion of the discourses; but though I
tried my utmost—and there were from eight to ten

speakers—I never caught more than the words, oft repeated, of '*Liberté et Patrie*,' when immense thumping and stamping, followed by cries of 'Bravo!' and occasionally, 'France!' with a menacing look towards that quarter, succeeded by an ominous silence. When any of the orators stopped for want of breath or ideas, they made a sign by holding up the left hand, and then the drums rolled, until they were in a state to go on again.

The distribution of the prizes which followed, was conducted with very little ceremony; each man who had been successful presented his ticket and received in return the article to which was affixed a corresponding number, without remark or comment, and the oddity and inapplicability of the rewards did not seem to strike any one of the spectators but ourselves. I saw a general of division—not quite *compos* through having assisted in emptying the casks I spoke of—riding away, decorated with a breastplate of six German silver tea-spoons fastened on a blue pasteboard, and a soup ladle and a broom slung across his charger's neck, seemingly as proud of his trophies as a Roman of his laurel crown. Many gallant officers passed me laden with saucepans, frying-pans, gridirons, candlesticks, warming-pans; indeed, there is no article to be found in the shop of an ironmonger that was not among the prizes awarded to valour that day.

As we rode home in the twilight the lamps were lighted, music and dancing were heard in most of the houses, the soft warm summer air floated over all; and as I turned back to take a look at the illuminations, a loud explosion, followed by the mounting of scores of rockets into the sky, announced that the official portion of the three days' fête was over.

CHAPTER IV.

Autumn—No accounting for Taste—Comparative Industry—
Communal Properties—Village Curés—Immorality—Pas-
tors and Flock—Fruit Gathering—Bien Cuit—Vendange—
Fisherman of the Rhone—Grape Cure—Dark Side of the
Picture—Dans la Cave—Conseil Municipal—Evil Commu-
nications, &c.—Fête-à-la-Champêtre—English Exclusiveness
—Wine Press.

AUTUMN is the season for fun and jollity among the
Swiss peasants, who have not much notion of any
enjoyment that is not partaken of out-of-doors.
During the spring and summer they are too busy in
their vineyards and fields, while in the winter they
shut themselves up like hermits in their rooms, with
large wood fires in their stoves, living in such an
atmosphere of bad smells—as poor families have
seldom more than one room, that serves for bedroom,
kitchen, and living room—that the wonder is they
exist till the spring comes round again. Rarely do
they open a door, as they generally have enough
provisions of all kinds stored up to last some months.
More than once I have penetrated into these hotbeds
of disease, and, as the belief is not uncommon that
the Swiss in general, and of this canton in particular,

are pretty clean, I will give an account of one which will serve as a fair specimen of many to be found in the French cantons.

The people who lived in the apartment I am about to describe were what we should call well-to-do in the world, having a shop for fruits and vegetables, and a *laiterie*, where they sold cheese and milk, and were doing a fair trade. There were two beds in different corners of the room of the style we call French, with full curtains of stuff—once green, but now so covered with grease and dirt that scarcely a trace of their original colour was discernible—slung through a ring in the ceiling. In another corner was a sink that appeared to serve for more purposes than the one for which it was placed there, so beastly was its condition; and in the fourth was a miscellaneous collection of pots and pans that would have been all the cleaner for a good washing. A greasy sofa was drawn near the stove, and on it sat the mistress of the apartment combing wool; two or three children, so begrimed with filth that they might be said to belong to any race but the white, were sitting on the floor making dirt confectionary with the aid of their spittle. The ceiling was hung full of sausages, bunches of herbs, maize, loaves of bread resting on sticks slung across from

wall to wall, and quantities of chesnuts and walnuts
lay on the beds.

The walls, that had once been coloured in the way
I have heard called slapdashed, were so begrimed
with fly-dirt that only here and there (probably
where some article had been hanging) a vestige
of former splendour remained. The windows might
never have been opened for half a century, to judge
from the spiders' webs that formed a blind almost as
thick, and of quite as good a colour, as the muslin
curtains. Filth of all kinds covered the wooden
floor that had evidently not known a broom for
weeks; but the smell! Oh! ye gods and little fishes,
it came not from this earth, I think! The living in
such close rooms, sitting so near the hot stoves, and
the neglect of necessary washings to the face, must
tend to make the women look so frightfully wizened—
like crumpled-up brown paper—at an age when our
countrywomen are still fresh and apple-cheeked.

It is not hard labour certainly that ages them so
prematurely, for I have never seen man nor woman
in this or the neighbouring canton of the Valais,
where they are even far less industrious than here,
who was what an English labourer would call very
hard at work. They work a little and rest a good
deal, a remark that applies to all kinds and classes

of artisans and labourers. To compare their industry with that of an English workman is absurd and unfair, as the cases have nothing in common, and the races are constitutionally different. The climate too renders it almost impossible to keep up that constantly sustained labour which an Englishman performs with comparative ease; nor indeed is it necessary, for the soil, being constantly renewed by alluvial deposits, is so rich that it requires but little working, and the glorious sunshine quickens into life and ripens, with a rapidity little short of the marvellous to those accustomed to the slow growing vegetation of more northern climates, the seeds and plants placed therein; and as the majority are tilling their own plots of ground, which are seldom of any great size, there is always 'time enough and to spare,' so that they have no need to hurry themselves. An Englishman could not be happy without work, he could not live idle; while a Swiss, like his neighbour the Italian, likes the *dolce far niente* existence, and only works because he knows that—his bit of land being often his only means of subsistence —he would starve if he did not.

Half the time he is in the fields is spent in looking about him, nursing his children—for as a man always takes his wife (not out of affection, dear

reader, but because he fears she will not have her
full share of the hard work if she remain at home)
it necessarily follows that the children must go too—
chatting with his neighbours, lolling lazily under
some tree, or, what is far worse, imbibing deep
draughts of that injurious white wine which weakens
his brain and nerves, and in the end renders him
more than half a *crétin*. Preparing the vineyards
in spring is the hardest work of the whole year, yet
that labour is not more arduous than the cultivation
of a garden, and is soon over, because here, unlike
France, they are rarely of any great size; and as to
the tying up and cutting they require afterwards,
I know many an English country gentleman who
performs for pleasure quite as laborious an occupation
on his espaliers and wall-fruit trees.

It is said that there are quite as many landed
proprietors in the Canton de Vaud as in Great
Britain; so it is not to be wondered at that we find
but few estates large enough to employ more hands
than the household living upon them furnishes; and if
this system of partition go on as at present, each man
leaving his piece of ground to be divided amongst
his children, to every one an equal share, the time is
not far distant when no one in the canton will
possess enough ground to be buried in. This reminds

me that the other day, going into the little cemetery,
there was pointed out to me the last resting-place of
a man who had been killed by the falling of a huge
piece of rock whilst ascending a mountain in the
neighbourhood. He lived long enough after he was
found to be able to express his dying wish, which
was that the rock which had crushed him should be
placed over his grave, and there it is, having been
transported with great labour and difficulty from the
place where it fell.

To return to my subject, however, I must say that
at present everyone seems happy and contented, and
no one has need to beg; for every citizen has a share
in the surplus revenues of the commune at the close
of every year, besides the right to send a cow to
pasture for so long as he likes on the public lands;
and a share in the wood, of which immense quantities
are felled every year, from the forests belonging to
the commune. These rights belong to rich and
poor alike, but the former usually waive their claims
in order that the poor may have more, and as they
are sure of these helps, in addition to what little
else they may possess, 'they prefer a dinner of herbs'
and idleness 'to a stalled ox' and industry. How
many times have I been unable to procure a washer-
woman or a man to chop wood, although I have

offered double wages, and to people that I knew
were living on what would starve an Englishman.
In winter, no bribe will tempt them to go out to
work, though the cold is something to be smiled at,
for, except in very rare winters, the snow seldom lies
more than a couple of days.

Since the expulsion of the Jesuits in 1847-8,
there are not so many fête days in the Vaud, and if
we compare the number with those of the neighbouring Catholic canton of the Valais, where the inhabitants are said to have four fête days out of the seven,
and the remaining three for cleaning out the churches,
we shall have reason to fear they may have a chronic
malady for want of a little recreation; though the
truth is, that—what with attending fairs, to all of
which they go as a sort of religious duty instead of
attending church, the number of days employed, I
had nearly written *wasted*, for the glory of the *patrie*,
in firing at a target, or the image of some obnoxious
Austrian, hundreds of which may be seen in passing
through the country, hanging outside the châlets, and
perforated in every part—the festivals of the church
and the seasons, there is at least one-third of the
year consumed in holidays, to say nothing of the
winter, when the men do little or nothing, with the
exception of an occasional excursion to the moun-

tains, for the purpose of cutting wood; the remainder
of his time being spent in the café house, or in amusing himself by giving black eyes to his wife for the
sake of exercise.

This, by far the largest wine-growing canton in
Switzerland, consumes all, or nearly all, it produces,
besides importing one-third more; and from these
two facts, one may arrive at a pretty correct idea
of the amount of drunkenness there is among the
people. Their morals too, in other respects, are fearfully low, and I am afraid of being accused of mis-
representation when I say, that the number of illegi-
timate children in this village is in the proportion of
one to five, a state of things not to be attributed to
the sin which has been termed 'the parent of all
other vices,' as in other cantons, where the inhabitants are very sober, the same deplorable immorality
exists. I have made every possible inquiry on this
head, before I placed on record a statement reflecting
so gravely on the character of a people ; and by one
whose position enabled her to be the best authority
on such a subject, and whose high respectability was
the voucher for the fidelity of her statement, I was
told ' there was hardly a girl in the place who had not
had a child, or a married woman who had not been
enceinte ere she became a wife.'

It appears to me that the want of intellectual food, and more liberal religious and moral instruction, is the great cause of this. The hot blood and unspent energy of youth must find vent somewhere, and, if not absorbed by having higher aims placed before it, will expend itself by grovelling in the dust. They have emancipated themselves from priestly domination; but what have they now? Curés who preach to empty churches, and, though good sort of men enough in their way, sadly wanting in that fervour, energy, and zeal necessary for obtaining a powerful and permanent religious influence over a people grown indifferent by reason of the rapacity, selfishness, and immorality of the 'blind guides' they have expelled. I am not speaking of the large towns, for with them I have nothing to do, but of the dwellers in out-of-the-way places, and the large population spread over the mountains, who, unless they descend to those villages in which the church is built, never hear the 'glad tidings of great joy' preached to them. 'Oh for a Felix Neff to labour here!' I often thought when I was so long among the simple kind peasants aux Plans, and saw they were like sheep without a shepherd. After leaving school, the only intellectual recreation they ever appear to indulge in, is the reading of the local papers full of cantonal squabbles in the café houses; their numerous holidays and idle hours are devoted by the young to amusement alone. Public balls, prolonged to break of day without any supervision of parents, accompanied by deep drinking among the male sex; mountain excursions, each lass with a lad, from which they seldom return till past midnight; long evening rambles in this seductive clime, that are kept up so long as the summer lasts; scores of young girls, singly or in parties, turning out of the village after sunset, meet with an equal number of swains, and wander up and down the mountains screaming, romping, shouting, and dancing, startling quiet folk like ourselves from our slumber, till the stars fail before the light of the sun.

I declare that I have not the faintest idea when the people here *do* sleep during the summer, or whether they ever go to bed at all. It is not improbable that like the dormouse they lay in a sufficient stock during the winter to last them till the cold weather comes again, and I don't know but what it is a good plan, in a country where the nights are almost more beautiful than the days, the sunset in summer being followed by a soft dreamy twilight, so bewitching and captivating, that it seems a shame

not 'to turn the night into the day,' and thus enjoy
them both.

But I have wandered far from the autumn avoca-
tions of the peasants, which might with more correctness be called amusements, for the work is so light
and so agreeable that from the beginning of September till the close of the *vendange* they look upon
it as a holiday and give themselves up to enjoyment.

When the season has been a fine one the walnut
gathering begins about the first week in that month,
and anyone ignorant of the habits of the people, who
during that time should enter any of the villages at
an early hour in the morning, would imagine that
an emigration of the inhabitants was taking place;
scores of whole families, down to the little baby at
the mother's breast, turning out with *hottes* on their
backs, and bearing long light poles 50 or 60 feet
in length in their hands, proceed to their little
properties, or the trees they rent, a custom common
enough here, and commence knocking off the walnuts
by means of these poles, a work that always seemed
to me rather troublesome from having to hold the
head back and stare upwards; giving to the gatherer
pretty much the same pleasing sensation about the
neck and eyes, as when one has spent a whole day
' *so* agreeably' in an exhibition of paintings.   The

poles, too, so thin and flexible, appear, like naughty overgrown children, to be quite beyond management; but the nuts fall off somehow, and are collected in sacks and *hottes* by the children, while the women sit on the grass, plying their knitting needles, without which they never move a step from home : whether in the railways, their carts, or going or returning from their field labours, they are always knitting stockings, almost a work of necessity here, as manufactured ones are frightfully dear, and of so poor a quality they are not worth the buying. The yield of nuts in some seasons is immense; and I have often thought that if we could have in England only what they leave on the ground we should be quite satisfied: here there is no necessity to buy, for anyone may have his fill for the asking. The oil that is expressed from the nut is very good and fine, and employed in cooking and a variety of other household purposes.

The apples in Switzerland, which cannot be compared with ours in flavour, for the reason that no one takes the trouble to improve the sorts, are gathered in the same manner, and this is why this excellent and useful fruit never keeps here. I have often remonstrated with them upon this practice of knocking off, and at the same time bruising the fruit, but they seemed to think that our plan of gathering them by the hand

G

was taking a great deal of trouble for very little profit; and as the uses to which they apply them are quite as well served by their present mode, I don't know that they would gain anything by spending so much more time over plucking them. The largest and best are cut into quarters and dried in the sun, in the same way as plums and cherries, for winter use, when they are stewed with water and sugar, and are, the cherries especially, very good, and make excellent cakes, as they call the large, round, open tarts, that are often a yard in diameter. These cakes are quite the standing article of confectionary here, and are made with a quantity of these fruits laid in circles on the paste lining the tin, a lot of sugar, pounded cinnamon, and dabs of butter are strewn over the fruit, and last of all some thick cream, and when baked the compound is not to be sneezed at. The greater part of the apples goes to make cider, which is none of the best; and when the crop is plentiful, quantities are given to the pigs.

From the fresh cherries they also make a peculiar kind of conserve, which is much prized on account of the healthful properties it is said to possess. The fruit when fully ripe is put in a canvas sack open at the ends, that are held by two persons who twist and squeeze them with all their might till the pulp is expressed. When some gallons of this pulp are ready, it is put into a large pan and kept slowly boiling the *whole night* and constantly stirred. No sugar is used; and when done it is almost black, with the consistency of clouted cream, and a taste that is neither tart, nor sour, nor sweet, nor bitter, nor, indeed, of any one flavour sufficiently predominant to enable you to form an opinion as to whether it is good or bad. It is called *bien cuit*, and may be made of apples, plums, or pears, but that from cherries is by far the best.

Pears are very abundant, and I have eaten one or two kinds equal to any I have ever tasted; but the majority are woolly and insipid, and serve only for baking, in which form the people are immoderately fond of them.

By the time the fruits are gathered the *vendange* comes, the glory of the year, the season of delights, the golden age; 'not that the rivers roll with milk,' but that the mountains run with wine, when high and low, rich and poor, meet together under the canopy of heaven to enjoy the pleasant time and crop the luscious fruit. On a day appointed by the local authorities of the district, before which no one is allowed to gather his grapes, under penalty of a fine, the roads are covered with people bearing tubs, baskets, *brantes,* and driving the long narrow carts,

drawn by oxen, laden with casks to hold the grapes
when crushed. All are dressed as for a fête, every
face looks happy; the children are laughing and
shouting, none but pleasant sounds are heard: the
song, à la Tyrolese, caught up again and again by
some answering singer, comes echoing from the hills,
and mingles with the ringing of the bells round the
necks of the patient oxen, as they bear their burdens
to the foot of the mountains, to rest under the shade
of the chesnut trees, till the work of the day is over,
while we ascend the narrow zigzag path that leads
us among the vineyards.

As we mount we meet numbers of men carrying
brantes filled with the crushed fruit, which they tell
us they are taking to the casks below; and as we stand
still to watch them in their slippery descent, we
think we should have to go through a lifelong
apprenticeship before we should be able to carry that
full burden down such a road without spilling a
good deal: and when we see them mount the ladders
reared against the casks, and bending sideways pour
the whole of the liquor into them without removing
the *brantes* from their backs, and even without
losing a drop, we are convinced that we could never
learn to do the same. As we meet and pass the
peasants, all have a smile and '*bon jour*' for each of

the party, but especially for M——, who is so beloved by them : no one fails to invite us to come and eat grapes with them, and lots of bunches are thrown into the hands of the children as we walk slowly on, for at present we have promised to eat as many as we can in the vineyards of Rapaz, the fisherman of the Rhone, who with his wife and two stalwart sons, with *their* wives and some six or eight children, we saw looking out for us higher up. Now we pass through the vines laden with purple grapes, that are not to be gathered for a week to come, as they are much longer in ripening than the white, which, though not so beautiful to look at, are far the best to eat.

This year the vineyards look lovely, as the latter rains have not only added to the plumpness and fulness of the fruit, but have preserved the foliage which the heat usually withers before the grapes are ripe. How beautiful are the rich purple clusters, as we peep through the vistas formed by the over-hanging branches! how tempting! how inviting! What charming contrasts between the blooming purple of the fruit and the fresh green of the leaves! What immense bunches! Many I am sure weighed a couple of pounds; and much as I liked demolishing them— an art in which I am not to be excelled—I enjoyed nothing more than sitting on the ground contemplating the riches hanging in such marvellous profusion from every plant.

As soon as we reached the kind folk who were eagerly expecting us, my children begged for scissors and began cutting away with the rest, never ceasing until the work was done. As for me, I had enough to do in looking after my baby, who toddled under the vines and made himself such a figure of fun with the sugary juice and rolling on the soil, that everybody laughed at him, which made the little fellow laugh too, until he fairly crowed with delight.

I should be afraid to tell how many I ate, I can only say that one's capacities increase with the occasion. At the commencement you are rather shy or modest, or whatever you please to call it; and after having eaten three or four fine bunches, everyone offering you the largest they cut, you think it is time to give over: but after resting a few minutes you see (or some one brings you) *the finest bunch you ever saw,'* which, of course, must be an exception to the resolve you have taken to eat no more; and when that has disappeared, you discover to your surprise that your appetite has returned, and, recollecting that *vendanges* are not held every day, you think you may as well have a few more while the opportunity offers: and so you set to for a good tuck in, and eat and come again, and make valiant resolutions that are broken as soon as made, and never have too many, though you are eating when the last grape is laid in the *brante*; and day after day, so long as the *vendange* lasts, this sort of thing goes on, and when all is over you are horrified to think you have swallowed as many as Robbin-a-bobbin could have done. It is really amazing how many you can eat, and without experiencing any ill effects: on the contrary, you are wonderfully benefited by them. The inhabitants look forward to the *vendange* as a time when they shall get rid of their ailments; and numbers of strangers come here at that season to undergo the grape cure, a very simple process, which consists in eating a large quantity before breakfast, followed by a walk, the two producing an effect similar to the purgative waters at Harrogate, and found to be very beneficial in skin diseases, and many complaints arising from a sedentary life.

At noon we all adjourned to a grassy slope on the mountain-side, and sat down on the grass to a frugal repast of bread, goat's-cheese, sausage, and wine, spread under the shade of a large cherry-tree, whence we had a distant view of the lake looking only like a

thread of silver along the horizon.   Grapes, as
children say, must go for nothing, for we were all
hungry, and fell to the bread and cheese with a
relish the finest entertainment in the world could
not have given us ; but no unnecessary lingering, the
grapes must be cropped ere the sun sink behind the
Dent du Midi, and we set to work again with might
and main to fill our baskets, emptying them as soon
as filled into the *brante* set upright in the path,
against which stands a man who smashes the grapes
with a long wooden mallet as they are poured in.
When the *brante* is filled to a certain mark, it is
lifted on his back, he passes his arms through the
leathern straps that hold it in its place, and while he
descends with it into the valley below, we cease from
our labours for a few moments, in order to watch the
busy *vendangeurs* around us.

What shouting and screaming there is as some
young fellow claims the fine, every girl has to pay,
for leaving any grapes hanging on the vines from
which she has been cropping ! How they rush and
hide among the bushes if the pursuer be ill-favoured;
and how quietly and coquettishly, with only a little
turning away of the head, the salute is received, if
he be not disagreeable to her !   Those who have
finished first, come and help the others, and it is

delightful to see the kind feeling and good fellow
ship that seems to animate everyone. We all leave
together, my children laden with two large baskets
full of the finest bunches the good-natured Rapaz
has been able to collect; but our present must be a
little diminished as we pass out of the vineyards
into the shade of the chesnut trees, where a dozen
or two of the poorest children of the village, each
with a basket, are collected to receive the contri-
butions of grapes, which no one refuses to give them.

It is impossible to say how many invitations we
accept for the morrow, but we do not forget that we
have promised to assist Rapaz and his family when
they cut the purple grapes, and then having said
'*Bon soir*' and shaken hands all round, a civility you
must on no account omit to offer to a Swiss peasant
unless you wish mortally to offend him, we wend our
way home after the bullock carts, and almost as lazily,
thinking over the happy day we have spent; but forced
to admit that it would have left a much more pleasing
impression on our minds, if it had not been accompanied by the drunkenness which seems so habitual,
that even the poor wives, who are the greatest sufferers
from the vice, tell you their husbands have taken
a walk *dans les vignes du Seigneur*—a favourite
metaphor to express that they are drunk—with far

more unconcern than if they were talking of the weather.

If a man come to reside here from any other canton, Berne for instance, where the people are more sober—and for two good reasons, first, that the wine there is three times dearer; and, secondly, that there are very heavy fines for indulging too freely in the pleasures of Bacchus—no matter how steady and industrious he has been formerly, he is sure to fall, and not by very slow degrees, into the same intemperate habits as those about him. Partly the vice may be said to spring from hospitality and goodfellowship, no one ever entering a house without being invited into the cellar, where you are expected to drink as much as you can; and it requires a much stronger *morale* than the people here are possessed of to be able to resist an invitation given with so much friendship and heartiness, especially as a refusal, however politely given, is sure to be taken as an offence. These cellar meetings generally end in all parties getting so drunk that they remain lying on the ground till they are sober again, often all night, no one in the house troubling themselves at all about them; and it is by no means uncommon, if you happen to go to a house and enquire for the master of it, to be told that he is *dans la cave,* which means that he is lying dead drunk on the floor of the cellar.

The higher classes, as they are called, are not a whit better than the lower in this respect, and occasions are neither rare nor far between when even the authorities degrade themselves to the level of brutes. Not many weeks ago the Conseil Municipal of this place, consisting of twelve members and the Syndic, met to consult on some matters of great importance connected with the well-being of the town; and, as the subject to be brought before the meeting was one of more than ordinary interest, they resolved to inaugurate the occasion by paying a visit to the cellar of one of the members hard by. When there they commenced drinking wine, using the same glass, a fashion quite *comme-il-faut* when they go to drink below; and this same glass travelled so fast round the circle and back again that at last all these dignitaries lay dead drunk on the ground. The next morning the first to awake from his drunken sleep was the secretary, who left the cellar and went to the Hôtel de Ville, where the Conseil holds its meetings when sober, and taking the minute-book, wrote down, 'That all the propositions submitted to the meeting the night before were passed *unanimously*;' and not the least laughable part of the story is, that the matter, whatever it was, that ought to have been laid before that august body, was actually carried out.

A poor and very decent Bernese woman, whom I had known some time, came to me just before the last winter set in, to say that she had at last prevailed upon her husband, who had always been a sober, industrious man previous to settling in Bex, to leave the place and return to his native canton; as she found that there was nothing but poverty and misery in store for her and her children, so long as they remained where he could get wine so cheaply, and was always being tempted from his work to drink by bad companions. She said she had gone eighteen leagues over the mountains to find a place to settle in; and having succeeded in getting him work in one of the villages high among the hills, she had returned to send him on with the four biggest children, in order to have him safe, while she remained behind to dispose of their few bits of furniture, and would follow in a few days with her two youngest little ones, the eldest of whom was not quite four years old. Much snow had already fallen on the mountains, and she was anxious to start before the roads were impassable. She would have to go by the way of the *Diablerets* over passes

5,000 and 6,000 feet high; and my heart bled for
the poor creature when I pictured her toiling up
those dreadful heights with her two babes, and big
with another child. Think of this, ye fine delicate
ladies! who are afraid to use the slightest exertion
when in that interesting condition; and yet this poor
soul would suffer far less than you, and be delivered
safely without the aid of an accoucheur, or a *sage
femme.*

Towards the close of every *vendange* a *fête-à-la-
champêtre* is given by M. Wagner, and three other
maîtres-d'hôtel, to all the visitors who may then
be stopping in the place. The site selected is one of
the loveliest imaginable for such a purpose, being a
smooth grass plateau, with two immense oak-trees
in the middle, on the summit of a hill, about two
miles from Bex, whence on one side you have a
view as far as the *Vallée de Dappes,* and on the
other along the Rhone to *Mont Catogne.*

Here, after a charming walk through the chesnut-
woods clothing one side of the hill, we found the
most lively and busy preparations going on for the
festival. Full a quarter of a mile of table-cloths
was spread under the shade of the trees, and on this
several waiters, our old friend with the queer nose
among the number, were laying knives and forks by

dozens, loaves of bread, hams, fowls, roast beef, pasties, such as are made nowhere so good as at Bex, and wine. A great wood fire was burning under the wall of one of the vineyards, at which two women were roasting chesnuts; while others were arranging some bushels of grapes in large flaskets, that were to do duty as dessert dishes. Every moment came fresh arrivals, and by one o'clock there could not have been less than 600 people assembled; the occasion being a favourable one for organising a number of private picnics in addition to the large one of the day.

Everybody seemed ready for their dinner, which passed off far more sociably and pleasantly than is usual with so mixed a company. Even the English lost their reserve for a time when the good wine, so liberally bestowed by M. Wagner, whose jolly face shone everywhere, had warmed their hearts; and it was actually an Englishman, who could not speak five words of French, that proposed his health, and though nine-tenths of the listeners did not understand a word he said, they applauded when he came to the name of ' Wagner,' and even tried to help us in giving three-times-three—that mystery no foreigner can understand; and I am sure no less than twenty people came and asked me what was the meaning of all that noise.

When this 'pleasing duty' was over, a number of musicians began to play, which set the feet of all the young people in motion. The little waiter, throwing his napkin in a tree and turning down his cuffs, asked M—— to allow him to dance with one of his daughters, a request willingly acceded to, as at this fête it is understood that all classes are to mix freely and dance with one another. French, German, Swiss, and Italian ladies danced with the peasants; but not one English. They all sat on a wall looking on with high-bred indifference, until one of the young ladies who lisped condescended to polka with 'her bwother.' M—— tried to talk them into a more genial mood; but 'They didn't wike,' 'They were twired,' 'It was so twoublesome dancing on the gwass;' and at last, out of all patience with their stiffness and exclusiveness, he caught up his baby, and executed a galope with him on his shoulders.

About five o'clock the company began to break up, and by six, M——, who remained to walk home with an English gentleman who was his frequent companion in mountain excursions, and whose agreeable wife must be mentioned as an exception to our national frigidity and pride, told me that at six there was nothing left of the fête, but 'the newspapers and chicken bones.'

Before I quit the subject of the *vendange*, I will
endeavour, for the benefit of the uninitiated, to give
a short account of the process employed in the wine-
making here, and a description of the clumsy old-
fashioned wine-press in common use. It is made
entirely of wood, and consists of two strong upright
posts, the one I saw being about twelve feet high
and ten apart, fixed in the ground, supporting a
cross beam with a screw in the middle. Between
the posts is a square trough on four legs, and in this
a perforated movable frame, for the reception of the
grapes, is placed, and then boards, whose dimensions allow of their being pressed into the frame,
and piled on the fruit till nearly on a level with the
screw, which is worked by two or more men, according to the pressure required. Each lot of grapes is
stirred up, and pressed three times; the juice, passing
into the trough, runs thence through a hole into a
large tub, which is again emptied into the barrels,
where it is allowed to ferment for ten days or a
fortnight before it is closed, and in six weeks they
consider it is fit to drink. The white grapes are
pressed as they are brought from the vineyards;
but the black, of which comparatively very few are
grown in the Vaud, are allowed to lie and ferment for
several days previous to the pressing, in order to

improve the colour of the wine. From the residuum a common sort of brandy is distilled, called *eau-de-vie-de-marc*, from the name given to the pressed grapes; and if kept some years—a rare occurrence in this country, as regards both wine and brandy—it has the flavour of good Cognac.

After the *vendange*, the chesnuts, which mostly fall off, have to be collected together, and then shelled; and to effect the latter, they are laid in holes scooped in the ground under the trees, in which a lot of combustible material, such as dried grass and fagots, has been placed, and after they have been covered with green pine branches, a light is applied to the grass and sticks below, and they are left to burn till the fire has spent itself, by which time all the prickly husks have burst, and come away easily enough. These fires are always lighted as near as possible to the trees, which, being prone to decay, are said to derive great benefit from the smoke. Scarcely ever do you see a chesnut tree without the main branches having been cut away from premature decay; and it is curious to notice the number of boards, that I at first thought were notices to warn off intruders, nailed like plaster over the wounds left by the branches having been cut or torn away.

H

CHAPTER V.

Pierrabessa—Salines—Strong-minded Women —Crinoline—
A Bad Road—Light in Darkness—La Grande Rencontre—
Fatiguing Ascent—Maison-de-Cuite—Cray-Fishing—Ducking
a Dandy—Valley of the Rhone—Encampments—Pests of
the Country—Vipers—Cure for Palsy.

THE first autumn I spent at Bex, not being in
very robust health, I was not able to take many
uphill excursions with the rest, and accordingly
revenged myself by exploring all the nooks and
unfrequented places I could discover in the valley,
and in this way saw so much that otherwise might
have been thought unworthy of a special visit, that
I had no reason to regret the circumstance of my
compulsory abstinence from more toilsome or more
exciting rambles. One day, in passing through a
wood about a league from the village, I remarked
with astonishment the immense fragments of rock
strewn among the trees, and whilst speculating upon
the how and when they came there, I found myself,
after reaching the top of a hill where the trees were
less dense, close to a stupendous mass of stone, and
of the most extraordinary shape. The part that

reared itself above the ground on which I was standing, was about twenty feet high; and on going to the edge of the hill, that seemed to make an abrupt descent on each side of the rock, for the purpose of examining it more narrowly, I found, to my alarm, that I was leaning on the edge of a precipice not less than fifty feet in depth, and formed entirely by the lower portion of the stone, that was cleft in two from the top to the bottom, the pieces standing perfectly upright, side by side, most probably in the position in which they fell. I found from inquiries that it was called the Pierrabessa or twin stone, and is certainly the most remarkable of those erratic blocks, so often met with in the Alps, supposed to have been left there by the retreat of an antediluvian glacier. I am not learned enough to give this on my own responsibility, and therefore think it better to state that this information was communicated to me by a queer old geologist and botanist in the neighbourhood, with whom I have had many a pleasant hour's talk.

I must not class my visit to the salines or salt-mines among the untrodden ways, as they are certainly the lions of Bex, and the source of any notoriety it may possess, the brine being brought thence through pipes for the use of the baths which,

like Parr's pills, are said to cure every disease under
the sun, and insure a long life.   In my life, I have
been some half-dozen subterranean journeys, and
frankly own that I never derived the least enjoyment
from any one of them·(not even excepting the
Thames Tunnel); and as I calmly review the matter,
I am afraid I must have been influenced by the
vulgar fear of being thought womanish and timid
(for in these strongminded days, nothing offends a
woman more than to be told she is possessed of the
attributes that belong to her sex and nature) if I
failed to accomplish what I was given to suppose so
many other ladies had done.   I am well aware that it
is very unfashionable to own to a dislike of anything
that is arduous, painful, or disagreeable; and that
to speak of experiencing unpleasant sensations from
remaining six hours underground, will appear absurd
and unmanly in the eyes of those gifted ladies who
believe, as one expressed herself to me, that 'though
the mental and physical powers of women are at
present inferior to those of men, there is little
doubt that, by a proper system of training, they
could be made equal, if not superior, to them;' and
it is no fault of mine, that my neglected education
leaves me only a woman, whereas if I had been so
fortunate as to have come into the world fifty years

later, I might have died an Amazon. I ought certainly to dilate on dangers and difficulties, borne not
only without murmuring, but with positive pleasure;
the guide should go into ecstasies at witnessing my
courage, and declare that no specimen of woman-
kind he had conducted through those labyrinths
had ever exhibited such cool intrepidity and unconcern: but truth compels me to say, that no
such delightful adventures came in my way. I was
only wet, dirty, miserable, and perhaps not in the
best of tempers with myself, for having been foolish
enough to undertake an excursion that was not to
my taste, though after it was over I was glad I had
been.

When we engaged a carriage to take us to the
entrance of the mines, about a league hence, the
driver said, 'Madame had better have as little
crinoline as possible;' upon which I rushed off to
the modiste's, and bought one of the tiniest dimensions for three francs and a half; over this I put
a grey linen skirt, and with my dress fastened up,
and a large Swiss hat, felt quite the thing; and,
presenting myself as ready, was not a little ruffled
in my self-complaisance by being told that my
crinoline was 'ridiculously large.' As we understood that we should have quite enough walking

in the mines, we thought it best to husband our
resources in that line until we reached the small
house near the wood, through which we had to
pass before arriving at the dwelling of one of the
overlookers, situated in a small clearing by the side
of a broad rapid stream, that was rushing and
foaming over its rocky bed, and carrying with it
thousands of logs of wood, to be collected lower
down in the river, for the use of the boiling-houses
that are more than a mile from the Salines.

At the entrance to the mines, one of the miners,
who take it in turn to act as guides to the visitors,
came forward with three lanterns, one of which he
gave M——, another to our driver, and the third
he kept himself; saying, with an awful squint at
my crinoline, that 'Madame would have enough to
do to get along,' and then, preceded by the rude
man and M——, and followed by the *cocher*, we
entered the gallery, which is about four feet broad
and seven feet high; but such a road! Along the
whole length of 6,600 feet, run wooden pipes, about
half a yard apart, which convey the brine from the
reservoirs to the boiling-houses. Upon each of
these pipes you place a foot, steadying yourself as
best you can, to prevent tumbling into the dirty
water that is flowing down the hollow way between,

a work of no little difficulty from the slipperiness of the pipes, wet with the oozing through of the brine. I did my best, however, and stepped out bravely, making a great noise with the heels of my boots, lest any of the party should discern the inward horror I had of putting my ankles out of joint, but unable to discover how it happened that, after stretching out my foot to take a long, valiant stride, it always came to the ground a short, timid one. Upon an average, I slipped off the pipes one step in six, splashing myself to the knees at each dip, and by the time we came to the first halting-place, I had knocked and twisted my ankles so unmercifully, that the fear I had entertained of being laughed at, especially by the man in the rear, who seemed to be afflicted at times with an inward choking that was rather suspicious, though it *might* have been produced by the damp, was lost in the pain from which I was suffering.

When we had traversed about two-thirds of this gallery, we were shown two reservoirs: the first circular, containing the weak brine, which has to pass through a process of concentration; the second square, and much larger, held the strong brine, which is conveyed direct to the boiling-houses without undergoing any intermediate process. A

little further on, where the gallery widened considerably, the guide held his lamp suspended over
the dark mouth of a pit, protected by a wooden
railing, and, telling us to look down, let fall some
lighted newspapers into the hole. I did as I was
told, and watched the flaming paper eddying round
in its descent, getting ' small by degrees, and beautifully less,' till there were left only the parson and
the clerk, and then nothing more; but though I
could not see it with my own eyes, I devoutly
believed all the man told me about the abyss;
namely, that it was of immense depth and extent, a
tradition existing that it had once been worked, and
yielded vast quantities of salt, and that it was said
there was still a large well at the bottom containing
brine, besides an exhaustless mine of rock-salt, about
a third of the way down.

After this we came to a turning on the right,
' which led,' I quote the guide, ' to a gallery
not now used,' and then to another on our left,
which was ' a ditto, ditto,' and to a pit that ' had
nothing more in it; ' and soon after the guide
stopped, and, holding up the light, showed us an
inscription on the roof, which said that in that
place, called ' *La grande rencontre*,' the workmen
employed in making the tunnel in which we were

standing, had met, having commenced at opposite ends. We then visited the galleries whence the rock-salt is obtained: and here the scene was busy and interesting; some were breaking into portable lumps the rock that had been extracted by means of gunpowder; others were wheeling it away to the reservoirs in the interior of the mountains, where it would be dissolved in water; while a third set were returning with the empty barrows. I can hardly remember into how many or what places we did or did not enter; I know that we ascended and descended a great many ladders, into chambers and galleries all having very much the same appearance; that once M—— disappeared suddenly from before my eyes into a hole, where the guide told me not to follow; and that, after leaving me standing at the mouth for a length of time that seemed interminable, he reappeared, and said he had seen nothing worth going down for; that then we turned into the main gallery or tunnel, and soon afterwards arrived at the bottom of a staircase in the rock Countruy, 762 steps leading to the upper mine of Le Fondement.

Here the guide stopped, and turning round, asked if we preferred returning the road we came to undergoing the fatigue of the ascent, which would bring us out at the top of the mountain. We chose the latter, by way of variety, thinking also that as we were in for it we might as well see all there was to be seen ; and, telling him to 'lead on,' commenced mounting the steps in the same rank-and-file order as before. This staircase and the upper passages were made a century ago, and before the practice of blasting the rocks by means of gunpowder was introduced at Bex, and consequently are extremely narrow : in some places I had to give myself, though none of the fattest, a good push to get through, and in others, where the steps were worn away, I had to haul myself up by clutching at M——'s coat, and scrambling anyhow I could along the black rocks down which water was trickling in all parts ; and from all these causes combined, I felt I was in about as dirty a state as could well be imagined. When we had mounted about halfway, the want of air, or fatigue, or perhaps both, brought on so painful and distressing a sensation at my heart, that I was unable to proceed, greatly to M——'s alarm, who, unable to get alongside of me, caught hold of my hat and then of my arm, holding me there until the spasm had passed. The guide said that it was not uncommon, even with gentlemen, to feel giddy and ill while ascending those stairs ; and as he afterwards told me that he had never known above two ladies accomplish the feat, I would fain believe that I was a bit of a heroine after all.

The upper mine is so very much like the lower that there is no need for giving a description of it, and I was not sorry, after threading another long and frightfully low passage, to see daylight peeping in at the distance. I had been stewed up so many hours in those dark places, that when I emerged into the sunlight, I felt like a friend of mine who, going to kirk in some village in the highlands of Scotland, had to listen to two services and two sermons in one sitting, as the minister came from a distance, and was anxious to get through his work without the interruption of the dinner hour, so as to get back home before dark; and such was the stupefying effect of the long six hours' preaching and singing and praying upon his brain, that when he got out of church again he actually believed it was the next morning.

As soon as I could see I cried out to M——, whom I had mistaken for a miner, 'What a mess you are in!' 'Ditto to you!' he replied, and going to a fountain, I saw that, black as were my clothes, they were not one whit blacker than my face. I made myself as respectable in appearance as I could by making a plentiful use of the clear cold water, in order that on our return we might be able to visit the evaporating

and boiling houses, the former filled with fagots
through which the weak brine filters three successive
times, the gypsum adhering to the twigs and presenting
a curious appearance. . In the boiling-houses I was
shown the salt ready for sale, of a quality and appearance much inferior to that we use for agricultural
purposes in England. The quantity of wood annually consumed at the *maison-de-cuite* is enormous,
almost incalculable. I tried to ascertain the exact
amount, but could not; and it is the great expense
incurred in fuel that renders the salt so high in price
—nearly five times dearer than with us. I was told
that salt brought from France was not only very
superior in quality, but could be sold at one-half the
price of that obtained from the mines here; and of
course I asked why they did not import all and close
the mines, when I was answered, with a look that
spoke the most touching pity for my ignorance, 'that
they were kept open for the national prosperity and
glory.'

One of our favourite amusements during the summer was cray-fishing, because to this we could take
all the children, who enjoyed the sport mightily.
As the fish don't bite till the heat of the day is
beginning to subside, we generally set off after an
early dinner, directing our steps towards some stream

that had a good reputation, not more than three or
four miles off, taking into our service one or two
lads on the way, whose use will be seen anon. As
soon as we reached our destination, our first care
was to cut a lot of sticks, fifteen or twenty, about
six feet long, with a slit in one end. Meanwhile
our Flibbertigibbets had been busy killing and skin-
ning frogs, one of which was inserted in the slit end
of each stick, which were then stuck in the water,
at some distance from each other, frog downwards
of course, choosing those parts of the stream where
the bed was stony, or shaded by bushes, the cray-
fish frequenting mostly those spots. Each person
should be provided with a small net fastened round a
circular wire inserted in a pole, and as soon as a fish
is seen clinging fast to the frog, a thing easy enough
to discover in the clear water, you gently insert this
into the stream with one hand, while with the other
you raise the stick, taking care to put the net in such
a position that if the fish loose its hold it will fall
into it. In this way you may catch some dozens in
an hour. Those who have never tried the sport can
have no idea how much fun and excitement there is
in visiting one stick after another to watch for victims—how everyone tries to catch the most—what
laughing there is when some fish larger than the rest

gives a nip with its claws to the catcher—how delighted everyone is (but the unfortunate) when a too ardent fisher gets a ducking.

On one occasion we were accompanied by Count T——, a Russian nobleman, who, turning out *en grande toilette* to catch cray-fish, was the subject of much raillery and merriment on the part of the young ladies, who one and all told him they hoped he would measure his length in the water before the day was over. M—— tried to persuade him to turn back and don more suitable garments, but all he could be prevailed upon to do was to turn up the hem of his trousers when he got among the rushes by the water-side. He was soon as deep in the sport as any of us, and far more eager, as it was the first time he had witnessed anything of the sort; and, like most beginners, he had better success than any-one else. The afternoon was half over, and there seemed no probability of the unkind wishes expressed towards him being fulfilled, when, stooping forward to seize a large one that he feared was about to escape him, he overbalanced himself, pitched head forwards into the stream, rolled over, and then lay on his back, where I declare I thought he was going to remain for the amusement of his tormentors, who were too mischievous to help him out, and only laughed at and teased him ten times more than before. What shouting and clapping of hands hailed him as he scrambled up the bank, the water dripping from his clothes, and shaking himself like a water-dog! what lots of pocket-handkerchiefs were in requisition to rub him down! and how he had to be trotted up and down like a horse, to keep him from catching cold! There is not much difficulty in getting dry, after a dip, under such a broiling sun, and I do not remember that any one of us ever caught cold from these impromptu bathings, or that Count T—— suffered any greater calamity from his, than the spoiling of his Paris clothes.

Sometimes we would take a carriage large enough to hold us all, as far as a little village about eleven miles off, in the valley of the Rhone, where there is capital fishing of all kinds, and then our preparations were more extensive, as we usually started early in the morning, and remained until sunset. We knew some good, kind people there, who had a small auberge, and to them we always wrote the day previous, so that boys and bait might be ready. To have seen our packing up before starting, one would have imagined we were going to encamp for the summer; first a large tent, which M—— had constructed expressly for these picnics, was made

fast to the hinder part of the vehicle; then a large
hamper containing provision and wine was stowed
somewhere under the driver's legs, enough fishing-
tackle of all sorts to have depopulated the Rhone
was laid in the safest place, a press for the flowers
that were to augment our botanical collection, and
books to amuse the idle, were placed under the
cushions, besides shawls and rugs to form a carpet
in the tent, and a bottle of ammonia in case of
stings from insects, &c. Without the tent it would
not have been possible to remain out-of-doors during
the middle of the day, as there is little or no shade
in the lowlands that border the Rhone, into which
flow the streams by whose side we pitched it.

All my life I shall remember with unalloyed
pleasure those happy days spent in the meadows
there, each one amusing himself according to his
taste, some looking for cray-fish, others angling,
collecting plants, flowers, and insects, or playing all
sorts of practical jokes on each other. When we were
hot or tired there was the tent to retire to, where
M—— taught them to make shepherd's pipes out of
the reeds, or the prettiest baskets with the bark of
nut-trees, and the long slender branches of the cle-
matis—'traveller's joy,' as we call it in the country
in England—that hangs in such marvellous profusion

from every tree and bush in Switzerland, and adds so much to the beauty of the woods and hedgerows; or, if it were autumn, he would send them to gather the stalks of the maize or Indian corn, and speedily we had a most musical fiddle, with strings and a bow!

There was one article *I* always took under my especial care, and that was a telescope, by the aid of which I could spy out all the châlets on the mountains, each in its little oasis of green, many perched on points that appeared inaccessible, until you searched further and discovered the little crooked path winding among the rocks. I could see the cows on the pasturages, and lower down the goats; the tinkle of their bells telling of their vicinity, even when the naked eye could not discern them. Amongst all these beauties and delights, must I say there were *désagrémens*? Without shawls, &c., we could not have sat upon the grass, every blade having its fellow grasshopper or cricket, millions and millions, hopping, skipping, and jumping, as no other creatures can, into your eyes and ears, banging against your nose, hopelessly entangling themselves in your hair, hiding in your clothes, where they remain until you take them off to go to bed, when dozens, some dead, but more alive, and as lively as

I

ever, drop on the floor, to reappear in the bed-
clothes next morning, and woe to you if, in the act
of sitting down, you happen to squash a few while
attired in a silk dress! They are of all colours,
some beautifully green, from the lightest pea to the
darkest olive, others scarlet and black, black and
yellow, blue, grey, brown, or wholly black, their
sizes varying as much as their hues; from the
myriads of large green ones a couple of inches long,
to the innumerable tiny creatures not much bigger
than a fly. No one can form the least idea of their
numbers without seeing them; to say that in the
grass they are as thick as bees in a hive, is no
exaggeration, and from their first appearance in the
spring, till they vanish at the commencement of cold
weather, they keep up an incessant noise night and
day; some make a whirring sound like a spinning-
wheel, but clearer, and more musical and pleasant
to listen to, especially as evening draws near, and
the other sounds of animal life are stilled; others
chirp like a bird, or click-clack like a watch.

Lizards are everywhere, but most where the sun's
rays fall fiercest, basking in the burning heat that
is their life; darting into their holes at your approach,
pretty agile creatures! many a one have we captured
and tamed, and one in particular, of the beautiful

green species, was so familiar as to follow my boys round the garden. They are the most harmless little animals in the world, and nothing can be more absurd than the alarm I have seen exhibited at the sight of them; my children nurse and fondle them like kittens.

In one of these fishing excursions, I was seated upon a shawl opened on the ground, watching the fishes, when I felt something creep up my arm under the large sleeve that I wore, and on searching to discover what was the intruder, found a large brown lizard, that had taken a fancy to the warm nest: and a woman at Les Plans told me, that one evening, after working all day among the hay, she returned home before her children, to prepare their evening meal, and whilst so occupied, felt a very strange sensation, as if some animal were running up and down her back; but as no one was in the house to look what it was, and to take off her garments was not only too great a trouble, but a luxury seldom indulged in, she contented herself with giving them a hitch now and then, till her daughter came home, when her dress was opened, and out jumped a lizard, she assured me, full twelve inches long.

I cannot say I admire the salamanders; they are so black, shining, and evil-looking, though I believe

they are harmless to man if not to lizards. The lads
who were with us caught several snakes, some of
which measured five and six feet in length; none
were poisonous, yet for all that, no one liked the
sight of them, and nothing could prevent the peasants
from killing them as soon as caught. Vipers are
numerous, but their retreats are mostly known; and
it is not often that you see them far from their dens,
nor do they show fight unless trodden on or attacked.
During all the time I have been here, I have never
heard of anyone being bitten by these evil-looking
creatures, of which numbers are killed every summer.
A chamois hunter, who lives at Frenières, about
3,000 feet up on the way to Les Plans, related to me,
that last summer, whilst getting in his hay, he fell
asleep in a corner of his field on a heap of dried grass
and leaves, and awoke fancying he felt something
move under him; being suspicious of the cause, he
jumped up pretty quickly, and on moving the grass,
discovered a nest of six vipers; five he killed with
the stick he had in his hand, and the sixth escaped.
An opinion prevails here, and, I believe, in some
parts of France also, that the melted fat of a viper
taken internally is a certain cure for the palsy. An
old fellow who lives like a hermit in a house he has
built himself at the foot of the Montet behind our

house, with no companions but a rabbit, that follows him everywhere, and a tiny dog, with a long bushy tail three times as big as its body, has killed scores of vipers in his life, and assured me he always preserved their grease for that purpose, but he could not tell me of any cures he had performed, though he had many to relate of the experience of others.

Such are a few of the drawbacks, if they can be called such, to the outdoor amusements in this lovely land, where, with a climate so delicious, the bare sensation of existence is almost happiness enough; where for seven or eight months of the year the radiant beauty of the day fades away, only to give place to the serener beauty of the night, that is scarcely less lovely; where flowers of rarest form, most dazzling colour, and most delightful perfume, gladden the senses at every step, and form a carpet brighter than the diadem of a queen; where every sound is replete with music, and every object, surrounded by such an atmosphere, a study for a painter.

CHAPTER VI.

'Charley'—Pedestrians—Les Bergères de Florian—Terrific Gale—'One Look was Enough'—'Beauty and the Beast'— Ascent of the Dent de Morcles—Guide—Bains de Lavey— Le Saut du Chien—Natives—Châlets de l'Haut—Alpine Dairy—Night in a Laiterie—Fleas—Chamois—Guide at Fault—Summit—Mind and Matter.

THERE are but few mountains in this neighbourhood that M —— has not ascended, and generally without a guide, though not always alone; though it is much more difficult to procure a good walking companion, than the numerous accounts of pedestrian excursions in the guide books would lead you to imagine. The majority of travellers do not walk, preferring the sitting to the upright posture, and the exercise of the gastronomic powers to that of the legs; and I have seen many a tourist come here, and remain several weeks, without extending his acquaintance of the place, or its environs, beyond the precincts of the hotel gardens.

I shall always remember one English couple, who used to sit, day after day, and week after week, on a seat, ' under a spreading walnut-tree,' in the garden facing the hotel; he with a newspaper, and she with

a novel, their backs to the sublime scenery, and their
four feet resting in a row on the low wall in front of
them, never conversing, rarely raising their heads,
and only moving when the bell sounded for dinner,
returning as soon as it was over to the same place,
the same attitude, and the same occupation. They
were of that class of persons who must be 'genteel
or die,' and the lady appeared to have carried this
principle to such an excess, that there would soon
be no more left of her, whilst the husband, whom
his wife called 'Charley,' was one of those stout
red-faced, red-whiskered young men, who, by sinking
their manliness in the endeavour to appear fashionable, lose the only pretensions to good looks with
which nature has endowed them.

It is not everyone who has 'Mont Blanc' burnt on
his alpenstock, that has been as far as Chamouni,
neither is it everyone who says he has ascended
snow-capped mountains, that has even reached their
foot. If the number of alpenstocks purchased were
a fair criterion for judging of the number of people
who put them to their legitimate use, I should not
dare to make the foregoing assertions; but as I see
that most of them serve only for helps in getting out
of the railway carriages, or ascending the steps of an
hotel, I am convinced that I am right.

Anyone new to the spectacle may be deceived by
the sight of parties of ladies—English of course; the
women of other nations, as a rule, don't walk—setting off in the morning to make the ascent of some
mountain 7,000 or 8,000 feet high, at an hour when
they ought to have been on the top, all got up so
prettily in fashionable walking costumes, looped over
the gayest petticoats, widened to the utmost by the
crinoline beneath, neatly-shod feet, very suitable for
a promenade in the parks, coquettish hats, inviting
the sun to kiss their faces beneath; while a prettily
painted tin box, for botanical gleanings, and a stout
alpenstock that might be going to do all the walking, complete a *tout-ensemble* at once effective and
interesting, reminding one strongly of Les Bergères
de Florian.   To see them set off under the guidance
of some son or brother of one of the party—generally a fair young man, with clothes a shade lighter
than his complexion—striding away at the energetic
pace peculiar to English ladies of the present day,
you imagine that they are going to perform wonders
before you lay eyes on them again; but if you
happen to meet them returning, you are struck with
amazement to find them looking just as fresh and
blooming as when they set out, no dust on their feet,
no soil on their gay petticoats, no weariness in their

step. I never could make it out, especially as those who *do* walk, and *do* scale mountains, never by any chance meet these showy parties of ladies up there.

Their botanical collections, too, are amazingly large, and have been procured in an inconceivably short time. I have known ladies exhibit pressed flowers they declared they had gathered not many days before, and take in high dudgeon the remarks of ill-natured individuals, who insisted that it was impossible to find such flowers at that time of the year; and coupling this with the fact that there is not a more thriving trade than the sale of plants, both dried and fresh, I don't *quite* believe all I hear about the frightful precipices climbed, and the dangers braved, to procure a fern or a grass. Still the best walkers are undoubtedly the English ; and among the men, one meets with many whose pedestrian powers might challenge the world.

M—— went many excursions with one of this class who I verily believe could have promenaded the globe without fatigue. Though rather a heavy man, he soon knocked up even those who had not above two-thirds of his weight to carry; and many is the unlucky wight who has had to turn back and retrace his steps alone, while the other has gone on his way rejoicing. You

could not name a mountain he had not ascended nor
a *col* that he had not passed over; the pleasure he
took in these feats being derived not more from the
scenery than from the exercise and the amount of
ground he got over. He was the only person who could
go 'in gleichem Schritt und Tritt' with M——; and
many are the anxious hours I have spent when they
have been benighted on the mountains, down which
I pictured them tearing at a tremendous pace, no
light, not even a star, to guide them, unless they
happened to possess a few lucifers in their pockets
with which they might be able to set on fire a
branch of pinewood.

Once they ascended the Chatillon, a mountain
6,000 feet high on the south-east side of Bex in a
wind that threatened to be the destruction of half
the village; but they had determined to go, quite a
sufficient reason for any madness on the part of an
Englishman. The violence of the gale was such, that
it often arrested their progress, tearing off branches
of trees and hurling them in their way, and creating
such a noise and uproar that they could not hear each
other speak, so that it was not without immense labour
and fatigue they reached the last pull before gaining
the summit. Here they described the wind as something awful, all their strength being required to keep

on their legs; but, believing that once on the top they should find a securer resting-place than the one they were on, they determined to persevere, the wind increasing at every step, cutting and blinding them with the sharp splinters of rock it blew in their faces. Keeping their eyes fixed on their feet, for they had no power to look ahead, they reached the top, to find to their horror that they were on a ledge of rock hardly broad enough to stand upon, descending on one side nearly half-way to the village of Lavey and on the other to the depth of several hundred feet. They took but one look, and then, with the quick instinct of self-preservation, threw themselves flat on their faces, clutching by the rock till a pause in the wind allowed them to creep backwards to some lower and less dangerous spot ; and since that time I have never heard either of them propose to ascend a mountain in a gale.

At another time M—— accompanied an elderly gentleman from London, who was ambitious of telling his friends on his return that he had accomplished so extraordinary a feat, to the Valleret, a mountain comparatively easy of ascent, and of about the same altitude as the Chatillon, but on the opposite side of the valley across the Rhone. M—— had been there several times, it being a favourite spot on account of the magnificent view you can get from it into Savoy, but on the occasion of which I am speaking it was late in the season, and snow had fallen so low as the pines that reach to within 700 feet of the top, and on emerging from the cover of the last wood, they saw in the snow, about 200 feet ahead of them, a bear reared on his hind legs, and rubbing his back gently against a pine that grew with some half-dozen others among the rocks. As they had no weapons, they did not waste much time in contemplating their unpleasant neighbour, who was fortunately too much absorbed in his pleasing occupation to notice them, and, thinking that discretion was the better part of valour, they turned on their heels without exchanging a word until they reached some châlets nearly halfway down the descent.

It was in one of these wretched châlets that they saw a girl, whom they described as so surpassingly lovely that, had the fact not been corroborated by the evidence of another gentleman (who, in speaking of the excessive ugliness of the majority of the Swiss women, said that the 'previous season he had seen a lovely exception, in a hut on the Valleret '), I should have been inclined to believe that the contrast with the bear (the last object seen) had heightened the effect of her charms. Being hungry they had opened

the door of the châlet to ask if they could have some
bread, upon which a girl, who was lying on a bed
as dirty as the room, came forward and told them
there was no bread to be got in any of the châlets, as
it was too far down to go and fetch it, but that she
could give them some boiled chesnuts which served
them instead the greater part of the year. M——
says that she was one of the loveliest creatures he ever
beheld, a sort of blending of the French and Italian
types of beauty, with a form that might have rivalled
Venus herself, but so extremely dirty, that when she
complained of being ill, and asked them to tell her
of something that was good for the headache, M——
told her that the fountain near the door contained a
sovereign remedy for such ailments, and that she had
but to drink some and wash herself well to prove the
truth of his words, which she accordingly did to their
infinite amusement, and not only came back cured,
but a thousand times handsomer.

It is a fact that amidst the prevailing ugliness and
deformity of the Valaisan women, you meet here and
there with a face of wondrous beauty, like a lovely
gem in a dark mine; but it is not the case in the
Vaud, where no women are to be found that, by the
utmost stretch of imagination, could be thought even
good-looking, though at the same time I must admit

that you do not encounter an equal number that are actually hideous.

It would be impossible to give an account of a tithe of the ascents M—— has made of different mountains since coming here; and indeed there must necessarily be such a similarity in the descriptions, all going up, up, up, and then down, down, down, with horrible precipices, hair-breadth escapes, enchanting prospects, &c., that I think one will suffice: and I have chosen the following, which he must relate in his own person, because it is one not often attempted, and I do not remember ever having seen it described.

'The *Dent de Morcles*, which constitutes part of the chain of the *Diablerets* and *Grand Muveran*, forms the boundary between the Cantons de Vaud and Valais, and, at an elevation of nearly 10,000 feet above the sea, is the most striking, if not the most beautiful, object to be seen from Bex. Thence its summit presents the appearance of two bare, dull grey peaks, rising abruptly and almost perpendicularly to the height of more than 1,000 feet out of the vast plain of snow that encircles their base. The nearer and lesser peak, by some eighty feet, has exactly the shape of a decayed tooth partly broken off, and is so steep that even in winter it is clear of snow a few hours after it has ceased to fall.

'Having ascertained from one of the boldest chasseurs in the Alps that to one possessed of a strong head an ascent of this mountain was practicable and not very dangerous in any part, save the lower peak, which I was warned not to attempt, I determined to try what could be done, and began looking about me for a stout active fellow, not so much as a guide, as to relieve me of the burden of carrying my knapsack. In general I trust quite as much to my own head and eyes as those of the guide, but this time, having heard that there were many tracks, and but one safe one, to reach the summit, I selected a young peasant who had more than once been pointed out to me as possessing a good deal of knowledge of the chain of mountains of which, save the *Diablerets*, the *Dent de Morcles* is the highest.   From his appearance no one would have imagined that he had an idea above his boots; his head was bent upon his chest, and he walked with a loose shambling gait that promised ill for mountain climbing: but for toughness and endurance he beat all I ever saw, trudging steadily on without uttering a word, never proposing a halt, and carrying my knapsack, which with painting materials, &c., could not have weighed less than forty pounds, for two days, without taking it from his back, and I believe would have slept with it there, if I had not insisted upon his unloading himself.

'We left Bex at 4 A.M., each provided with a stout alpenstock, and full brandy flask; and taking the high road that leads to the village of Lavey, about four miles off, celebrated for its thermal waters (accelerated by coal), where my guide, thinking, I suppose, that it was his last chance before coming down again, turned into an auberge, 'according to custom' he said, which externally presented the appearance of a cowshed, and internally a retreat for insane and afflicted persons, as I found even at that early hour a miscellaneous collection of crétins and drunken Valaisans assembled. My guide having called for a bottle of the nectar of the district, which gave me a better opportunity of hearing the sound of his voice than he had hitherto afforded me, it was placed on a long, dirty, deal board by a little woman with filthy clothes, red eyes, and the never-failing ornament of a goître.

'Having paid fifty centimes for the liquor, which the disgusting appearance of the hostess disinclined me to share, I was walking out to breathe the fresh air, when, observing that he had poured out two glasses, of which I was expected to empty one, and reflecting that the exterior of the landlady could not very well affect the interior of the bottle, and also that in all kettles there is some good tea brewed,

I raised the glass to my lips, and swallowed something, that made me feel as if I had been pickled; it was so sour and rough that my tongue was like a rasp, and my throat smarted as if a mustard plaster was in it—a sensation I did not lose till I had swallowed some snow I found lying in a hollow some hours later.

'[*Mem.*—Never to believe that the wine of the country will prove Chablis, because the guide smacks his lips over it.]

'I held my peace, however, lest my mule with two legs should not do honour to the house by following my example of abstinence, a circumstance I had no reason to be afraid of; for not only did he finish the bottle—thinking, I dare say, that I was drinking glass for glass with him—but he begged to be allowed to pay a turn, a courtesy I was compelled to decline, as I was already experiencing effects similar to those produced by a dose of Epsom salts. So I told him we must be off, as we had a tough day's work before us, and I wished, if possible, to reach the châlets where we were to sleep, in time to take a few sketches before sunset.

' As soon as we got out of the village, we turned off the main road, and struck into the low scrubby woods that are the only vegetation to be seen on

K

that barren and inhospitable rock, following a steep
and tortuous footpath winding in a remarkable
manner along the side of the mountain we had to
surmount before arriving at the village of Morcles.
In some places the roads had been destroyed by
avalanches; and where this was the case, we had to
use great precaution to avoid slipping down the
slides made by their fall. As the day advanced, the
heat became excessive, and we could plainly tell
that, when we should emerge from under the shadow
of the huge rock round which our way wound, it
would, as a peasant once said to us, "be hot enough to
melt the horns of a herd of bullocks." Several times
we crossed the pretty stream called the Avençon of
Morcles, which, tumbling and foaming along in its
steep descent, forms a succession of miniature cascades, and lower down takes an unbroken leap of
sixty feet over the rocks, and makes the pretty
cascades of Pisse-Chêvre behind the baths of Lavey.

'After two hours' walking, we reached a sort of
platform, where I was warned not to approach too
near the edge, as it projected considerably over the
frightful precipice below. This place is called "*Le
Saut du Chien*," from a dog having leaped over while
in pursuit of a hare that led the way. I am inclined
to think that every mountain in Switzerland has its

saut du chien, as every hill in England has its lover's leap; though my companion stoutly denied this impeachment, declaring that the place we were on was, like the old Eccles cake-shop, the " Original never removed." There was so lovely a carpet of grass and flowers in this spot, that I could not resist the temptation of throwing myself down for a few moments to enjoy the prospect.

'Right below me I could trace the valley of the Rhone, from Martigny to Lac Leman. To the left were Mont Blanc, Mont St. Bernard, the glacier and Gorge de Trient, the Fall of Sallenches, or Cascade Pisse-Vache, as it is more commonly called, and an almost countless number of Valaisan villages. Conspicuous from its extraordinary position, the two ends of the bold arch resting on the bases of the *Dents du Midi* and *Morcles*, which there leave only just room enough for the river to force its way through, was the old Roman bridge of St. Maurice, with the fortifications, ancient castle, and guard-houses at either side. In front of me towered the mighty *Dent du Midi*, its immense glaciers and cruel-looking peaks, that have from time to time been the cause of so much destruction and desolation in the smiling valleys beneath, now lighted by the glorious morning sun, that, while it gave a bronze

tinge to the naked rocks, threw a shower of
diamonds on the snow. Lower down than the
snow, the eye could trace the graduated scale of
vegetation, beginning with scrubby, isolated shrubs
and patches of scanty verdure, increasing in number
and size as they neared the pines, gradually softening
into the oak and beech-woods, to be succeeded by
the rich green of the chesnut and walnut-trees,
that reached to the fields full of the numberless
crops of varied colours that, from a bird's-eye view,
make an Alpine valley appear somewhat like our
great-grandmothers' best patchwork quilts.

'To the right of the *Dent du Midi*—to my thinking
one of the most beautiful mountains in Europe, as
in its triangular form it presents to the eye the
exact model of what we imagine a Swiss mountain
ought to be—lay the town of Monthey; and I could
follow, in all its windings, the zigzag road leading to
Champéry, through the lovely valley *De l'Abondance*, its sides covered with thousands of châlets,
its green pastures, limpid streams, and air of thriving
plenty, presenting a picture worthy of the Arcadian
age.

'We continued our route through a narrow gorge
till we reached the village of Morcles, which consists
of from fifteen to twenty châlets of the rudest pos-

sible construction, lying in a hollow from which there is no view save of the rocks by which they are surrounded. The village is almost choked up with débris of all kinds that has fallen from the mountains; and from this cause, and the dilapidated appearance of the dwellings, that are perched here and there wherever a hold could be got on the solid ground, some leaning a little on one side, some on another, it presents exactly the appearance of a place that has been shunted there by an avalanche.

'For nearly a quarter of an hour we searched about for one of the human race who could tell us where we could procure something to satisfy our hunger; but, seeing no one, we addressed our questions to two fowls, that presented the same decayed appearance as the habitations, but without meeting with any response, as I found they did not speak the language of the place; and on searching further, happening to look through a gate that appeared to lead to nowhere, I saw what at first I believed to be a pig sitting on its haunches, but what on a closer scrutiny I found to be a real native, who condescended to answer my enquiry, four times repeated, by telling us that we could get bread and cheese at a house just underneath our feet: and as we thought that scrambling down the loose stones, indicated as the path by a jerk of his thumb over his shoulder from our intelligent acquaintance, was a tedious mode of locomotion, we jumped on to the roof and dropped to the ground in front of the open door, to the alarm and astonishment of an old woman bent nearly double with another goître and more dirty rags about her, who was making soup in a kettle like a witch's cauldron. She was so deaf, that I had to shout with all the force of my lungs, "I want some *milk* and *bread* and *cheese*," before she replied in a very low voice, that "if we would go through a door to the left we should find a room to sit down in, and she would bring us what we wanted there." After we had appeased our hunger on the hard black bread and still harder cheese, that had to be chopped, not cut, and were smoking our pipes, I remarked that after all one might have a worse place to sleep in, as it was tolerably clean and furnished with a large bed, besides sundry articles of men's wearing apparel of all shapes and sizes, suspended from a beam, that might possibly come in useful; but no sooner had the words left my mouth than I felt something walking over my feet, and, looking down, I saw no fewer than eight mice quietly partaking of the crumbs that had fallen from our feast.

' After an hour's rest, we started again, much more

refreshed by the copious draughts of water we had imbibed from the fountain near the door of the châlet than by the sour wine at Lavey. The heat was soon insupportable; and the road soon ceasing to be a road at all, we were obliged to follow the bed of a torrent so steep, so choked up with immense rocks and trunks of trees, that we had the greatest difficulty in making our way, crawling on hands and knees, and leaving a good deal of our epidermis on the sharp projections. The footing was often so insecure, through the looseness of the stones, and the decayed nature of the blocks of wood that had rested there perhaps for ages, that in a few seconds we often slipped back a distance it had taken us a quarter of an hour to mount. We were soon wet through with wading in the water and stumbling into holes where the water was deepest, and were not a little pleased, after scrambling up a horribly steep and dark ravine, to find ourselves at the entrance to a small wood, through which a narrow path, like a sheep-track, led us to the bed of another torrent, this time a dry one. This sort of progression, *à la qua-drupède*, with now and then a rest in the shape of a march upright when we came to a thicket or more level bit of rock, lasted till we reached the *châlets de l'Haut*, where we were to sleep.

These châlets are really sheds for the cows that
are sent there for summer pasturage; and in one of
them, not one whit better than the rest, live the men
who have the care of the cattle, and the making of
the cheese and butter. For this trouble they are
paid six francs for every cow, besides a percentage
on the produce of the dairy. When the cattle first
go up to these pastures, usually the end of May or
the beginning of June, the yield of milk from each
cow is ascertained as near as possible by weighing it,
and at the close of the season, never later than the
beginning of October, the cheese and butter are
divided accordingly. These beautiful pasturages
abound all over the Alps, and have been the means
of affording many a welcome refuge to weary
travellers.

'There were two rooms devoted to dairy purposes;
in one the cheese and butter were made, and in the
other they were stored; but if my readers are pic-
turing in their mind's eye a delicately sweet, clean,
bright dairy, such as we so much love to see in England, they would be wofully disappointed could they
be transported into one of these mountain *vacheries*.
In this one, which was a fair sample of all I have
ever seen, all the light came from the door, and
there being no chimney, merely a hole in the roof,

the walls were begrimed with the smoke ascending
from a wood fire required for the cheese-making, made
between two stones on the floor, that was formed of
rough lumps of rock stuck in anyhow, many with
spaces between full of water or whey. There was
no furniture of any kind, not even a stool, and I suppose none was needed; for as soon as the work is
done, the men creep up a ladder like those to hen-
roosts, slide into the loft, which is not nearly high
enough to kneel in, and lie there till work begins
again. The dairy utensils, all of wood, were beautifully clean, and the milk and cream of a richness
and flavour far superior to any I have ever tasted
at Bex.

'The men were very civil, making up a good fire
to dry our clothes; and when that operation was over,
I went outside, as there were still two hours more
daylight, to take some sketches and enjoy the magnificent sight of a sunset amongst the mountains. The
view from this point was immense; the whole ramifi-
cation of Mont Blanc, lighted by the Alpenglühen,
appeared as if by one bound you could clear the
space between and alight on the summit of 'the
monarch of mountains,' though the distance could
not have been less than thirty miles. Lac Leman I
could trace to Génève, and by a shortening effect of

perspective all the hills directly below me appeared
level with the valley, and immensely increased the
apparent extent of the plains bordering both sides of
the Rhone. When I had gazed my fill, I rambled
round the châlets and made acquaintance with a lot
of goats, amongst which I was astonished to find
some with four, five, and even six horns. When I
got back to the *laiterie*, I found my guide fast asleep,
stretched full length on the uneven floor before the
fire; and not succeeding in rousing him by shouting,
I tried the experiment of a *coup de pied*, on which
he turned round and said quite simply, "You woke
me by coming in;" a remark that convinced me he
had not felt the kick, and must be endowed with the
skin of a rhinoceros.

'We had a good supper of delicious cream, cheese,
and bread; after which we all squatted round the
fire—a luxury always very acceptable at that altitude
after sunset—for half an hour, talking and smoking
our pipes, and then crept to our dormitory above the
cowsheds, where the shepherds told us we should
find some fresh hay. We threw ourselves down
without undressing, intending to start at two o'clock
so as to reach the summit by sunrise; and no sooner
had my head touched the hay than I was asleep, and
dreamt that scores of people with goîtres were prick-

ing me all over with pins, the heads of which were formed of smaller goîtres: and at the moment of intensest agony I broke away from my tormentors, and awoke to the reality of my dream in the shape of myriads of fleas, feasting away on my body as if they had not every day an opportunity of tasting foreign dishes. After several fruitless attempts to sleep, I crawled down and lay before the fire, where I managed to get some very unrefreshing sleep. As for my guide, he slept like a dormouse; and soon after two o'clock I had to renew my experiment of the preceding night, which had the effect of making him rise so quickly that he bumped his head against the rafters and bobbed down again on the hay, where he lay for full five minutes in utter bewilderment.

'After swallowing a bowl of milk, we started in good earnest, soon leaving the châlets far behind us, and taking a narrow path in better order than the one we had traversed the night before, leading among fallen rocks and scrubby bits of almost lifeless trees, in half an hour we were ahead of the last signs of vegetation, and thence we traversed the side of a range of nearly perpendicular rocks, where in some parts the ledge that we had to walk on was little more than a foot broad. On our right were precipices, and on our left our shoulders touched the wall of rock not less than a hundred feet high. We advanced slowly and with extreme caution until we gained a platform, where we stood still for a few moments; and whilst there I saw on a rock to my left some hundred feet above me what at the first sight I believed to be a goat; but almost before I could call the guide's attention to it, I saw it leap from its place on which it had been resting over a gap not less than twenty feet broad and alight on the rock the opposite side; a feat that told me at once it was a chamois, even before the guide shouted it out to me.

'From this platform we kept along a goat-track for about half a mile, and then all traces of footpaths, even of animals, disappeared. At this point, being rather at fault, I thought I might as well test the much-talked-of abilities of my companion as a guide; for hitherto I had led the way while he had resolutely kept in the rear, without hazarding a remark as to whether I was going right or wrong: so, turning to him, I said, "Where next?" to which he replied by shaking his head, and then, after a long pause, during which he scratched his head and stared up at the sky, he let fall the words, "The path is gone." There was no help to be got from him, so I resolved to put into practice the first geometrical axiom, and turning myself towards the summit, I signed to my man, guide no longer, to follow; and up we went, climbing on our hands and knees, making use of all sorts of projections to assist us in our ascent, often pausing for want of breath, not daring to look behind, but keeping our eyes on the summit, red with the eastern glow.

' About an hour of this desperate exercise brought us to the last rock, round which we turned and scaled with more ease, possibly because it was the last, than I had imagined possible, and we were on the top of *La Pointe au Fâvre*, eighty feet higher than its fellow peak, which gives the name of *Dent de Morcles* to the mountain. There we remained only long enough to trace out the road to be taken to reach the lower peak, a more difficult task than the one we had accomplished, but presenting no such formidable dangers and difficulties as I had been led to expect. Descending from our elevation as rapidly as we could, we found that in order to cross the chasm between the two, we must pass along a narrow ridge of rocks with scarcely room to place one foot after the other, where, with the *glacier de Martinet* on one side, and multitudes of ragged peaks broken by the thawing of the snow on the other, if one lost his balance the

other could not have been of the least assistance to
him.   Each one took care of himself, I keeping my
eyes on my feet till about two-thirds over, when
feeling a giddiness coming over me, and knowing
that I must conjure up a strong will or be lost, I
looked resolutely down on each side of me, and the
result proved that determination was all that was
needed to overcome the vertigo.   After some ten
minutes of this tight-rope dance, we reached the end
of the ridge; and then there was only about 200 feet
of easy climbing straight ahead, and our feat was
accomplished.

'We threw ourselves down ; I to regain my breath,
as for the last half-hour I had been sensible of an
increased quickness of respiration: and I may remark
that it was after I passed the elevation of 6,000
feet, as near as I could guess, that I first felt this
unpleasant sensation, which continued until I was
within 1,500 feet of the top, when it left me, and
returned as I was climbing the last peak.   Notwithstanding that the sun had risen a couple of hours
when we reached the top, I felt it piercingly cold,
as soon as the glow produced by the severe exercise
had passed away, and I was compelled to swallow
some brandy before I could enjoy the sublime scene.
My companion, who like myself had not eaten any-

thing that morning, set himself immediately to work to diminish our stock of bread and cheese—an occupation which he appeared to think far more sensible than getting into ecstasies with the scenery; and doubtless he was right, as far as he was concerned, for he had more than once seen pretty much the same from a lower elevation, and would doubtless have many opportunities of doing so again, whilst I might never more have a chance of beholding a prospect that, in my opinion, is unrivalled even in Switzerland.

'The first object my eyes rested on was, as usual, Lac Leman, like a sheet of burnished gold, with the Rhone issuing from it at the further end, running its course, now hidden by hills, now reappearing, until it was finally lost in the mountains of the Jura. Two thousand feet below me on the right was the *Lac de Fuilli*, black and gloomy, in a hollow on the top of a mountain, like an extinct crater; further on towered the Grand Muveran, with its three glaciers, looking massive enough to crush the world. At its foot, the lovely valley of *Les Plans*, and the village of Frénières, lay smiling in their verdant oases of emerald green; and next to the Grand Muveran, the Diablerêts, the highest point, the Oldenhorn, wrapped in its eternal white shroud, frowned in stern and savage grandeur upon the desolation and ruin made by their fallen brethren in the valleys below. Mont Blanc, lighted by the morning sun, looked one smooth mass of snow; and the mighty Rhone, on the near side of the lake, seemed so shrunk in volume, that, as it rolled its slow course through the dimly-lighted valley, I could compare it to nothing but a single grey hair in a thick black wig—a very mundane comparison to suggest itself on those heights; but it came, and the reader can make a better if he please.

'After remaining on the top nearly half an hour, we commenced our descent by a path I had discerned leading by the *Lac de Fuilli*, that was quite as grim and dark on a near inspection as at a distance; thence we passed at a rapid rate down some steep rocky declivities, through some pastures, a wood, the bed of a torrent, down some more rocks, then through another wood and another pasturage, and by some châlets, into a better path, and finally reached the village of Outre-Rhone about two o'clock. There we had dinner, doing justice to the homely fare afforded by the little auberge, my appetite being no longer disturbed by the contemplation of the sublime, and arrived at Bex, nine miles off, soon after five.'

CHAPTER VII.

Picnic—A French Countess— Christening a Cascade—Fré-
nières—Les Plans—Pension Bernard—Search for Snow—
Snowballing in June—Exciting Pastime—The Lost Child—
Happy Valley—Interior of a Châlet.

WHEN I look back on past events, my life appears
as a varied landscape, in which the mountains, the
most prominent features, correspond to those bright
and happy portions of my existence on which the
memory first seizes; the chasms and abysses so deep
and sombre, to the dark and troubled times from
which my thoughts involuntarily shrink; and the
level plains, to those more tranquil periods, during
which my existence moved on without variation or
disturbance. Some few days there are, brighter
and happier than any others, that are more clearly
defined in my remembrance, like the mountain-tops
that are the first to hail the rising sun, and the last
to wish him good-night; and most assuredly, of all
these, the one on which I love most to dwell, is a
day spent in a picnic *aux Plans*, 'the Elysian

L

fields,' as my children have christened the place, where afterwards we spent the golden time of the mountain summer in such perfect happiness, that to speak of it calls up the extremest sensations of pleasure and pain ; for, in the recollection of such a time, there is always mingled the apprehension that days so bright can never come again.

Before I give an account of our long sojourn there, I must let my readers share this picnic, the most enjoyable of all the many we have enjoyed there. It is not always that our good intentions with regard to picnics are crowned with the success they deserve; there are so many conflicting elements that come into opposition, or are cruel enough not to take into consideration all the trouble and concern you have undergone to arrange the affair ; such as the weather, which is decidedly unfavourable to such parties, and must, I think, be a member of some so-called religious sect, opposed to rational amusements amongst the people; the tempers, tastes, and health of the company; the falling lame of one or more of the horses as you are just on the point of starting ; besides many minor annoyances, such as the hamper containing the champagne, or the ham that was to have flavoured the cold chicken, having been left behind through the carelessness of a

domestic, or a little jealousy among the ladies: but this
time all went merry as a marriage bell—a simile that
does not hold good here, where they ring none on such
occasions. The weather was superbly lovely; nothing
was forgotten, because we helped ourselves; everybody was in health, good temper, and high spirits;
and even the little baby, who must go everywhere,
and might have been voted a nuisance by crusty old
bachelors and antiquated spinsters, only added to the
general enjoyment by his merry tricks and good-
humour.

Crowded picnics being a nuisance only second to
crowded dinner-parties, I never invite more than
six in addition to our own rather numerous family,
and on this occasion we had but four, the two Counts
L—g, *père et fils*, who had been summoned, the one
from Lisbon, where he was attaché to the Prussian
embassy there, the other from his estate in Silesia,
to see the brother-in-law of the elder who had been
taken seriously ill at the Hotel in Bex, and being
a millionaire, was worth looking after; and the Count
de C——, with his new young wife, dressed *à la
Louis Quatorze*, the gayest of gay Frenchwomen, who
had a mortal dread of horses in any shape or place,
and as she couldn't walk or wouldn't walk, from dis-
inclination or coquetry, or a spice of both, was con-

stantly jumping in and out of the carriages, now
riding a little, now walking a little, now leaning on
one gentleman's arm, now on another, then enticing
her husband to carry her a *little bit,* and saying and
doing such grotesquely absurd things in her real or
affected alarms, that it was impossible not to laugh
at her, and like her too, as she was the best-tempered
little creature possible. The count, whom she had
married after a seven days' acquaintance, the alliance
having been arranged by the heads of the respective
families according to the French mode, had lately
purchased an estate in the neighbourhood, about a
mile and a half from Bex; and as she usually
visited us every fine day, and dared not for worlds
venture in the carriage, her pedestrian powers,
though still nothing to boast of, had considerably
improved since making our acquaintance. With
the exception of the Countess and the baby, which
she nursed as a child would a doll, exclaiming,
'*Qu'il est joli!*' '*Qu'il est charmant!*' 'Leetle
darling!' all the English she had learned, to every
one who approached her, none of us made much
use of the carriages during the ascent to *Les Plans,*
which occupies three hours when there are no unnecessary delays.

The morning was too fresh, too beautiful, the

scenery too *riante*, to permit us to be idle, and there were too many lovely flowers to be gathered and delicious strawberries to be eaten. How lovely the Avençon looked! Not the Avençon of Morcles, but of La Varraz, a snow-fed stream and the most picturesque in the world, rushing, foaming along; now forming the most enchanting cascades over the huge rocks that lay in its course, now white as the snow from which it springs; there widened to the dimensions of a goodly river, and here narrowed almost to a stride by the contracting of the gorge through which it forces its way. It is our companion all along the route, nearly on a level with us as we leave the village; but as we turn round the mountain among the beech and chestnut woods, we hear and see it hundreds of feet below, winding in and out until it meets us again at Frénières more lovely than before, when we again say good-bye to it for a time, but without losing the sound of its musical murmuring, and cross it once more as we turn into the valley of *Les Plans*.

The boys had their butterfly nets, and many a lovely prisoner was caught that morning, that met with an untimely fate, to have its beauty preserved and admired after death, an enviable immortality for a butterfly. I have quite forgotten to mention three

very important members of our party, who certainly
were not the least amusing nor the least admired,
namely, two Mont St. Bernard dogs and a little
Spitz that we had brought from S——, who was so
fond of the strawberries that it was always a race
who should reach them first. Sometimes we called
a halt to count and collect our scattered forces:
for though the road is a good one, the precipices are
steep; and among such a mad-cap company, one
might have taken a fancy to a roll head-over-heels,
or a bath in the Avençon.

When we were about two-thirds of our way to
Frénières, we stopped at the pretty waterfall that has
been called after M— since our first visit to Bex,
for the purpose of rechristening it in due form, and
drinking to its prosperity in the pure element; but we
all sobered down a little when we passed from under
the shade of the beech woods, and had to trudge the
long reach of level ground, with the sun shining
full upon our heads, that extends for nearly two
miles before and after reaching the village of Frénières, though there are some delightful resting-
places by the way even there: one a fountain with
two streams of water; one slightly warm, at which
the most timid water-drinker might slake his thirst;
the other icy cold, and said to be the purest stream

in the district; and another, a clump of cherry trees with fruit as sour as the morella, and for that reason all the more acceptable to hot thirsty travellers.

There is no more lovely collection of châlets in the Alps than those that form the village of Frénières; and nowhere do I remember having seen the rich brown of the wood of which they are constructed contrast more finely with the grey rocks and dark pine forests than at this spot, where everyone must stop to admire, and envy the lot of those whose ' lines have been cast in such pleasant places.' After passing the saw-mill beyond the village, you are sure to meet numbers of women and children with baskets full of the most tempting raspberries they have been gathering on the hills cleared of timber, and are only too glad to dispose of at the low prices asked, 3*d.* and 4*d.* for a basket holding from two to three quarts. We laid in a stock of fruit from these Pomonas, and were not sorry to enter the pine-woods soon after, where we found Count Fritz, who with our youngest girl had gone ahead of us since the cascade M—, seated on an immense rock in the midst of a splendid waterfall, the melting of the snows greatly adding to the beauty of an object that in the fall of the year cannot boast of enough water to drown a kitten.

About half a mile further, we came to a place

where there is a stout rail fastened from tree to tree
to prevent persons falling down a frightful precipice,
narrow, but 200 ft. deep, and as straight as an arrow
down to the river: and here the two Counts L——
commenced upheaving stones, which they rolled to
the edge, and then pitched into the abyss beneath.
This pastime was quite a passion with them both,
and it seemed quite as impossible for them to
pass a precipice without stopping to crash some
rocks down it, as for Lulu, our Spitz, to see a
mouse and not kill it. It was quite delightful to see
the eager boyish zest with which they searched for
the biggest rocks they could move; the excitement
with which they followed the huge mass as it smashed
along, and at last leaped into the torrent. At the
bridge of *Les Plans*, the road divides; the right-
hand branch continuing to ascend the sides of the
mountain till it reaches the Plateau of the *Pont de
Nant*, where we were to dine: the other, crossing the
bridge, passes in front of the châlets which form
the hamlet of *Les Plans*, and again joins the main
road after forming a semicircle of about half a mile
in length.

I must not stop now to describe *Les Plans*; I should
linger too long, and we were all ravenously hungry:
so, after leaving the carriages at the châlets, with

directions to the *cochers* to follow with the hampers
as quickly as possible, we resolutely shut our eyes to
the deliciously cool-looking *pension* of Madame
Bernard, that seemed to invite us to enter and dine,
and set off at a *one-o'clock pace,* as I have heard it
called in Manchester, to get over as quickly as possible the mile and a half of hard walking that still
separated us from the *Pont de Nant and our dinner.*
But by the time we reached the last strong pull of
five minutes' hard climbing, more than one was
inclined to think it would have been better to have
yielded to the seductions of Madame Bernard's cool
shady dining-room *out of doors,* as you see them in
many a mountain châlet.

Up the steep bit we went, scattered over the hill
like a flock of goats ; and even the little countess,
inspired by the examples around her, valiantly
clutched an alpenstock, and vowed she would ascend
unhelped and alone ; but, alas for the instability of
all human resolves, and of a countess's in particular !
she had not achieved half the distance to the top,
when she uttered a piercing scream. Her long dress
was fast in the ground with the point of the alpenstock
stuck through it, and she could not move a step.
Down rushed the gentlemen, and after an infinite
variety of stratagems she was set free, and carried,

nolens volens, to the platform where the rest of the
party were already seated on the soft turf, cooled by
the sight of the glaciers, and discussing which was
the most convenient and agreeable spot to dine in;
as if anyone ever dined on that plateau but at the
picnic stone, to which we old frequenters of the place
led the rest; and then snow must, be procured to ice
the champagne, when it arrived; and accordingly
Fritz and the boys set off up the narrow valley to
the right, where they were sure they should find
some *in no time*.   I said nothing to damp their
ardour, but as soon as they were off, I told Count
L—— that, on my last visit there about a month
before, I had seen in a hollow of the rocks, not a
great way off, a large quantity that had collected
from the falling of avalanches, and that if he would
take a basket, I was sure he would be able to fill it,
and be back again almost before his son was out of
sight.   So off he set with the rest of the children in
high glee at the idea of stealing a march on Fritz;
and in less than a quarter of an hour I saw him
returning with enough to supply a Lord Mayor's
feast, which he exhibited in triumph to the ' boys,'
who did not come back for nearly an hour, after
having searched in all the nooks and crevices without discovering any but a very small quantity, and
that awfully dirty.

But all this time no dinner came. 'The drivers must be getting drunk.' We had been there an hour, and no signs of them, and we were just sending off Count C——, who, being the fattest, had most need of exercise, in search of the hampers, when we caught sight of the men in the road below, walking as leisurely as if there were no appetites to be satisfied. Away we all ran to quicken the approach of the eatables; and what a rush was made on the cold sausage and mutton when they were unpacked! I was obliged to keep guard with a large knife and fork to prevent it being devoured before the cloth was laid, and get M—— to distribute lumps of bread and cheese to take off the edge of their appetites before attacking the meats. The champagne had been delivered over to the tender mercies of Count C——, and when all was ready we fell to with appetites that would have seasoned a horse. What a merry dinner that was! Never was there a more joyous one, and everything was *so* good. The burgundy just suited the cold mutton and chicken; whilst the champagne agreed with the sausage; and the punch, concocted by M——, was just the thing to aid digestion after the quantities of bread and cheese with which we finished up the meal; after which we fell to eating the snow in lieu of ices, and

then, as the gentlemen would keep all the cold coffee
to themselves, we began snowballing in June; a sport
that was kept up for full seven minutes, and then
was terminated by everybody laughing till he was
too weak to play any more.

Then the cigars and pipes, the countess smoking
her cigarette, were brought out, and a rest of half an
hour prepared us for a walk we proposed to take to
the *châlets du Nant*, as if any of us ever entertained
the slightest idea of being able to keep up an even
amount of energy, in the gay humour we were all
in, sufficient to carry us over a league of the
roughest ground imaginable; but no one, of course,
expressed a doubt of their capabilities, and would
not, I am convinced, if a proposal had been made to
scale the Grand Muveran before sunset! Everybody wanted to carry the baby, who had partaken
of the chicken in the shape of a drumstick, and the
contest ended in Count L—— carrying him off in
triumph on his shoulders, looking like a Hercules
with an infant Cupid. ' *Quelle horreur!* ' screamed
the Countess, as she stumbled among the rocks
with which the narrow valley, sometimes little more
than a gorge, is everywhere strewn; giant Titans
that have lain there for ages, some half buried in
the earth, and covered with the loveliest verdure,

mosses, flowers, fruits, the scarlet strawberries peeping out so invitingly from the green, forcing us to
linger and gather; sometimes the path, which the
feet of generations had worn in and out among the
rocks, wherever they were so fallen as to admit of a
passage, led down to the stream, with the pretty
name of *Eau Claire*, which joins the Avençon below
the *Pont de Nant*; and of course everybody wanted
to drink, being thirsty after the sausage; and some
mischief-loving child sprinkled Count Fritz's face,
who returned the compliment in kind, which led
to everybody sprinkling everybody; and then the
Countess, being 'used up' by her protracted exertions, and having exhausted her stock of exclama-
tions, declared she could not move an inch further,
in proof of which she sank down all of a heap;
and then the good Count L—— proposed to carry
her Lady Lancheon fashion, and after a seat had
been constructed, she was lifted on to it by Fritz,
and transported gaily enough till her two bearers
began to think it no joke carrying eight stones on a
rough road up a rising ground, with the thermometer
at ninety degrees, and a halt was proposed, and we
set to picking strawberries, while the elder Count,
who had spied out a hill covered with loose boulders
that were just the thing for rolling, crossed the

stream by a bridge of snow formed by an avalanche,
and having ascended the mountain opposite to a
considerable height, commenced his favourite pastime. To have seen him striding away at such
a tremendous rate up those steep places, among
loose stones, catching here at a bush, there at a
firmer piece of rock, one would have imagined he
was under thirty, instead of nearly sixty, and we all
agreed that we should like to know his secret for
preserving to that age a frame so vigorous and
elastic, a face without a wrinkle, and hair unstreaked
with grey. 'Look out there below,' he holloaed
out in English, as he discharged one stone after
another, and hurled them down the hill, tearing up
the soil, sometimes splitting other stones in their
course, or stopping short against a tree, but oftener
leaping with tremendous bounds into and over the
stream. After about ten minutes of this exciting
game, he mounted still higher, and disappeared in a
wood ; when Fritz, the best of sons, took it into his
head to go in search of him, if the girls, who were
always up to any amount of mountain-climbing,
would go too, the rest promising to wait till they
returned, which one of the party was very near
doing pretty quickly, having rolled back many yards,
without further damage than a few scratches ; and

before they were far on the ascent there was the Count again pushing before him a stone large enough to crush a house, with which he was to give an effective finale to the exhibition.

By the time all were collected together again, we discovered that the sun no longer burned so fiercely, and that if we were to make any stay at *Les Plans*, it would not do to have any more lingering in the narrow valley, and we accepted without murmuring the excuse afforded by the Countess's inability to use her feet, and turned our faces homewards, though we stoutly persisted that, if it had not been for *that*, we should have reached the pasturages and drunk our cream. But where was my eldest boy ? Not two minutes before, I had seen him stepping from rock to rock, collecting plants and insects. ' He could not be far.' · ' No harm could have come to him.' ' He was so careful, and there was no deep water near.' Such were the consolations uttered in my ears as some ran this way and others that, shouting his name, no answer but the echo coming back to us ; and just as our alarm was becoming serious, appeared the kind Fritz with the lost child, who, it seems, had lingered behind, occupied in his absorbing pursuit, and, not hearing of our change of plans, had gone on towards the châlets, until he began to think we were long coming up with him, and was retracing his steps, when he met Count Fritz; but, alas! he must be punished for lingering—he had been admonished not to do so before, and this threatened painful termination to our day's pleasure was near casting a cloud over our happiness, when our united pleadings effected a sort of compromise—the question to be settled by a jury on our arrival at *Les Plans*.

The discussion was hardly ended by the time we reached the picnic tone, the countess managing, with the aid of two gentlemen and a stick, to crawl all the way, and even ventured to return thence to the hamlet by a much more difficult but more picturesque path than the one we took in going, leading by the bank of the Avençon. *Les Plans* was bathed in a flood of golden sunlight when we reached it, and we were glad to sit down on a bench under the overhanging roof of Madame Bernard's beautiful châlet. We declined the good old lady's hearty invitation to enter, preferring to sit outside and inhale the fragrance of the little garden that separated her châlet from that of her neighbour's, a venerable but active octogenarian, who was busy among the bachelor's buttons, fuchsias, sweet williams, and lavender-trees, with which the borders were filled. As we looked on the lovely scene, the little plain, nowhere half a mile broad, so brightly green, nestling among the mountains, the châlets so picturesquely placed in an irregular semicircle almost at the foot of the hills, covered with richly-wooded pastures that bound it to the north; while, on the opposite side, the Avençon, fringed with trees, forms a graceful curve within the boundary of the mountains, that seem to touch the skies,—we said to one another that no sweeter spot could be found on earth.

At the eastern end rise the Argentine and the Grand Muveran, its glaciers of *Plans Nevé* appearing to touch the woods, filling the space between the hamlet and the *Pont de Nant*; while to the west, if you mount a gentle rising, you can see far, far away, over hill and dale and river, till the eye can see no more. 'Let us come and spend the two hottest months of the summer here,' I exclaimed to M——. Why not? 'The next châlet was to let,' said Madame Bernard; and away she trotted across the garden to speak to the old lady who was now examining her fine stock of bees that sent forth a ceaseless hum, and speedily returned with the intelligence that we could inspect the châlet, which we almost filled, as everyone must give an opinion upon its merits. It was pronounced 'delightful,' 'so primitive,' 'so pastoral;' there we could at last realise our long-

M

cherished dream of living *à la Suisse.* The long,
low, narrow, dark kitchen, extending the whole
length of the dwelling, with an immense flat stone
laid on the ground in lieu of a cooking-stove, at
which it was impossible to distinguish fish from fowl,
was pronounced superior to all modern inventions.
What soups we could concoct there! what pâtés in the
tourtières! What darling bedrooms, two leading out of
the kitchen with roofs not six feet from the floors,
and tiniest articles of pine-wood furniture! What
fun to go out into the court, ascend by a ladder to
the remaining bedrooms, two leading from a balcony,
while a passage, so low that your head described a
right angle with your feet in walking through it,
conducted to the others that looked over the plain
across which the people were coming to milk their
goats. There were enough rooms, and one to spare
for visitors; the Countess would come and play the
Phillis if we could find a Corydon. There was abundance of everything; a stack of wood, and all so clean,
that before we set off on our return to Bex, we
had agreed with the owner to take it for the remainder of the summer, our engagement to commence in a fortnight.

Then Madame Bernard brought some wine to
drink all sorts of good wishes for our stay there, and

a jury was empanneled to try the little truant, who defended himself and was acquitted, on pleading that he had not been *behind* but *before*; and when that was over, the carriages were ready, and there was a contest with the Countess, who dared not go home unless we allowed her to have a seat in our vehicle drawn by a sober old horse, whose steadiness she had once before tested; and accordingly she mounted by the side of M——, declaring she dared not allow anyone else to drive her, and in her fear holding his arm so tightly, that it was pinched black and blue for a week after. The pedestrians reached Bex before us who were in the carriages; and as we gave our charge into the hands of her husband, who was awaiting our arrival on the steps of the hotel, she kissed us all on both cheeks, and vowed she would buy the ' *bon cheval*,' that had brought her down so safely.

CHAPTER VIII.

Strange [Laws—Debtor and Creditor—Prince Vladimir—
Prince and Principle—Better than a Duel—Suspicion—
Affecting Leave-taking—Dupes—'A Leaf from Charivari'—
Rather cool.

AMONG the queer laws in this canton, those relating to the recovery, or rather non-recovery, of
debts are not the least curious; and when one has
learned how next to impossible it is to force payment, one wonders still more at the extraordinary
amount of credit a stranger can have among the
people, who every season lose what to them are
considerable sums, from the cupidity of dishonest
travellers, who, aware of the laxity of the law in this
respect, come here expressly to take advantage of it:
and the most astonishing fact of all is that the
sufferers never appear to grow any wiser from experience, but allow additional bills to be run up by
the very individuals from whom they have been
unable to obtain payment of former accounts.

Usually, the utmost that is done in the way of

endeavour to recover a debt is to ask for the money, *and very politely too*, without the shadow of a threat, that every debtor knows is writ in water; but if a creditor *is* so cruel as to take the case before the Court and judgment be given in his favour, the law enacts that he can apply for an order to seize either the person or the effects of the delinquent: but there are so many tedious delays and difficulties in the way of getting the order, and when got it is so easy to be evaded, that most people prefer to wait and trust a little more, in the hope of matters mending, to proceeding to extremities, which after all is only throwing good money after bad. But supposing that an order *has* been got to seize the effects of a debtor, he has only to protest against the seizure, and the affair is quashed, until judgment has been given against him a second time: and this farce can be repeated once more before the unfortunate creditor can touch a sausage, or, if he have a fancy to securing his person instead of his goods, the arrest must take place after sunrise or before sunset— a regulation, one would imagine, made expressly to allow the rogues plenty of time for escaping to the neighbouring canton of Génève, where no one can touch him, or if he take it easy and surrender, the creditor has to pay a franc and a half a day so long as he remains in prison ; and then, when the term of his incarceration is expired, he walks out, and the poor creditor cannot afterwards touch a *centime*.

Hotel-keepers incur the heaviest losses; and the only consolation they ever receive is in being told by the Court, 'that if they had not trusted so much, they would have lost less ; that it was simply *un abus de confiance,* and they ought to have presented their bills earlier, and then they would have known whether the person in question intended to pay ;' a proceeding that would not be productive of the desired result if all landlords were as kind and as tenderhearted as my friend Wagner, who, especially if the poor devil pulled a long face, would be likely to trust him ten times more, and lend him a hundred francs into the bargain. If an hotel-keeper have a suspicion that all is not right with a visitor, he has the choice of two alternatives : one, to turn him out of his house and lose all chance of getting his money; the other, to seize his luggage. And it must be stated, that if the *suspecté* has a wife, she can save whatever she claims as her own from getting into his hands, and send off as quickly as possible to the principal town in the canton for an order from the Tribunal Cantonal, authorising him to detain it until his bill be paid; but if this order should not arrive in twenty-four hours from the moment of seizure, the owner can claim his goods, and be off, blessing his stars that at last he has found a land where rogues go free.

Since coming here, I have seen and heard many cases of swindling, of such cool, unblushing, barefaced impudence on the one side, and so much easy, unsuspecting, simple confidence on the other, as could not be equalled in any other country in Europe. One of the most amusing was an affair that happened last summer but one ; and I have selected it from among many others, as it seems to illustrate more things than the unworldliness of the cheated. Not many weeks before our picnic at *Les Plans*, I was passing in front of the hotel with M——, and, seeing him raise his hat to a dark, short man, wearing a red fez, whose age could not have exceeded twenty-three, was told that it was a prince of Montenegro, brother to the Prince regnant, whose reverses, together with the sufferings of his brave people, were just then exciting a good deal of public interest. Naturally, I was curious to know why this Prince Vladimir was absent from Montenegro at so momentous a time—a question that, it appeared, had been asked by others as well as myself—and was always met by the reply, 'that from a very early

age he had always held the severest republican sentiments, and had preferred to resign his right of
succession to the princedom, and leave his native
country for ever, rather than abandon his principles.'

All this was very fine, and the bait took immensely;. never was there such a noble young man,
quite another Brutus—doubly admirable for such
sublime abnegation, after having been reared in the
lap of despotism! He was very fond of talking of
his good friend Lord Derby, with whom he boasted
he had travelled in the East; and as to crowned
heads, there was not one in Europe with whom he
was not on the most intimate terms, and whose
genealogy he could not give you to the remotest
generations. So interesting a prince beat all the
princes of all the fairy tales put together; how
could he fail to be immensely popular? Fine and
titled ladies languished for his smile; fair English
girls thought themselves only too happy to be
favoured with a *billet doux,* slipped under their
plates, appointing the witching hour of twilight for
an assignation. Staid, heavy, middle-aged, official
Herrn, with sentimental Frauen, found themselves
suddenly bereft of those pleasing attentions they
had been accustomed to receive from their gentle
partners, who were now always engaged riding and

walking with the patriot Prince Vladimir. Poor fellow, he was like a cat in a tripe-shop, quite *en embarras de richesses*, having the pick of all the ladies, who chimed so pretty a chorus in his defence against the envious insinuations of Count T——, who one day, when the Prince was absent, ventured to say he was not quite sure of his being a prince at all, and backed up his assertion by quoting M—— as one who held the same opinion.

This was repeated to his Highness; who, the next time he encountered M—— in the coffee-room, stalked up to him, and, bowing profoundly, said, 'I understand, Monsieur, that you have had the goodness to observe that you do not believe that I am the Prince of Montenegro, and I shall be glad to be favoured with your reasons for entertaining such an idea.' 'Certainly,' replied M——, bowing also. 'My reasons for thinking you are not the Prince are, simply, that I have never before seen royal personages eating and drinking at the same table with common travellers in the restaurant, in preference to taking their meals with the rest of the company at the table-d'hôte, nor using their fingers in lieu of a pocket-handkerchief.' 'Monsieur,' exclaimed the Prince, in a furious passion, advancing with his hand in a menacing attitude, 'if you were

not a married man, I would call you out.' 'Pray
don't let that be any impediment,' said M——, 'for
it certainly would not prevent my killing you; but,
before I do that, I will show you something else;'
and, letting go the arm he had grasped to arrest
the threatened blow, he took hold of him under the
arms, lifted him off the ground, and gave him so
tremendous a hug, that his Highness roared for
mercy. This squeeze so effectually cooled his warlike ardour, that no more was heard about fighting;
and a few days after he walked up to M——, holding out his hand, begging he would accept his friendship, and allow him officially to present the Prince
of Montenegro to Monsieur D——. To which
M—— made answer, 'Allow me to return the compliment, by presenting Monsieur D—— unofficially
to the Prince Montenegro.' After this affair, the
Prince frequented the table-d'hôte, and was no
longer to be found mixing with the occupants of the
restaurant, becoming doubly popular, spending large
sums, that is, running up large bills, in ices and
champagne, with which he liberally treated the
visitors, organising picnics on a grand scale, and
creating an unusual animation in the photographic
trade, from the number of portraits presented to
him, as *gages d'amour,* by his fair admirers, who,

as he shrewdly observed, 'must be dazzled by his title, for he was sure he had no good looks nor fine manners to recommend him.' Monsieur Wagner did not take quite so good-humouredly as usual the well-meant warnings of officious friends, who thought he had better look a little after the state of the Prince's pecuniary affairs, as rumours were oozing out of his owing various little bills for perfumery, toilette-wares, and various knickknacks in which great people indulge their fancies, besides some spiteful tales of his having borrowed money, and largely too, from more than one fair friend.

At last, when he was beginning to be openly laughed at for his credulity, and had had a three months' visit from the interesting stranger, who talked of 'living and dying in the free air of this republic,' without seeing the colour of his money, Monsieur Wagner did tell him, as politely as if he were taking a great liberty, that 'he should be obliged if his Highness would settle a portion of his account, as he had some pressing payments to make.' Upon which Prince Vladimir flourished before his eyes a letter from his Princesse Mère, in which she gave him the sorrowful intelligence of his brother's illness: and following it up by exhibiting a telegram he had that morning received from Kossuth, Mon-

sieur was quite satisfied that he was what he pretended
to be, and retired quite ashamed of himself. Though
his Highness could speak and write most modern
languages, his correspondence was so voluminous
that he needed a secretary, who was soon found, a
Monsieur C., giving up an excellent situation as Chef
de Gare, to accept the more brilliant one of 2,000
francs a month. It would be laying claim to too
much penetration and foresight, to say that we had
doubts respecting so distinguished a personage, when
so many wiser and nobler people came to grief.
But I may mention without presumption that when,
three or four weeks after engaging his secretary,
whose office appeared to be a sinecure, he was setting
off for a three days' séjour at Génève, in order to
meet his suite, who were to return with him, we
did venture to say that we thought it probable we
should never set eyes on him in Bex again. His
departure, though but for three days, was described
by an eye-witness as 'intensely interesting, quite an
ovation;' ladies in tears waved their handkerchiefs,
waiters stood bowing around, and Monsieur Wagner
respectfully attended him to the door of the omnibus
to wish him 'bon voyage.'

There could be nothing wrong when he had left
his luggage behind him; and, moreover, Monsieur

C——, his secretary, being a fast friend of Wagner's, would soon report if matters began to look suspicious. At the end of the three days, the secretary returned to prepare apartments for the suite, whose non-arrival still detained the Prince in Génève, and he had sent on Monsieur C—— to announce his speedy return, and see that Monsieur Wagner had all in readiness for his reception, as a prince attended by a magnificent suite was a very different person from a prince *incognito* and alone. There was some talk in the village about the disappearance of a wealthy widow of fifty, who had been missing since the day the Prince departed for Génève; but no one ever dreamt of coupling her flight with his, until it was discovered that she had been seen promenading with him more times than was prudent, and had converted her property, one of the finest in the village, into ready cash a few days before she left. Still the illustrious personage was expected back hourly. But, alas! the hours grew into days, days into weeks, and no tidings of him. The poor secretary was nearly mad, for, besides the loss of his situation, he had lent his Highness 1,000 francs. Monsieur Wagner consoled himself by thinking of the luggage, which was opened after three months, and found to contain three paletots, four old shirts, and one red fez. But they were not the only losers. Many a lady, whose gay attire had made her the envy of others of her sex, was forced to practise rigid economy for a length of time before she could make up the losses she had sustained through obliging his Highness with various sums at different times.

The week after the Prince left Bex, a cartoon styled 'A Leaf from Charivari' appeared at the hotel, in which the leave-taking with the fascinating stranger was so broadly caricatured, and had so painful an effect, that many ladies, and not a few husbands, lost their appetites, and, soon after discovering that the air of the place did not agree with them, took their departure, greatly to the relief of the host. The buxom widow, who was supposed to have accompanied the Prince, returned to Bex fifteen months after, minus most of her cash; but as she never complained, and always declared that she had been visiting some friends in England, who had advised her investing her money in the funds, *where she had lost it*, no one had any business to enquire further.

Nothing more was heard of Prince Vladimir till a year after, when a lady, who had been staying at the hotel when the events related transpired, met him in Marseilles; and he had the cool effrontery to en-

quire after ' le bon Monsieur Wagner, et tous ses
amis de Bex.' That the successful adventurer *was*
a Prince of Montenegro, there seems little reason
to doubt, not only from the numerous telegrams
addressed to him by noble and distinguished personages, but from enquiries made afterwards. But the
same enquiries elicited that his 'darling republican
principles' had made him such a naughty boy at
home, that his papa had sent him abroad to mend
his morals and manners, to find, I doubt not, like
many more parents who have tried the same dangerous experiment, that it is about the best way to
make bad worse.

CHAPTER IX.

Starting for the Mountains—Swiss Champagne—Setting to
rights—Beginning Life in a Châlet—The Swiss Hero—
Danger of Fires—Use of Flies—Impromptu Dinners—
Rambles and Scenery—Evening—Goats' milking—Raspberry
Mountain.

THOUGH it was midday, when all 'the village seems
asleep or dead,' half the population turned out to
see us set off for our summer's stay at *Les Plans*.
What an exodus it was! First walked the girls with
alpenstocks and various minor articles of luggage;
then followed a large wagon piled with hampers,
boxes, baths, &c., drawn by two fine horses belonging
to a wealthy farmer of Frénières, the *beau fils* of the
old dame who owned *our* châlet; next came the
carriage in which I and the baby were seated, forming but a modicum of the baggage with which the
remainder of the vehicle was crammed—bread, potatoes, hams, sausages, groceries, cooked meats, baskets,
shawls, umbrellas, camp-stools, easels, and a collection of miscellaneous articles that would have done
honour to a broker's shop; crowning all was a large

cage in which a green parrakeet screamed fearfully in its terror at being jolted up and down: at the back was fastened the baby's carriage, that, from tumbling on its sides, was minus all its paint long ere we reached *Les Plans*. . Our St. Bernard dogs, as usual when starting, bayed and howled as if an army of robbers was approaching; while the little Lulu, who had a weakness for little boys' legs, kept up an incessant skirmishing among the people until she had received a kick from a man whose son's trousers she had torn.   M—— and the boys came last, to see that nothing fell from the baggage, the garçons being useful in scotching the wheels when we halted in steep places.   As we passed the hotel, out came Wagner and his wife, followed by the waiters, to wish us '*bonne santé*;' and even the visitors opened the closed shutters of their apartments to see what was the cause of the unusual excitement in the village.   'Mind you don't starve us,' was my parting injunction to the host, as, knowing the difficulty of procuring fresh meat at 4,000 feet above the level of the sea, we had made an arrangement for him to supply us with any cooked eatables that were transportable in hot weather whenever he sent up a carriage with excursionists.   From almost every house came people to gaze at our cavalcade, and many were

N

the stoppages made to be shaken by the hand and
receive the polite expressions of good-will of which
the French language is so prodigal.

The day was insufferably hot, the commencement
of five weeks of the most scorching weather I have
ever known, even at Bex; the horses were maddened
with the flies that bit them till the blood ran on the
ground, and for the first two miles the poor tortured
animals could not go many paces without stopping
so abruptly that I was nearly pitched on their backs
in their desperate attempts to get rid of the pests.
Their tormentors did not leave them till we got
within the shade of the woods, long before which
the horses were so covered with boughs that they
were like Macduff's army coming to Dunsinane.
Through the weight of our luggage we were much
longer ascending than usual, but no one, however
hot and tired he might be, found the way too long.
There was always a shade on one side of the road at
least, lovely rills and fountains of iciest water at
which to drink, and fruits for those who would take
the trouble to gather them.

At Frénières we halted for half an hour before the
house of Monsieur G—— to feed his horses, ourselves
preferring to sit in the meadow under the cherry
trees, from which the owner slashed down the fruit

for us with his whip, to entering the house, though it was so clean—generally speaking, one finds a marked improvement in this respect as one mounts higher—that it was almost too great a temptation to resist; and when asked to descend into the cellar and taste Père Giraud's champagne *à la Suisse,* we did not wait to be invited twice: and I advise my readers, if ever they are in Switzerland and tempted in like manner, to yield to the soft impeachment. This wine, being put into the casks and closed up before the juice of the grapes has undergone any fermentation, is so effervescent that it cannot be bottled, but is drawn as wanted from the barrel, which is made of extraordinary strength and covered with iron to prevent bursting, as instances are known of their exploding and causing death to persons who happened to be near. I sat down on the steps of the cool cellar whilst I drank my rosy champagne, and learned what I have related about its manufacture.

As soon as we passed the saw-mill, everybody rushed off right and left in search of raspberries, returning with such marvellous accounts of the quantities seen and eaten that I hardly could believe them, until higher up I saw the heavily-laden bushes hanging over the rocks where they had been cut away to form a road. I don't think I ever felt more glad than

when we crossed the rude little bridge and turned
into the peaceful valley: the prospect of spending a
considerable time there with those dearest to me
among the pastoral simple peasants; the tranquil
aspect of the spot, its green plain looking greener
and fresher than ever now the hay was gathered; the
rustic châlets, each with its little plot of garden,
some as blue as the heavens above with the borage
that the people prize for its healthful virtues; the
hush, the quiet, the repose, not a sound being heard
above the murmur of the Avençon,—were so captivating, so soul-subduing, that for a few moments I
knew not whether I was experiencing more of pleasure or pain.

Our approach roused the citizens from their afternoon's torpor, for assuredly no one had ever before
seen 'such a getting up' there.   Worthy Madame
Bernard hurried across to help us; her son, with
half a dozen others, lent a hand to the unloading; old
Madame Giraud, who was to live during our stay in
a tiny room like a box she had built at the back,
lighted a fire, and set the tall coffeepot-shaped
kettle on to boil in readiness for tea: one of the girls
unpacked the provisions; another carried the other
articles, as we turned them out, into the respective
little chambers; a third held the baby, while the

boys transported the eatables into the cellar, 'such a jolly place they had found full of rubbish,' of course entered from outside and as far as possible from the door of the house—for the benefit of the health of the provisions, one would suppose. Many willing hands make light work, and by the time *goûter*, that is tea, was ready, we had stowed all away save the cases, that were to find places under the tremendously high beds—so out of keeping with the low ceilings—to serve in lieu of chests of drawers. The bedroom opening out of the kitchen near the fire, and appearing from its worm-eaten floors and walls to be far more ancient than the rest of the house, contained a large old-fashioned buffet, which had to do duty as wardrobe, linen chest, and store-room for groceries, preserves, &c.; and as, next to the kitchen, it was by far the largest apartment in the building, the big bath was placed there, a man named 'Christ,' a baptismal appellation not un-common among the Bernese, having been engaged to fill it twice a day, and bring as much more water from the fountain in the centre of the valley as we should require for other purposes; his wife too would wash for us, and the rest of the work was to be done by ourselves.

The fire, as I said before, was made on a large

rough stone raised about eight inches from the
ground, and it had been a matter of no small
speculation amongst us as to how any cooking, save
by boiling, was to be done there; but we found the
most cunning devices in the way of pans, tourtières
with hollow lids in which are put red-hot embers,
for cooking stews, ragoûts, cakes, &c.; skeleton iron
stands, some shaped like the old-fashioned articles,
for keeping buttered toast warm, our grandmothers
called spiders, once so common in everybody's sitting-room in England—others formed of an iron ring
on three legs attached to an upright bar resting on
the edge of the stone that supported the immensely
long handle of the frying-pan fitting in the iron ring
over the fire.   There were pans in brass and iron
and copper of every imaginable size and shape, and
all with three legs! and when I saw that all the
little stools for sitting round the stone, and all the
coffee-pots, and teapots, and jugs, had three legs too,
I began to think that there was some mystery in
the matter, and on seeking for an explanation was
told there was an order of freemasonry among them.
At first we were a little puzzled, not to say bothered,
with our new-fangled culinary articles, and our
gipsy's fire; but by dint of a little endeavour, and
the occasional calling in of the old lady, who was

proud to be appealed to, we were soon 'to the manner born;' and before a week had passed there was not one of us who did not vote ovens a bore, and would not have exchanged our big stone, on which we could make half a dozen wood fires if needed, for the finest kitchen range ever invented.

We dined in the kitchen near the door, it being the only unoccupied place in the châlet large enough to seat us all, and 'Madame's bedroom,' said the old dame, curtseying, 'is the best for a salon,' when we needed one, as it contained a sofa stuffed with grass and covered with an old yellow and scarlet chintz, a barometer long ago spoiled, a chest of drawers minus all the handles, and eight coloured prints, with narrow black frames, of scenes in the life of their great hero—'Tell shooting the apple from the head of his child;' 'Tell escaping;' 'Tell shooting Gessler,' &c.; in all of which he was represented as a pink-cheeked man with fat short legs cased in yellow pantaloons, and stout body clothed in blue coat with brass buttons and red waistcoat.

Long before going up to *Les Plans*, we had agreed that as it was to be a holiday, a time of enjoyment for each and all of us, no more work was to be done than was necessary for the comfort of all parties in the house, that early rising was to be the order of the

day, and that if visitors came they were never to
interfere with our occupation or previous arrangements.

As soon as we had taken our first meal in our
new home, we sauntered out to take a survey of the
little hamlet, that seemed quite transformed in our
eyes now we had taken up our abode in it. We
no longer regarded the gardens for their beauty alone;
it was of far more importance to discover if good
vegetables and salads grew in them; and the lovely
châlets covered with roses and fragrant honeysuckles,
once contemplated only as adding greatly to the
beauty of the landscape, were now criticised by us
matter-of-fact housekeepers, who lived in one of the
same, as to the number of rooms they contained,
their dimensions, &c. As we strolled up the rising
ground from which you have a view of the valley in
which Bex lies, we found many more châlets than
we had seen before nestling in the hollows or among
the trees, and my lads ran to give me the joyful
intelligence that they had discovered a cobbler at
work in one of them, an artisan whose good offices
were generally needed before those of any other
handicraftsman.

 That night, as we were preparing to go to bed,
amid much laughing and merriment, while arranging

a procession by candle-light to see the majority of
the household out of doors before shutting up, the
old lady came in to beg 'that we would not carry
any lights across the yard, but make use of the lanterns,' of which some half-dozen were hung against
the wall—a necessary precaution where fires are of
such frequent occurrence and the buildings are constructed of wood. In all the towns in this canton,
a person found walking in the streets with a lighted
lantern of which the glass is broken has to pay a fine
of six francs; and in St. Maurice, where the houses
are packed very closely together, no one is allowed
to have a fire burning after seven o'clock P.M. When
we came to compare notes next morning, we found that
each one had encountered the same difficulties in the
shape of the height and hardness of the beds and
lowness of the roofs. I, for one, had quite a sore
cranium, with bumping against the latter in getting
in and out of bed, before many days were over, a
misfortune it is impossible to avoid; and the grass
mattresses—the only *down, up* there—though sweet
as a nosegay, are as hard as the boards to lie upon,
and I don't see but what the latter would do as well
but for the name of the thing. I had been told that I
should be almost eaten alive with all sorts of insects
in the châlets; but, with the exception of fleas, which

were of a size and number to delight the most ardent
tamer of those active little bloodsuckers, I saw
none to complain of. Want of cleanliness was certainly not the cause of their populousness, for no
Dutchman's dwelling could have owed more to soap
and sand and elbow grease than Madame Giraud's
châlet ; they are in the wood, and indeed most places
in hot weather, and great is the annoyance they
cause to those luckless individuals for whose skins
they evince a decided preference.

Grasshoppers no one heeds, as they only bite your
clothes, evincing a great partiality for white garments,
in which they bite innumerable little holes no bigger
than a pea. The obstinate flies visited us after a few
days, and then there was no need of a tocsin to wake
us in the morning ; there was no sleep for anyone
after the sun had risen and roused them up. You try
every imaginable dodge to frighten them away; duck
under the bed-clothes till you are nearly smothered,
and think biting from flies preferable to death in
the blankets; cover your face with your handkerchief,
fight frantically in your half-awakened state with
pillows or anything you can lay your hands on,
always fancying in your dozing rage that *one* detest-
able individual is the cause of all you are suffering,
and only consoled by the thought that when you *do*

catch him, *he* will catch it too; then slumber off again
through sheer exhaustion, to be thoroughly awaked
on feeling the smarting of a hundred stinging you at
once, and at last jump out of bed anathematising the
whole race, to discover, on approaching your open
window, that they have done you good service in getting you up, and believe that at last you have found out
the use of those creatures you had before been accustomed to look upon as sent only to plague poor man.
Would it not have been a sin and a shame to have
remained in bed on such mornings as we had up
there, each one more glorious than the rest? How
deliciously fresh and cool the air blew in at the doors
and windows! while down at Bex we knew the
people were half dead with heat that had burned up
all vegetation, and at *Les Plans* the pastures were
green as in spring. We had heat and sun enough too,
and found it pleasanter after eight or nine o'clock to
sit sewing or reading under the low eaves that keep
the rooms always cool, besides affording an agreeable
shade to the benches beneath, than taking active
exercise.

Everybody was up and astir between four and five;
when what a making of beds, and plying of brooms
and dusters, grinding of coffee, boiling of eggs, till half-
past six! at which hour we breakfasted with appetites

sharpened by exercise, the open door affording us a
peep at the valley, looking so bright and blooming
that it might have been made over again during the
night. When breakfast was done, one *sided all away*,
while another made preparations for dinner, as,
though Monsieur Wagner did not forget us, there
was always soup to make, salad to gather and prepare,
vegetables to stew—not boil in water, as is the ordinary
mode in England; and when *Les Plans* was not the
rage among the visitors, and no supplies coming from
Bex, we had to depend upon our own resources,
we had always the best dinners, and the most amusement, as the one whose turn it was to perform the
duties of *cuisinier* was bound to invent a new dish.
Perhaps some time the world will be gratified with a
new edition of ' Cookery by a Lady,' with thirty new
recipes from *Les Plans*. I remember that once
M—— improvised what was to be kept a profound
secret between him and the cook till dinner-time,
when there appeared an immense dish of potatoes,
in each of which a hole had been made and filled
with cheese; they were then roasted in butter, and
pronounced worthy of Soyer; but the quantity of
butter used was so enormous, that as it was never an
easy article to get, we begged him not to interfere in
the culinary department in future.

If we were minus the meat, we had always the soup to fall back upon, with dessert of raspberries and strawberries mixed with wine . and sugar, and cakes fried in the tourtières ; and with such appetites a king would have envied us our dinners. Our hunger was frightful, nothing appeased it ; and how good everything tasted ! None of us will ever again eat anything so good as the potato-soup, cold sausage, and cabbage salad. I never can forget the positive enjoyment it was to eat anything and everything ; dry bread was as good and better than the richest delicacies ; not one of us had a moment's illness ; we were busy, happy, and well, and to have remained in that state would have been to have realised the dream of an Arcadian age.

M. generally sallied forth with knapsack and easel on back as soon as breakfast was over, to some spot among the mountains, where he would remain sketching so long as the sun kept above the hills ; and as it was always my office to take him his dinner, I had the most delightful walks and rambles among the woods skirting the Avençon, and always preferred the old road by the river to the newer one higher up on the mountain-side, on account of its leading me for about a mile through the most charming and fascinating scenery it is possible to imagine. Nature

has been almost too prodigal of her riches in most
parts of this lovely land, but nowhere more so than
in that favoured spot. What lovely glades! What
splendid groups of beech trees and stupendous pines,
through which the sun slanted so richly on the soft
carpet of grass and mosses lying between the rocks
and stones beneath, giving a deeper ruby to the
strawberries that contrasted so charmingly with the
rich green! How the river rushed madly along, ever
and anon receiving additional force from the torrents
pouring into it from the sides, over which the path
was carried by means of rustic bridges formed of
trunks of pine trees, that added to the beauty of the
picture! The purple mountains seen above the giant
pines towering to a height that made me dizzy to
look up at; the peasants in their picturesque dresses,
among the hay in the meadows sloping down to the
opposite bank; the gorgeous butterflies, splendid
flowers, delicious perfumes; the pure air, so warm,
yet never oppressive, combined to form almost a
Paradise upon earth.

Very often we spent the whole day out of doors
among the peasants at work in the fields, or lending
a hand, and mouths too, to lighten the crops of late
cherries on the trees. Higher up on the slopes, we
wandered far among the woods and pasturages that

cover the swelling hills, reading, sewing, or playing
à volonté, the children amusing themselves by flying
down the smooth grassy slopes in the large wooden
sledges used for conveying grass from the mountains,
till we caught sight of M—— returning, when we
would descend and relieve him of his burden, those
who had been at home eager to show him the delicacies prepared for the evening meal, freshly-gathered
raspberries and strawberries, garnished with their
own lovely tendrils and green leaves, amber honey
in the comb, and cream from the dairy in the mountains.

When tea was over, it was time to go and meet
the goats, that every morning, as soon as it is light,
are taken from each hamlet and village by the
shepherds, whose duty it is to look after them, to
feed upon the grass growing among the rocks in
places inaccessible to heavier cattle, where they
remain until evening, when they are driven back to
their homes, to be milked and housed for the night.
As these pretty animals are very fond of salt and
fresh green leaves, we never omitted filling our hands
and pockets with a stock of both; and great was the
fun when they rushed up to us, knocking over *their*
little ones and *ours*, in their eagerness to get first at
the dainties. What butting and fighting there was

among the herd; and how they struggled to get free from the grasp we laid on their horns to pull them into the little wooden sheds where they were tied to be milked! All the peasants possess one or more goats; and a pretty sight it is, to see them returning from the milking, with their bowls filled with the frothy liquid, that, to my thinking, is much pleasanter to the eyes than the palate, though I know many who are not of the same opinion. Everybody knows how healthful it is, and numbers of people come into the mountains in summer for the sole purpose of drinking it. The little round goats' cheeses are palatable when neither too new nor too old, and that is the highest praise I can bestow upon them, as nothing can disguise either the taste or the smell that savours too much of an old dish-cloth to be agreeable.

Many an afternoon we spent on a hill cleared of large trees, but covered with raspberry bushes, to the left as you approach the Pont de Nant, pitching our tent on a level sward at the foot for baby and his guard, while the rest mounted to pluck the delicious fruit whose fragrance scented the air long before you came to them. As without seeing I never could have credited the quantities that grew there, I don't expect that any description I can give will convey to anyone more than a very imperfect idea of their profusion. My readers must imagine a hill as high as the Wrekin, if they have seen it, so thickly overgrown with raspberry bushes to the top that you have some trouble in forcing a way through them; fancy also every bough so laden with ripe fruit that they were bent down by the weight, and fell off by thousands as you touched them; and even if they are able to picture all this, they cannot taste how good they were, how much superior to any grown in gardens; nor will it do to mention how many we ate besides the basketsful we took home for tea, and boiling for puddings and cakes. In an hour you may have bushels, if you have but hands enough to gather them; we used them for syrup, preserves, creams, and anything we could think of, and after all large quantities were thrown away.

CHAPTER X.

Neighbourhood of Les Plans—Martyrs to Custom—Grion—A
Short Cut—Draught at the Fountain—Visitors—Novel Specu-
lation—Châlets du Nant—Moraines—Glacier de Martinet—
Swift Descent.

IN the immediate neighbourhood of *Les Plans*,
there are so many beautiful and remarkable scenes
and places to be visited, that, as a painter said to
me, 'a long life would not suffice for seeing all;'
and one is only puzzled to know where to begin.
There are the glaciers of *Martinet* and *Plan Nevé*,
the *Diablerets*, the *Grand Muveran*, the *Argentine*,
the *Chamossaire*, *Chatillon*, and a dozen other mountains and glaciers; the châlets of *La Varraz*, *Anzien-
daz*; and I know not how many more romantically-
placed hamlets and villages, far higher up than the
one we were in, besides waterfalls and gorges. All
must be seen; and of course when you first go up, you
intend to leave nothing undone, but at the end of your
stay you discover that the life lower down has been
so charming and attractive, you have dawdled away

your time without accomplishing half the programme. 'And why'—I have often asked myself on hearing people refuse to engage in some amusement they liked, because, as they have said with the air of a martyr, 'they must go up this or that mountain'—'need so many travellers over-exert and exhaust themselves by toiling over difficult and dangerous places, when they prefer less laborious excursions that are generally productive of more pleasure, and profit too?' For if you are a botanist or entomologist, you will not find the rarest plants and insects where eternal winter reigns.

I believe that a good many of those who travel in Switzerland, are very much like persons in society, who *ennuient* themselves by going to, and giving, a certain number of dinner and supper parties every week, for the sake of keeping up their position, as they term it; for I am morally certain that it is only the silly dread of not being in the fashion, of not doing as others of their acquaintance have done, that makes them worry and torment themselves, in endeavouring to get through a certain amount of climbing before they return home, instead of enjoying themselves according to the bent of their inclinations. They forget that it is not everyone who can surmount precipices without being

seized with vertigo, and perilling the lives of others
besides themselves, or can go through great pedestrian feats without succumbing to fatigue ere half
the toil is over.   Mountain excursions are the most
exciting, invigorating exercise in the world for those
who like them, and have head and strength equal to
what they undertake.   But they are nothing but a
toil and a bore to such as have no taste that way,
and who, moreover, are often serious drags upon the
enjoyment of those who do derive the most intense
gratification from them.

I am pretty strong and a good walker, but I
always had enough of seven or eight hours' walking
under that broiling sun, for it is precisely at that
time of the year when the heat renders the body
least capable of violent exertion, that these journeys
must be made, or not at all; if one could only take
them in the winter it would be a different thing
altogether.   Certainly I never felt so near *caput*
with the heat, as the day I accompanied M—— to
Grion, a large village splendidly placed at an elevation of 3,500 feet, on the side of a very steep
mountain, about three hours' good walking from *Les
Plans*.   We started early, with the intention of
resting there during the greatest heat of the day,
but found so many beauties on the way that it was

past eleven before we reached the little auberge of the Croix Fédérale, where we paid five francs for two boiled eggs, a small bit of bread and cheese, and a draught of milk, in a room so redolent of curl-papers that it might have been a barber's shop; and, as I had left my baby at home, we had only time to get cool before returning.

There are two good pensions, or boarding-houses, in *Grion*, which is celebrated for its pure and bracing air, and is the starting-point for excursions to the *Diablerets*, *Sion*, and other places of note. The châlets are very superior in construction and size to any others I have seen in the Vaud; though to the painter and lover of the picturesque, they are less attractive than those more rudely put together. The fountains, too, are larger, roofed with pine, and paved round—a great improvement on the lakes of mud in which one usually sees the women standing. Washing and scouring of all kinds, is done at these fountains—for this reason, that as there is never any water in the interior of the dwellings, it is much easier to take Mahomet to the mountain, than to bring the mountain to Mahomet. They are the gossiping-places of the villages: thence emanates all the scandal, and there your servants become worse than bad. From morning till night they are surrounded by

women rinsing and blueing clothes, washing salads and
vegetables, scrubbing pots, pans, pails, and everything
that can be taken out of the houses to be cleaned ;
what cannot be moved, stands a good chance of never
being cleansed at all.

I never saw a village so bare of trees as *Grion* ;
through the whole distance of the long narrow street
I did not see one : but the châlets are built in such a
manner, with deep overhanging roofs and open courts
surrounded with balconies, where the inmates sit the
whole summer day, and there is so much shade from
the great high mountain that shoots up almost perpendicularly behind it, and there is always so cooling
a breeze morning and night blowing over the snow-
capped mountains that lie on almost every side of it,
that it is not nearly the hot place the first view of it
leads you to imagine, and is a very delightful spot to
spend a few weeks in. To the botanist it is particularly
attractive, for in its neighbourhood are some of the
rarest and most beautiful flowers to be found in the
Alps.

Before starting on our return, we received many
warnings from the landlady on the danger of a *coup
de soleil* if we set off to walk such a distance when
the heat was greatest; but as I was in a manner compelled to get back soon, we did not pay much atten-

tion to her advice, especially as she had so shamefully overcharged us for our luncheon. Having been told that there was a much shorter and shadier route by way of *Frenières* than the one by which we came, we begged the loan of her little daughter to put us in the right road; and as we followed her active feet across the street, she disappeared so suddenly by the side of a châlet, that I involuntarily quickened my pace, fearing she had rolled down the steep declivities, but found to my relief that, instead of following the narrow path carried backwards and forwards like a W to facilitate the descent, she was only clearing the intervening spaces in a succession of leaps, that would not have disgraced a chamois.

This short cut by *Frenières*, like all short country roads, proved half as far again as the long one. The heat was appalling; every inspiration seemed to fill us with fire; we met no one; the hay-fields were deserted, the peasants having gone in the cow-sheds or under the shade of the trees to rest until it was cooler; and from having passed a good many other tracks, we were not certain we were in the right one— a very pleasant reflection when you feel that you are ready to sink every step you take. The whole distance is a succession of abrupt ascents and descents; there is not a step of level ground save in one part, and very little shade, and the whole of that line of hills, after leaving *Grion*, is so destitute of water, that we walked for two hours without finding a drop.   At every step, the heat and our thirst seemed to increase together, until at last I·trudged on after M—— with scarcely any feeling in me, save that my brain was on fire; and on emerging from a wood, that had afforded some protection against the burning sun, on to the open meadows, across which our road lay for half a mile or so, with the sun blazing full on our devoted heads, I was so overcome, so blinded, that if M—— had not turned round and said 'he was done up,' I don't think I should ever have summoned up resolution enough to go on.   His saying that, roused all the energy left in me; to stay there was madness, with no water and no shade.   'Push on, push on,' was all I could say.   The grass in the meadows seemed on fire; only the grasshoppers had any life.   At last we passed a shed, from the top of which two legs were dangling that served as a bell-pull to rouse the owner, and ascertain if there was any water there.   'No, none was to be got till we came to a small fountain further on.'   Then there was water in the vicinity.   Our spirits rose, and in less than ten minutes, on turning round a corner, we caught sight of a white cottage, and beyond it the fountain.   To see it gave me strength to reach it, but I had none to drink, until I had plunged head and hands in, to stay the throbbing of my brain. I shall remember the draught at that fountain as long as I have life.

At *Frenières* we halted a few minutes, and then, instead of following the usual route, which would have brought us to *Les Plans* in little more than an hour, we took the advice of an old man, to discover, for the second time in one day, the fallacy of believing old roads are shorter than new ones; and in lieu of a good broad one of easy ascent, we had to scramble over rugged paths through brushwood, and up places, that would have been inaccessible but for the flights of rude steps hewn in the rocks, upon which the sun struck so fiercely, that they burned our hands as we touched them in our ascent; and when we reached the summit of the last eminence and saw *Les Plans*, lying so green and fresh below us, we threw ourselves on the ground with feelings akin to those the traveller experiences in the desert, when he sees, afar off in the horizon, the lightning that is the precursor of the life-reviving shower. I did not have the predicted *coup de soleil*, but my eyes suffered terribly, and for many hours scarlet was the predominant colour in everything I looked at, and my face was a few shades darker than a Red Indian's, till I got a new skin.

We had no lack of visitors to occupy our spare

bedroom, besides those who came for a few hours to
see how we were getting on; and it was really laughable to see and hear the surprise of some of the
latter at finding that we were actually existing, and
very happily too, without the accessories of civilised
life. M——'s walking friend came with his pleasant
wife to look in upon us, and seemed to envy us our
pastoral life so much, that I think he would have
imitated our example had he not made other arrangements. The first inquiry made by one of our London
friends was, ' whether we had a good cook ; ' and I saw
that I and all my household rose immensely in his
estimation, when I assured him I had two very excellent ones, whom I would show him; and, opening
the door of the kitchen where my eldest daughters
were concocting a gooseberry dumpling, I said, ' There
are my two cooks.' For a moment his face looked so
curiously puzzled that I burst out laughing; when
he turned round and exclaimed, ' By Jove ! I should
like a pudding made by such cooks.'

The first friend who remained any time with us
was the Hon. H—— B——, the kind old gentleman
whose philanthropy and benevolence have made him
so well known in German Switzerland. As he was
at Bex for his health, we invited him to spend
a few days with us in our châlet, in the hope of

benefiting him by the fine air of the mountains, and
the more selfish one of desiring to share, some time
longer, the pleasure of his kindly society. The girls
had decorated his little room, as tastefully as they
could, with flowers and all the little knickknacks
they happened to have with them; and when, on the
third evening after our arrival, we saw his venerable
figure crossing 'the valley, we all ran out to meet
him, and welcome him to our mountain home. If
ever he see this book, I am sure it will give him
pleasure to read of those days of pleasant intercourse,
to the happiness of which, his genial temper and
cheerful conversation added not a little. Then we
had, for · *too* short a time, the dear friend whose
name I suppress, because he is the last man in the
world to wish to see it in print with a eulogium
tacked to it. But who that has had the privilege of
meeting him at Bex, or elsewhere, will not recog-
nise the portrait of one who, under an almost child-
like gaiety of manner, could not conceal a hand and
heart ever open to melting charity, and that broader
charity which hopeth all things, and maketh all the
world akin? If more of his cloth were like him,
there would be fewer of those so-called religious dis-
sensions, which so deform and disgrace the Christian
Church.

Some weeks prior to taking up our abode at *Les Plans*, M. Wagner had communicated to us, with the air of a person who felt he had got on the blind side of his victim, that he had purchased, for the astounding sum of twenty-four francs, the glaciers of *Martinet*, *Plan Nevé*, and one other whose name I have forgotten, with the intention of transporting the ice to France, where, through the unseasonable mildness of the preceding winter, it was then selling at a fabulous price.   I declare I thought he was romancing, as I could not believe anyone in his sober senses, least of all a Swiss having a knowledge of the locality, could dream of transporting immense quantities of ice from a height of 7,000 or 8,000 feet, without roads, down steep impracticable places, where no beast save a goat could get a footing; but M—— assured me that it was no joke, for Wagner believed it not only possible but very feasible, and talked of altering the path, that he persisted in thinking existed as far as the *Glacier de Martinet*, with very little labour and expense, so as to make it available for mules and carts. I heard no more of this gigantic scheme till about three weeks after our removal to *Les Plans*, when one splendid morning, about five o'clock, we were surprised to see his jolly countenance looking in at the upper half of the kitchen door.   He was on his way to visit a portion of his ice estates, and in the highest possible spirits, talking of commencing operations in a week or ten days, and was quite huffed if anyone threw cold water on his ice.

He was accompanied by an old gentleman, his cousin, who owned the pretty property I have spoken of at the commencement of this book; and when I saw that our stout and rather apoplectic host and the heavy venerable Monsieur V—— actually intended ascending to the *Glacier de Martinet*, and returning to dinner at one, I began to think that perhaps the project of bringing down the ice was not so impracticable after all; and as I was quite sure that where they went I could follow, I proposed to accompany them along with M——, whose opinion must be given before Wagner could decide upon any line of action. We had only time to swallow a cup of milk and run off, M—— shouting out to our eldest boy, who was not quite dressed, to follow as fast as he could, while we called at the next châlet for the son of Madame Bernard to act as guide. Following the old road, we crossed the oft-frequented spot of the *Pont de Nant*, and kept along the narrow valley between the *Grand Muveran* and *La Varraz*, that I have described in the account of our picnic, until we reached *Les Châlets du Nant*, where we had a

capital breakfast of cream, milk, and bread, with the
addition of sausage and cold beef fished from the
pocket of M. Wagner.

These châlets are almost at the extremity of the
valley, in about the wildest and dreariest spot
imaginable. The pasturages are small and flat, and
covered with rank coarse herbage; the mountains
closing up the valley are bare, bleak, and of a savage
wildness that strikes a chill into the heart, even when
the sun shines brightest. Innumerable torrents formed
by the melting of the snows and glaciers pour down
their sides, bringing with them quantities of loose
shale, dirt, and stones, with which the valley outside
the pasturages is covered. Not a tree, save two or
three half-dead firs behind the châlets, is to be seen,
presenting altogether as complete a picture of a
valley of desolation as one can imagine existing.
Sitting on milking-stools, we ate our breakfast outside in the pure morning air, watching the gambols
of the cows as they were turned out into the pastures after milking, H—— having a fight with a lot
of pigs that wanted to share his meal. I never met
with animals so impudent as they are at these mountain pasturages. Accustomed to be petted and caressed
like children by the men and boys who have the care
of them, they have no *mauvaise honte*, but smell

at and gambol round you, and often follow you a long way, before you can get rid of them. Sometimes they are rough and rude, and it requires some address to keep watch on all sides as you pass through a herd careering backwards and forwards like a lot of wild buffaloes.

At eight we left the châlets, picking our way over the streams that intersect the valley in every direction, the millions of bright blue gentians affording a delightful relief to the eye from the dull grey of the ground we were walking on, until we reached the foot of the mountain on which the glacier lies.

Everyone is deceived by the apparent nearness of glaciers, and this time it was difficult to believe that what appeared within rifle-shot would take us four or five hours to reach; but I was soon convinced of my mistake, when I found that after an hour's walking we actually seemed to be farther from it than when we began to ascend. Scrambling up loose shingly places, jumping from rock to rock, wading through torrents, was capital exercise for the legs, though rather fatiguing to our two stout companions, who were generally in the rear; and I noticed that M. Wagner no sooner reached the part where it was necessary to make a little use of the hands and knees, than he ceased all mention of the ice question, which until then had been the chief topic of conversation. As his thoughts must necessarily have been occupied in taking care of himself, I don't mean to insinuate that his silence proved he had relinquished his scheme; but I know that if I had been in his place, and undergone the frightful exertion and fatigue, the ascent appeared to be to him, my most sanguine hopes would have melted away long before I had got half-way to my property. I never saw anyone take less kindly to climbing, or suffer more from the heat. To have seen the perspiration pouring from him, you would have imagined he was fast wasting away, if you had not noticed that all the time his face became redder, and his bulk seemed to increase with every desperate effort to keep up with us. Now and then he would drop down on a stone like a man dead beat, wiping his steaming head and face with his handkerchief, till the water fairly dripped from the calico; then, roused by our laughter, he would again start forward with a determined earnestness that sat so comically on his goodnatured face, that we were often compelled to stop for the sake of indulging in a hearty laugh at his expense. His cousin, though an old man, did not appear to suffer at all, but walked at a quiet regular pace, habitual to those who have had much experience in mountain excursions.

The mountain was so grey and bare, that there was very little on the way to call forth our admiration, save where now and then in the sheltered valleys we came upon large patches of flowers that absolutely dazzled us with their brilliance. We gathered quantities of that most beautiful flower, the *Aquilegia Alpina*, of such a lovely blue, with petals so transparent, their graceful heads hanging from the tall stems by such slender filaments, that I wondered they ever came to flower's estate in that sterile spot. What masses, too, of that magnificent flower, the *Gentiana purpurea*, we saw wherever there was shelter!—while the *Rhododendron ferrugineum,* so often called the Alpine rose, and the sweet-scented yellow violets, were commoner still.

We crossed several valleys partially filled with snow, though their sides were pastured for cattle, and at a higher elevation traversed large wastes covered with the loose slate and rubbish washed from the moraines, of so insecure a footing, that ascending slopes formed of it was like climbing up a shivering mountain. M. Wagner had many a roll backwards, to the great delight of our St. Bernard dog, Lionne, who would scamper after him, barking with all her might till he came to a stop, when she would stand quite still while he picked himself up, and then

P

bound back to follow us as before.   The sagacious
creature evidently thought he was not a man to be
trusted with the care of his limbs.   We were on the
ice, and had walked some distance before I knew it.
' *That* the glacier ! ' I exclaimed, pointing to hillocks
of dirt and splintered rocks stretching on all sides as
far as I could see.   Where were the ice and snow I saw
looking so white from below ? and I began to think I
had gone through a good deal of exertion for very
little, until I was taken to some rents in the ground,
and, looking down, saw the immense yawning cre-
vasses with sides of ultramine, and heard the continual
cracking of the ice, like the straining of a ship in a
heavy sea; more than once experiencing a sensation
as if the ground was moving from under me.   As
we proceeded, we came upon parts where the ice was
cleaner, with large patches of snow blown into heaps
by the wind; and near the centre of one of the most
extensive of these ice-plains was a solitary hill, apparently entirely composed of the same slaty shingle,
not less than two hundred yards long and fifty high,
looking like an island in the sea.

On this hill we rested till our friends came up to
hold a consultation about the best means of disposing
of this fine property to a pecuniary advantage; and,
as we watched the ' melancholy slow ' approach of

M. Wagner, I observed with alarm that, three or four times, he bent down with his head very near the ground, as if he were ill; and I was not much less apprehensive on the score of his health when M——— told me, he was only drinking, as for a man, who for years had evinced almost as great a dislike to cold water as if he had been afflicted with hydrophobia, to be suddenly seized with so violent a passion for the pure element, was almost as alarming an indication of disease; and when, at last, on reaching a rill more seductive than the rest, he threw himself flat on his stomach, and, plunging his face in, drank at the icy waters till I had fear of the supply being stopped, I began to think it was all over with him, until I saw him rise from his recumbent position, walking the remainder of the distance with a firmer step, and heard him declare that ' never in his life had he tasted water so good, for that the more he drank the more he felt he *must* drink.'

After full half an hour's discussion as to *how*, we never got as far as *when*, the ice was to be hewn and taken thence to Bex, we came unanimously to the following resolutions:—1st. That the distance was too great. 2ndly. That there was no road for beast or vehicle. 3rdly. That to make one would take half a century, and cost as much as the piercing of the

P 2

Simplon.   4thly. That granted it *could* be brought
down, to transport it such a distance in the intense
heat of summer, would be to run the probable risk of
finding it ice no longer on its arriving at Bex.   And
that, 6thly and lastly, the ice was much better where
it was, both for M. Wagner's pocket and the pleasure
of future tourists.

Our descent was accomplished rapidly enough, for
when we came to the sloping valleys of ice, of which
we had some half-dozen to cross, we eschewed the
trouble of using our legs, and, sitting down, gave
ourselves a shove, and were at the bottom before we
could get our breaths.   The alarm of our poor dog was
distressing to witness.   She dared not follow, and yet
was so fearful of being left behind, that in her excitement she had not the sagacity to make a détour, but
in the end, after a good many extempore rolls and
upsets, she squatted down on her haunches and succeeded in reaching us; and I must not forget to
record that from some cause, possibly from both
having undergone grievous sufferings during the
excursion, she conceived a violent liking for M.
Wagner, which exists to this day.

We did not get back to dinner at one; on the
contrary, the sun was declining as we descended
from the *Pont de Nant,* and when we came into the

narrow road leading to the goat-sheds we found our children feeding the pretty frisky creatures, the tinkle of whose bells had been such pleasant music preceding us nearly all the way from the *Châlets du Nant.* M. Wagner lost his fondness for water long before reaching *Les Plans,* and revenged himself for his abstemiousness by diminishing the stock of Madame Bernard's white wine before he returned to Bex.

CHAPTER XI.

Superstitions—Sunsets—Louise—The Avençon—The Young
Tailleuse's Story—Drowned Dead—Fête of Mi-été—Dogs
and Cows—Chevrier—Colony of Artists—Fight with a Bullock—Critics—Ahead of the Blooomers—Winter and Summer—Seven Days' Rain—Night at Story-telling.

HAPPY as were all the hours that flew, alas! too
swiftly, at *Les Plans,* none to me were so delightful
as those of evening, when the hush and repose of
twilight came over the happy valley, and my thoughts,
released from the occupations and excitements of the
day, had leisure to dwell upon the enchanting sights
and sounds around me. The peasants, returned from
their daily toil, were seated in groups on the grass,
or, imitating our example, wandered up and down
among the châlets, enjoying, though with less emc-
tional sensations, the seductive influence of the hour.
I think I hear them talking, as with hushed voices
they recounted to each other the tales of a superna-
tural character, of which they are so fond; of the en-
counters, each one having some individual experience
to relate, with the spirits of departed acquaintances,
that haunt the spots where, during life, they have

committed some crime, until they meet some unlucky mortals who, ignorant of their condition, address them three times, and are henceforth compelled to bear the burden of the sin, until such time as they too are fortunate enough to dispose of it to some one else in the same manner and place.

Though professing themselves Protestants, they have an unconquerable dread of the monks, who are supposed to possess the power of exorcising demons, and of inflicting the most fearful torments, even unto death, upon anyone who may have been guilty of any sort of offence towards them; and endless are the tales of persons wasting away and shrivelling up from the effect of the spells thrown around them, by these powerful ministers of the devil. Most of the peasants believe in the existence of a spirit, half fairy, half imp, that is kind or evil towards them according to their conduct in life. If they are well-behaved and industrious, these creatures, they say, sometimes visit their houses during the night, and, after finishing any work that has been left undone, leave all clean and in order; on the other hand, if they have been idle, dirty, and wasteful, they may happen to find a double amount of disorder reigning in their dwellings when they rise in a morning. To provide for the material

wants of these nocturnal visitors, who from this trait
are evidently somewhat of the 'earth earthy,' the
peasants place the first spoonful of everything they
cook, on a plate that is kept expressly for their use;
for, should they receive a visit when these rites of
hospitality have been neglected, they would immediately be afflicted with 'cramp and side stitches,'
and all sorts of aches and pains, as punishment for
their carelessness. Though many persons are supposed to have seen these spirits, no one has been able
to render an account of their make and shape, for
the very good reason, that the presumptuous mortal,
whose curiosity has induced him to request the favour
of a sight of them, no sooner has his wish gratified
than he dies.

All the mountaineers that I have ever talked with,
are more or less superstitious; and, spending as they
do the greater portion of their waking existence in
those elevated solitudes, without any occupation save
watching their flocks and herds, they have abundant
time for indulging their own thoughts, and fostering
that vein of superstitious imagination, which in them
seems inborn. As I listened to their narratives, recited
with a simple earnestness and good faith that took
away every disposition to smile from the listener, I
felt that, if I had been born and lived among the

grandest and sublimest scenes of nature, and had no other teacher, I should have been like them.

How long we used to linger outside ! Always it was too early to turn in; the golden sunset, the rich purple stealing over the mountains, the shadows of coming night on the valley, while all the peaks were blazing with the Alpenglühen—all, all were lovely; and never can I hope to convey to anyone the · fascination of the time and place. How delicious were the moonlight rambles by the Avençon, looking more beautiful than ever in that light, and the long restings by the way on the little bridge, to watch for the first star appearing above the Javerne ! What long talks with the peasants and joyous games with the children ! And how we always felt it a shame to shut ourselves up in the châlet, although we remained out after all the rest of the people were in their beds !

One evening, as we were sitting on the bench outside, suddenly there rose high and clear from the summit of the opposite mountain, a woman's voice, singing a Tyrolese air. No singing that ever I listened to, not even the dulcet tones of the Swedish Nightingale, thrilled through me like that song—so pure, so fresh, so joyous: it seemed the very inspiration of the spirit of the mountain echoes, that took it up one after the other, till every rock was filled with the melody. For full half an hour the girl sang, while every eye was strained, but in vain, to discover the rock upon which she had perched herself. I guessed the singer could be no other than our neighbour, the goodnatured Louise Moreillon, who with her father had gone that morning to make hay high up on the mountains; and I found I was right, for when she descended the next day she told us that, after having finished their work, they had lighted a fire to cook their supper, and while the soup was boiling she had climbed up a peak, whence she had a good view of the valley, and, knowing it was the time when we should all be out of doors, had warbled away for our amusement.

When the peasants go up to cut the grass growing on these little pasturages, they usually remain, unless bad weather set in, until it is dried and stored, sleeping on the sweet hay in preference to being stifled in the little low châlet, where they keep just so many household utensils as are necessary for cooking their food. This roguish-looking black-eyed Louise was the kindest and best-natured Swiss lassie I ever knew, always ready to lend a strong arm and a swift foot to help us, and ever on the look-out to spoil the children by giving them cakes and honey, or leading them off to assist her in gathering cherries for her mother, who found, to her cost, that very few ever made their way into her kitchen.

Louise, who was stout, strongly-built, and not bad-looking, though she *did* lack the ornament of a goître, without which no Swiss woman can be considered handsome, did not, to judge from her exterior, waste much time in the mysteries of the toilette; her usual summer attire consisting of a coarse linen chemise, with sleeves reaching to the elbow, and a black cotton skirt that descended a very little lower than the knees, coarse black stockings, and heavy shoes. This dress was worn alike by mother and daughter, with this difference, that the elder lady wore her chemise open to the waist, displaying a brawny chest tanned to the colour of a rhinoceros by exposure to the sun and air, and did not appear to appreciate the blessings of clean linen quite so much as her daughter, who was never more happy than when playing with our children, going at full speed down the hills on a sledge, with one of the boys on her shoulders and another on her knees, or taking them to paddle in the Avençon, where they would have been well content to have remained all the hot summer days, had we not been warned to beware of the deep holes lying between the large rocks and stones. It is precisely where the river is most beautiful that the danger exists, and towards the middle of the day, when the volume of water is much augmented by the melting of the snow, a child might easily be taken off his feet and carried into one of these deep places. Every summer, casualties of this kind occur; and when one sees that from its rise, near the glacier of *Plan Névé*, passing through four or five villages till it empties itself in the Rhone, it is entirely unguarded, one is not surprised at the number of little children that have lost their lives in its waters.

I was much affected one day as I listened to a tale told me by a pretty young girl who had come from Bex to sew for us, and was standing watching the lads jumping in and out of the water. Seeing that she looked melancholy and had tears in her eyes, I asked what ailed her, when she related the following touching story:—' Often as I pass the river, I never see it without a shudder coming over me, on account of its having been the death of my only little brother, whom I loved better than all else in the world. It is now nine years ago, but seems but yesterday; for the after-troubles it brought on us in my father's death, and my mother's ill-health and incurable melancholy, are, as I may say, with us still. My brother, who was seven years old, was the youngest child, and a great favourite with all of us, on account of his being so gentle and obedient; indeed, he was so loving and so good that my mother often said 'he was too good to live.' (In what Christian country does this same ignorant idea not exist?) If he had a fault, it was in being too yielding to the wishes of his companions, whom he did not like to disoblige.

'One afternoon in May, after an early spring that had been unusually hot, and the Avençon in consequence was much swollen by the quantity of water pouring from the mountains, he was returning from school with his usual companion, a schoolfellow who lived near us, when they were met by another lad, who asked my brother to go along with him to execute an errand he had been sent by his mother to a house near the side of the river. At first Pierre— that was my brother's name—refused to go, saying he wanted to get home to his mother; but on being pressed, consented, giving his satchel to his friend to take care of till he came back. As he did not come to *goûter*, my mother sent to the boy who generally walked from school with him to ask where he was, and, hearing he was gone an errand with another lad, she did not get uneasy till it grew dark, when she persuaded my father to go to the house where lived the parent of the boy who had taken him off.

These people said they had seen nothing of my brother, and did not think he could have been with their son, who was playing outside, and had been home some hours. But on his being called in, and asked where he had left Pierre, he answered, quite carelessly, "Oh, he has fallen into the water"—the first words he had ever uttered to anyone on the subject. Search was made all along the river as far as the Rhone: but it was of no use; there was so much water that he must have been carried away long before he was missed, and a few weeks after we heard that the body of a child, so disfigured as not to be recognisable, had been cast ashore in one of the Valaisan villages and buried there. The bad lad's account of the matter was, that as they were returning he saw a scarlet poppy growing on a rock in the river, and as he wished to have it, Pierre offered to get it for him if he would hold his hand, and that, while doing so, he let go his hold, and my brother tumbled in the water; and then, instead of calling anyone to his assistance from the houses close to the spot, as any other boy of nine years old would have done, he went quietly home, and never seemed to have thought about the matter, till my poor father came to make inquiries.

'No one believed this tale, because it came out

that he had told a lie in saying to Pierre that his
mother had sent him an errand; and as he had been
heard to say "he would do for my brother," of whom
he was jealous at school, we never doubt that he
pushed him in; and so hateful was the sight of him
to my father, that he told his parents "he should
certainly kill him if they did not keep him out of
his way;" so they thought it prudent to remove from
the place till my father's death, which happened five
years after. He had always been a sombre melancholy man, and to work and save to educate my
little brother, and make something better of him
than the drunken people around us, was all he cared
to live for; and when he was gone, his only wish was
to die too. My mother has never known a day's
health since; and my younger sister, who was called
the handsomest girl in the village, died of consumption, brought on, the doctor said, by the hardships
and poverty we had to pass through after father's
death. The boy who caused all our troubles is now
grown up, and lives in B——, as wicked a man as he
was bad as a boy; and whenever he passes along the
street, and happens to meet the boys going or returning from school, they shout out, "There goes the
fellow who killed little Pierre." '

To all the dwellers in the mountains, quite the

most important event of the whole year is the Feast
of Mi-été, which is held on the first Sunday after
Assumption-day, August 15; and as, the year we were
there, the 15th fell on a Sunday, more than ordinary
preparations were made for celebrating the favourite
fête. I had noticed a great bustle and excitement
going on in the little hamlet several days, before I
inquired the reason why all the housewives were up
to the elbows in flour, and rushing here and there
in their eagerness to borrow or exchange tins to bake
their cakes in. Mère Bernard had a grand heating
of her brick oven, erected in an outhouse for the
benefit of the Plans world in general and herself in
particular. Her cook, who suffered a chronic martyr-
dom from the old lady's weakness for railing against all
such ' bêtes,' as she termed servants, was very nearly
reduced to a skeleton with so much additional work
and bother in the hot weather, and actually flew for
breath and refuge into our more quiet domicile. The
price of butter rose twenty centimes in the pound;
and even Madame Giraud tried her hand at a tremendous raspberry tart, which the lads, who had
been witnessing the whole operation, declared would
turn out a ' regular stunner.'

There is a particular sort of bread appropriate to the
occasion, made of dough mixed with butter, sugar,

and aniseeds, and baked in the shape of crowns, rings, and other devices.

This festival is not celebrated in the villages or hamlets, but in the cow châlets on the pasturages; and it is to serve the double purpose of a holiday, and of examining into the condition and yield of their cows and goats, that the peasants commemorate this festival, which always lasts a night and a day, as they go up on Saturday afternoon and return at sunset on Sunday. They take no eatables with them save the sweet bread made for the day; cream, milk, butter, and cheese, being supplied to them at the châlets. I saw scores of families, some numbering as many as five generations, passing through *Les Plans* on the Saturday, and pleased myself by fancying the numbers of people that were thronging all the mountain-paths that day.

We shut up house and ascended to the châlets of *Richard* early on the Sunday, and after a very long, but delightful walk, reached the outskirts of the pasturages, where, through having our dogs with us, we had rather an exciting scene. You come upon these pasturages very suddenly, after passing through a small wood of firs, and we had not time to call off the dogs before we were in the midst of the cattle. In a moment the whole herd appeared

Q

roused to a pitch of madness; roaring and bellowing, with tails erect, they careered after the mischievous dogs, who enjoyed the sport too much to desist, and were evidently determined to give them as much annoyance as they could. Now the cattle formed a phalanx to resist the charge of the two dogs, who were more than a match for 200 cows; then they retreated to a more distant part of the pasturage, as if to deliberate on a future line of action, returning more furious than before. There were several bulls among them that were disposed to be wicked; and as there was no possible way of reaching the châlets save by passing through the whole lot, we placed the little ones on the side furthest from danger, and taking advantage of a momentary lull, marching as closely and quickly as we could, with M—— brandishing a large stick, we got half through the infuriated animals; when the shepherds, hearing the row, came to meet us, and conducted us safely to the enclosure surrounding the sheds, on the other side of which we found more than a hundred people assembled, of all ages, from the infant in arms to the great-grandmother.

The married ones were seated on the grass, the women chatting and looking at the sports, while their lords and masters smoked and slept; children were playing, as children play all over the world, turning head over heels, duck and drake in the streams, or wading across them minus shoes and stockings, while the elder lads and lasses were dancing the polka as vigorously as if the thermometer were at 40° instead of 80°. The musician was an old blind fiddler, a genus that seems peculiar to no country, seated in a sort of pulpit bowered in pine branches and flowers, and surmounted with a flag bearing the inscription one reads on every bridge, prison, and guardhouse in Switzerland, of ' Liberté et Patrie.'

The shepherds took us into the *fruitière*, and filling two wooden bowls, one with milk and the other with cream, gave each of us an oval ladle, telling us we could have as much more as we liked—a piece of information they must have regretted giving us when they saw we emptied five or six of them. We had not neglected to take a store of the sweet bread to eat with it, and no fare could have been more agreeable or appropriate to the occasion. Of course the children danced with the peasants, and when they were tired we rambled to the extremity of the plain, and, leaving the baby playing on a carpet of gentians, in care of one of his sisters, the rest mounted the hills in search of flowers and strawberries, and came

upon such a wilderness of bilberries of extraordinary
size and flavour, that they tempted us to eat until
the sound of the goats' bells told us how swiftly time
had flown while we were scrambling and eating, and
warned us it was time to return.

The young people being all eagerness to follow
the flock, and assist in driving them as far as *Les
Plans*, we said a hasty 'adieu' to the revellers, who
were also commencing preparations for departure,
and came up with the *chevrier* and his goats as soon
as we entered the wood.   The men chosen for this
employment are mostly half-witted fellows, not much
better than crétins, who are incapable of learning a
trade; and the great lanky half-clad fellow before us
appeared inferior in intelligence, to the bright-eyed
agile creatures, bounding from rock to rock, over
which he was set as guard.   At *Les Plans* we found
they were anticipating a ball to wind up the festivities, and the largest cart-shed in the place was being
swept and prepared for the ball-room; but, alas!
Louise Moreillon was the only young unmarried lady
in the hamlet, and as, with the utmost good-will, she
could not dance with all the beaux at once, they
proceeded on to Frenières, where there was a more
plentiful sprinkling of belles, and so we were disappointed of our village ball.   However, we had the

old fiddler, who sat himself down in front of Mère Bernard's châlet, and played the most indescribable dance-tunes till he and the fiddle got drunk together.

That same evening, as we were watching the people returning, we saw a stout elderly gentleman standing in the little plot of garden that separated our châlet from Madame Bernard's, whose appearance and attitude, with his hands under his coat-tails, was so decidedly English, that I claimed him at once for my countryman, in spite of M——'s whisper 'that he was a captain of gendarmerie;' and furthermore decided in my own mind that, that fine good-humoured countenance, seeming to smile benignantly on all mankind, could belong to none other than 'a fine old English gentleman who had a good estate.' At *Les Plans* one gets acquainted without the ceremony of an introduction, and he and M—— had no sooner entered into conversation than they discovered, to their mutual satisfaction, that they were brothers in art, and before they separated had surveyed the valley from I don't know how many points of view, and agreed to commence painting it at an early hour the next morning.

He proved to be no Englishman, but a Monsieur G——n, one of the veterans of the modern Genevese school of painting; and the wound inflicted upon my

self-conceit, by discovering that my penetration had
been at fault in mistaking him for a *real John Bull,*
was partially healed when I found that all his tastes
were English; that he had the most unbounded
admiration for our country, her laws, institutions,
government, &c.; that he was sending his sons to be
educated in England, and emphatically declared
that had he been ten years younger he would have
gone to reside there and constituted himself an
English citizen.

Artists are like bees; wherever there is one, others
are sure to cluster round him; and in three or four
days we had quite a colony of the same located here
and there in the hamlet.   Mons. G—— was the guest
of Madame Moreillon, our neighbour; two were at
Mère Bernard's; a fourth, a very tall lanky man,
looking as if he had run to seed, managed to compress
himself into a room not nearly so long as himself,
built by the baker as a lean-to against his own
dwelling; while the fifth, a diminutive man, with a
face that reminded me of a lean mutton chop, his
person cased in a suit of white jean that long before
the end of his stay was the colour of his palette,
and who never moved a step without being followed
by a hungry-looking lad he called ' my pupil,' from
having more than once appeared with unmistakeable

agricultural tokens about him, was strongly suspected of sleeping in a hay-loft. Each morning, so long as they remained, they all started off in search of the picturesque, working away till twelve, when a man took them their dinner, after which they painted on till the light served them no longer. Mons. G—— was appointed 'Master,' with the title of 'Brigadier,' through M—— having mistaken him for a captain of gendarmerie; and few men could be found who so happily unite the qualities that make him the most cheerful and sociable of companions, with those that not only render him the most untiring and industrious of workers, but inspire an almost equal amount of energy and industry in those who have the happiness of working with him.

There were two parties from Lausanne, a Mons. B—— and a M. Gui. The first, a middle-aged bachelor, with a pair of spectacles so much too large for him that they were always just on the point of tumbling off his nose, was the most comical-looking man I ever saw; the sight of his face was quite enough to have provoked a saint to laughter; the mischievous twinkling eyes being in keeping with the mouth, that always looked as if it were about to open and say something diverting. A very plain and clumsily-made man, he pretended to be excessively vain of his person,

and frightful were the convulsions of laughter into
which he threw his hearers, as he recounted, in the most
dolorous tones, the unavailing attempts he made
each morning to conceal his baldness and increasing
corpulence; while the numberless jokes he perpe-
trated concerning his ' fine classical education,' showed
that he did not care to conceal the fact of his having
been the architect of his own fortune and position.

Mons. Gui, who is Director of the School of Design
in the Museum at L——e, was a quiet subdued-look-
ing small man, with hair cut so close to his head that
for some time I thought he wore a brown silk skull-
cap. His features were such a motley assemblage
that you might have fancied he had picked them up
in different parts of the world, and the whole face
had no one particular expression save that of extreme
goodness and benevolence. The world said he had a
skeleton in his house, in the shape of a shrew of a
wife; but it was hard to believe that any shrew could
be long untamed by the side of a man whom our
close and still-enduring intimacy showed us to be
the kindest and most unselfish of human beings.
The tall gentleman, who came a few days after the
rest, was a stranger to them all: but as he announced
that he came from Paris, talked in the most glib and
fluent style about rules of art, and criticised the

performances of the others that were hung outside
to dry, he impressed each and all with the idea that
a 'Daniel come to judgment' had fallen among
them; and even Mons. G——n owned to having
experienced a nervous fluttering about the heart, and
an unwonted trembling of the hands, the first morning they all six sat down, under the shade of their
holland umbrellas, with the new-comer. There was
not one that did not glance furtively aside to see
how he handled his pencil, and it was not until Mons.
B——, who was made the scapegoat of the party,
had succeeded by stratagem in gaining a near view of
his performance, and given a sign agreed upon by the
rest, that composure was restored. The best description I can give of it is in the words of one of my
children, who, seeing the same painting hung up to
dry, said, 'Some little boy has been amusing himself
by trying to paint.'

Though working hard—it was no merit to do so
under such a 'brigadier'—they were merry as
schoolboys, finding amusement in everything, even in
the very interruptions and accidents they occasionally
met with. Mons. B—— had an ungovernable dread
of horned cattle, and never sat down to sketch without glancing round to see that none of his enemies
were in sight. On one occasion, as he was seated at

some distance from the rest—he liked to be singular even in the matter of taking a sketch—a bullock, full of the playfulness common to the race when let loose, or possibly endowed with more elevated tastes than its fellows, gradually approached nearer and nearer the unlucky artist, upon whom it appeared to have fixed its eye since his first entrance into the field. Poor Mons. "B—— brandished his painting-stick and bawled for help to his recreant friends, whose enjoyment of the scene increased in proportion to the terror of their comrade; but the animal, discovering the weakness of its adversary, was not to be turned from its purpose of seeing what he was about; and at last, when, after upsetting and inspecting his knapsack, the pertinacious brute came snuffling at his canvas, the scared artist seeing no help was to be got from his friends, who were enjoying the fun too much to move to his assistance, fairly took to his heels and made for a tree a few yards off, up which he climbed with an agility not to be expected from one of his heavy make, leaving a clear field to his victorious adversary.

The 'Brigadier' met with a more serious accident, and, though he made light of it, M—— always said he had had a very narrow escape of his life. The two had been painting the upper reach of a waterfall from a ledge of rocks about half-way up, and were returning, picking their way down the steep wet stones, when M——, who had lingered behind to alter the strap of his knapsack, lost sight of his friend, and, on reaching the bottom, found him stretched, apparently lifeless, on the ground, his left arm doubled under him, and blood flowing from his face. Fortunately, M—— never left home without a bottle of ammonia in his pocket, and lost no time in applying some to his head and face, and as soon as he discovered signs of returning animation, forced a dose down his throat, which operated so powerfully, that in less than half an hour he was able to limp slowly home, with no bones broken, but terribly crushed and bruised, the skin torn off half his face, and a sprained hand.

As the six large holland umbrellas looked at a distance exactly like an encampment, it was natural that tourists, *bent on seeing everything*, should have the curiosity to approach them for the purpose of ascertaining the reason of so unusual a sight, and endless was the fun they had, in listening to the comments, mostly English, bestowed upon their performances. One gentleman, who talked so learnedly and pompously about parallel lines, just proportions, tone, finish, cottony clouds, that they set him down for an

art-critic to some provincial newspaper—pointed out
to the admiring auditors of his party, that the painting on which the artists were engaged would be
much improved by the addition of a stream of water,
in a part where it must have been represented as
flowing up a hill; another held forth on the absurdity
of going so far out of the way to seek for subjects,
when so inexhaustible a field lay around them nearer
home, and wound up his discourse by pointing out a
large lettuce, of which the leaves were turning reddish,
growing in a garden near, as a true and proper
subject for a painting.

There was a French authoress, whose name I have
forgotten, staying at Mère Bernard's, while these
artists were there, who took every possible opportunity of endeavouring to convert them to her views
respecting the rights of women, on which subject, I
was told, she had written more than one work. Being
one of those ladies—I beg pardon for making use of
so feminine an appellation, but until the sect invent
a new one I can do no other—who stalk about the
world *with a pair of trousers in perspective*, she had
already so far advanced in emancipating herself from
the trammels of female dress, that the above-named
nether garments were all that was wanting to complete
a costume at once rakish and manly; though fairness

compels me to add, that I do not ever remember to have seen anyone of the stronger sex habited in a red flannel shirt so unmistakably in need of the washtub as this talented woman wore; and the hat, tied round with a bit of narrow black ribbon, set on her closely-cut hair, would have been mended by a little use of that feminine instrument, a needle. Upon the principle that extremes meet, or perhaps judging that he would offer the least resistance to her theories, she attached herself pertinaciously to Monsieur Gui, for whose peace of mind it was perhaps fortunate that his wife came over from Grion, and carried him off as unresistingly as a hawk does a sparrow.

Until the beginning of September, the weather (except for an occasional thunderstorm, sometimes preceded by a violent wind, that, when the painters were on the *Pont de Nant,* more than once played sad havoc amongst their traps, upsetting the easels and even their owners by its force) continued magnificent, everything one could wish, when one of those startlingly sudden changes in the midst of summer heat, experienced only in elevated regions, put a stop to sketching, painting, picnics, rambles, and all other occupations and amusements we had been indulging in so delightfully out of doors.

I remember that I was standing watching the progress of a thunderstorm, that appeared to be sweep-
ing upwards through the opening into the valley on
my right, when Madame Bernard, who had been
gazing towards the heavens with a very lugubrious
expression on her countenance, joined me, and, on
my remarking that I thought we were in for a
violent storm, shook her head, and said, 'Oh,
madam, that storm will last a week or more.' I
laughed, and told her she was not politic to predict
weather that was sure to clear her châlet of visitors ;
but she stuck to her opinion, and added, 'she had
seen it coming on some days, and it was no use trying hiding the fact from herself or others, as it
wouldn't stop it.'

The old lady was right ; but it proved a more
serious affair than even she had anticipated, for before
the sun shone again, we had winter, with the flowers
in full bloom.   For seven days we were imprisoned in
our châlet, and during all that time it rained in
torrents or snowed.   Never in my life have I seen
rain to equal that ; it was like a waterspout, and the
clouds driven before the terrific wind filled the
valley till you might have fancied an army of loco-
motives was puffing away there.   Going out was
impossible ; for even supposing that you were tough

enough to brave the soaking you got in a couple of minutes, there was no making head against the wind, and after the third day's rain the cold became so intense we were almost frozen. Still we hoped on, and every night on going to bed talked of plans for the morrow if it were fine; but the aspect of affairs grew worse instead of better, and we began to think we had been foolish not to have returned to Bex as soon as the rain came on. The fourth day the snow was so low as the pine-woods, and shudderingly we watched it come lower and nearer, until, on the fifth night, the shepherds who had been out to look after the cattle reported it was on the *Pont de Nant*; and on the sixth morning the children knocked at my bedroom door and shouted out 'there was a white world,' and that 'a lot of men, wrapped in skins and sacks, and carrying implements for clearing away the snow, were setting off for the mountains to bring down the cattle.'

There was a stove in each of the bedrooms leading from the kitchen, and if we had been able to heat them, we could have made ourselves comfortable enough, and waited without impatience for the passing away of the storm; but unfortunately we had no more wood than was sufficient for cooking purposes, and no more could be got while the bad weather

lasted. When we were looking out the things before
leaving Bex, I was unmercifully laughed at, because, having heard that however hot it might be
during the day, the nights were often cold in the
mountains, I had placed some half-dozen blankets
among the articles I deemed necessary to take with
us to *Les Plans*. ' As if anyone ever heard of such
hot things as blankets ever being wanted during
summer in Switzerland!' was chimed in a chorus, as
the offending articles were thrown contemptuously
aside; but happening, when all was packed, to see
that the bath was not full, I smuggled in three or
four of the forbidden goods, and I know who had
most reason to laugh when everybody was shivering
and wishing 'they had but thought of bringing up
the blankets.'

Though we pitied ourselves, compelled to be shut
up almost without employment, we were far more
sorry for the artists who congregated together in
Madame Bernard's room, opposite ours, as if in a
community of misery there was consolation, and
were fast approaching an alarming state of melancholy and inanition. We lent them all the books,
and they were not many, that we had brought with
us; held frequent conversations, all on the state
of the weather, from the windows; sent them the

ruined barometer, in the hope that, as it always stood at 'fair,' it might tend to enliven them a little, *et fîmes tous notre possible* to prevent their setting off in a frenzy of madness and leaving us alone in our misery; our efforts being seconded by Madame Bernard's unhappy cook, who, having been engaged for three months, was fearful of having to bear a double amount of scolding if the visitors departed, and placed such tempting dishes before them, that, joined to the want of exercise, it would not have surprised me to have heard of a plethoric seizure. I must do the unfortunates themselves the justice to say, that for four or five days they did all they could to amuse and blind themselves to the fact, that it was all over with painting at *Les Plans* for that time at least, essaying a variety of experiments to keep themselves in practice till the weather should take up, which, according to M. Bernard, who never thought like anybody else, was to be every following morning.

On the second morning of the rain, I saw the whole party seated on the bench by the side of our châlet, where they were protected from the rain by the low roof, sketching away at Mère Giraud's bee-house, all other objects being shrouded in impenetrable mist. And certainly no one would wish to see

R

a finer example of the pursuit of knowledge under
difficulties; for the rain having meandered among
the pebbles paving the walk, had filled the holes
worn by the feet of sitters, and compelled them to
sit with their legs on the bench, like Romans at a
banquet minus the cushions; and having, of course,
brought no winter clothing with them, they were
enveloped in all the habiliments belonging to her
defunct lord and master, that their hostess could
furnish, some of a date prior to this century, as it is a
common practice for the well-to-do peasants to provide themselves with so large a stock of clothing
that it is impossible to wear it out in a lifetime, and
it descends to one generation after another without
undergoing the slightest alteration. I gave them all
the tables and low stools I could spare; and there for
two successive days they painted away at the bee-
hive, which must have been capable of as many
variations in perspective, as a leg of mutton is in
cooking; for there were views of 'The Bee-hive from
the right,' 'The Bee-hive from the left'—The Bee-
hive from the middle of the bench, from the top,
from the bottom, in oil and water colours; besides
sketches of the same in chalk and pencil by the sad
pupil.

When night came, they caricatured each other,

and painted Mère Bernard as Macbeth's witches, or
any other ugly old women of whom history makes
mention. But these occupations came to an end, like
everything else, and on the fifth morning, hearing
they had lost their appetites and were talking of
making their wills, I proposed they should come across
and have a night at story-telling, with a bowl of punch
to wind up. But here a difficulty arose in the shape
of want of habiliments; for though *à faire la toilette*
was unknown at *Les Plans*, it was necessary to have a
more complete costume than ' a straw hat and cigar,'
which, I have somewhere read, is the summer costume
of the Nicaraguans; a plight, it appears, our friend
with the white suit was nearly reduced to, his wardrobe having been so saturated by repeated wettings,
that he had sat nearly the whole of the day wrapped
in a counterpane! However, this obstacle was got over
by M—— sending him one of his suits, which, though
a world too large, was made presentable by turning
up the cuffs of the sleeves and the hems of the
trousers. As our room was not large enough to seat
them all, even if we had possessed seats enough, we
placed the least children on the bed; and having
installed the Brigadier as ' president,' the question
was ' who should begin ;' a query sooner asked than
answered, for the four walls appeared to have had

so quieting an effect upon their tongues, and made
them so bashful to boot, that nearly an hour was
spent in fruitless endeavours to overcome the repug-
nance of each gentleman to speak first.

The matter was ended by M—— proposing to make
the punch, in the hope of unloosing their tongues;
and while the brandy was burning, the children began
talking of a walk they had had a few days before
in the woods on the mountain facing our châlet, to
see a poor charcoal-burner, the smoke from whose
fire we saw constantly curling above the trees. And
this made M—— say that the mention of a charcoal-
burner reminded him of a perilous adventure that
had happened to him many years ago when travelling
in France, which he would relate to us if we would have
no more light than that the spirit afforded; a pro-
position received with acclamations by the small fry,
who, like most children, delight in a tale of horrors,
though it may send them shivering with fear to bed.
And then, having extracted a promise from Mons.
B—— that he would narrate the next tale, he told
us the following story :—

CHAPTER XII.

First Artist's Tale—Adventure in the Jura—A Dark Night —Half-way House—Something Wrong—An Attack—Retreat of Robbers—Escape—Conclusion.

'SOME fifteen years ago, as I was travelling in the Département du Jura, I found myself, towards the close of a day in July, at the little town of Lons-le-Saulnier, where, as my purse was never very heavy in those days, I took up my quarters at a second-rate hotel, called "La Croix Blanche." After despatching my dinner, I strolled through the town to see if it afforded any subject for my pencil, and then turned into a coffee-house where strangers usually assembled of an evening.

' On entering, I found that, owing to a concert being held there, it was impossible to obtain a seat, and, after searching in vain over the whole establishment for one, was returning, pushing my way through two rows of tables, when I felt some one give a very ungentle tug at my coat-tails, and, turning round, beheld the well-known faces of my brother and brother-in-law. As we had not met for some years, I was induced for once to depart from the rigid rule of economy I had laid down for myself, and change my hotel for the more fashionable and expensive one " de la Couronne," at which they were staying; and before separating that night, I had agreed, as they were travelling with their carriages of the sort generally used by merchants on their journeys, with a place behind for stowing goods, and a seat in front-capable of holding two or more persons, not to part company with them so long as our routes were the same. As they had a good deal of business to transact in the town, it was five o'clock in the afternoon of the next day before we left Lons-le-Saulnier, intending to reach Bletteran, which, we were told, was not more than five or six hours' ride distant, about midnight. Each of them had a fine powerful horse; and as my brother had a friend with him, I occupied the vacant seat beside my brother-in-law.

'I must tell you that in that part of France are vast forests, in which at that period (and, for aught I know, may be still) were living hundreds— report said thousands—of men employed in charcoal-burning, who appeared to have very little that was human about them, save the form. They led the

most lawless, desperate lives, robbing, plundering,
maltreating, and even murdering, any traveller they
could fall in with; setting at defiance all law and
authority, for their dense forests are more impreg-
nable strongholds than the stoutest castle. But of
this we then knew nothing, and journeyed on in the
highest possible spirits, at the idea of spending a few
days together.

'About three hours after leaving Lons-le-Saulnier,
the road entered one of those interminable woods; and
we could not have proceeded above half a league before
one of the sudden storms common in the mountains
of the Jura, obscured the lingering remains of daylight. The darkness soon became appalling; you could
feel it; and as we were not able to see an inch in
advance of us, we thought it better to trust to the
intelligence of our horses than our own blinded
vision, and, slackening the reins, we let them go as
they would. ·

'In spite of the obscurity, the animals went at a
tolerable pace. They were old travellers, and not to
be daunted by a little; but we seemed to get no
nearer the end of the wood, that, revealed to our eyes
now and then by the lightning, looked denser and
denser, and we began to fear that, in the darkness,
the horses had turned into one of the by-roads

leading from the main one, when, after having been, as near as we could guess, from two to three hours in the forest, we saw a light in front of us, and in a few seconds drew up before a white house, in a clearing on the left side of the road. My brother, being in advance of us, jumped down, and knocking at the door, which was opened by a wrinkled old woman, inquired if we were in the right road to Bletteran; and on being answered in the affirmative, with the additional information that it would take some four or five hours more to reach the place, he thought it best to ascertain if we and our horses could have food and lodging there for the night. Finding that we could, we at once decided to remain, as the animals were getting tired, and none of us relished the idea of two more hours' journey in the wood, the house, the old woman told us, being stationed about half-way through.

'At one side of the house was a long high wall with a door large enough to admit carriages; and having followed the old hag, who preceded us with a lantern and opened the gate, we asked her if there was no one to rub down our horses and give them their food: upon which we learned, to our surprise, that in that lonely place there were but two women, herself and a servant-girl, and that our horses would stand a good chance of getting nothing to eat if we did not attend to them ourselves. She said we should find plenty of hay and straw in a loft she pointed out to us, and then, giving us the lantern, walked off to prepare our supper.

'Before proceeding further, I must endeavour to give you some idea of the construction of the building in which we were destined to spend so eventful a night—a night that, so long as we live, will be freshest of all we have ever passed, in the memory of everyone of us. It had two stories, the lower one consisting of a large kitchen with two entrances, one from the road, the other from the stable-yard, and a small room leading from it at the back, used as a bed-chamber by the women: opposite the front door was a flight of stairs, having the wall on one side and boxed off by wood on the other, leading to a bedroom extending over the small one below and the stable, which filled up the square of the building, and was entered from the yard; and over the kitchen was a place for drying and storing linen, &c., reached by some steps over the front entrance.

'On entering the kitchen, we found the old woman busy cooking an omelette, which, she told us politely enough, was all, save bread and cheese and wine, that the house afforded for our suppers: and, whilst eating it, she let us know that she had a husband, who was often from home, and was then gone to some fair, a good distance off, and would be absent three days. Supper over, my brothers went to water their horses, and give them a feed of the oats they always took with them on such journeys : and while they were gone, the old woman having mounted up-stairs, I opened the front door and walked out into the road to see if the storm had passed over, when, to my surprise, I was joined by the servant, a rather good-looking girl, with whom we had been joking about the impossibility of her finding a husband in a hole like that. On attempting a renewal of the *plaisanterie*, I saw that she hardly seemed to notice what I said, and, not caring to have all the conver-sation on one side, was moving away towards the entrance to the yard, when she touched my arm, and said in a whisper, "Mind you shut your door to-night," and then, as if fearful she had said too much, exchanged a few jesting words and disappeared quickly into the house.

'When I joined my brothers in the stable, I re-peated to them what the girl had said; at the same time giving my brother a caution about the careless habit he had of wearing the leather belt, in which he carried his money, outside his shirt, where it was exposed to the view of everyone, instead of next his skin, telling him that I had more than once seen the woman's eyes fixed on it during our supper. They laughed and made fun of me, saying that artists were always scared at their own shadows; and as the girl had spoken in a tone half jesting, half earnest, I thought that very likely they were right, and determined to think no more of the matter.

' On re-entering the house, we asked to be shown where we were to sleep; and the girl, taking up a light, preceded us up-stairs, and along a narrow passage, that turned first to the right and then to the left, into the bedroom I have spoken of, and, setting down the candlestick containing the smallest bit of candle on a table, said, " Good-night," and left us. As soon as she was gone, my brother-in-law, according to his invariable custom, endeavoured to secure the door, but found there was neither lock nor bolt, though there were marks of there *having been* both ; and, coupling this with the servant's words to me, the singular circumstance of finding only women in a place so very far from any other habitation, and the smallness of the candle, that was declared to be the only morsel in the house, *he* too began to have suspicions that all was not right, and determined to make the door as secure as he could. For this

purpose he took a chair, and breaking off the two
hind legs, placed two of the ends in the iron sockets
of the empty bolts, making the others fast with
stout cord to the large iron hinges, one sees on all
the doors in French country-houses. He then looked
to the priming of his pistols, which were double-
barrelled ones, and placed them on a chair by his
bedside; and though my brother looked on with a
scornful smile at our preparations, saying that he
had travelled for twenty years and was not dead yet,
I fancied that, as I was getting into bed, I saw something shining, very like pistols, on the *commode* at
the foot of his bed, which made me think that he
thought more about the matter than he cared to own.
I should tell you that my brother was one of the
most powerful fellows I ever knew, nearly six feet
and a half in height. He had the stature and strength
of a giant, but he was rash and unthinking, and I
had far more confidence in my brother-in-law, who,
though a very fine man, was inferior to my brother
in brute strength, but had a much clearer brain and
cooler blood.

‘ There were three beds in the room—one behind
the door, occupied by my brother's friend—another
near the wall on the right, in which I and my
brother-in-law slept—and a third, placed across the

little low window opening in the middle, was taken
possession of by my brother, because it was in the
most airy situation. Whatever our suspicions, they
certainly were not alarming enough to prevent our
going fast asleep, and we must have been more than
an hour in bed, when I was aroused by hearing a
noise like some one pushing against the door; but, as
it ceased before I could be said to be broad awake,
I thought I had been dreaming a reflection of my
fears, and was dozing off again, when a loud crash,
followed by a dull sound as of a heavy body falling,
made us all spring from our beds, and, by the light of
the moon struggling through the clouds, I saw my
brother kneeling on his bed, his face towards the
window; and though the light was but feeble, I felt
horribly certain that there was blood on his right
hand, that was clenched and extended before him.
Without changing his position, he told us, in a few
hurried words, that as he was turning round in bed he
caught sight of a face looking in at the window, and,
without a moment's reflection, had struck at it through
the glass, knocking it backwards and cutting his hand
in the act. The words were hardly out of his mouth,
before another face appeared and shared the fate
of the first; but by this time my brother-in-law had
seized his pistols, and, thrusting one into my brother's

hand, suddenly opened the window, and seeing
several men on the ladder, with seven or eight more
below armed with hatchets, he waited until those
ascending were on a level with the window, when he
gave the ladder a tremendous push backwards, my
brother at the same moment discharging both barrels
of his pistol among them; and while stretching out
his hand to reach his own, my brother-in-law shot
off the one he held, and was followed up by my
brother firing all his four barrels at the murderous
crew.   During this time I guarded the door with a
stem of the broken chair, while our friend tore open
one of the beds and set fire to some of the straw
to give us a light.   When my brother fired off his
last pistol, my brother-in-law, who had been quietly
reloading, placed himself by the side of the window,
expecting a fresh attack; but after an anxious sus-
pense of several minutes, during which we could distinctly hear the groans of more than one wounded,
growing fainter as if retreating to a distance, he
ventured to look out, and saw that our foes were no
longer there.

'Though we were rid of our assailants outside, they
might be in the house; and for this reason we thought
it prudent to remain where we were a short time
longer, before descending to see what had become of

our property in the stables. After listening intently for ten minutes or so, and hearing nothing, we determined to make an attempt to get below; but, believing that the men were most likely lying in ambush in the crooked corridor, it was necessary to arrange our plans with caution as well as boldness. Having been twitted as a coward the night before, I went first, holding a loaded pistol in each hand, followed by my brother with two bunches of lighted straw twisted in lieu of torches; then came my brother-in-law with two more pistols, followed by our friend with more torches. At two yards from the door was the elbow in the passage where we expected the villains would be secreted; and I told my brothers that if they saw me raise my pistols from the horizontal position, they must be prepared to fight for their lives. As noiselessly as we could, we undid the fastenings of the door, and threw it open. In one stride I was at the turn—it was empty; in another I was at the stair-head. My brother threw a torch into the kitchen, and down we ran, my first act, after ascertaining that the kitchen was clear, being to look under the stairs; my brother directing his attention towards the doors, to see that no one entered, while the others searched the little bed-room, that bore marks of having been recently slept

in, but was now untenanted. We then secured the
front door, and opening the one leading into the
yard, rushed out in a body, hoping by that means
to scatter our enemies should they be collected
to attack us; but all was quiet as the grave, and
on entering the stable we were no less surprised
than rejoiced to find our horses and carriages untouched. We then began to breathe; and as the
morning was breaking our spirits rose, and I suggested that while two were putting the horses in the
carriages, one should accompany me to search the
cellar and loft, as it would be a piece of good fortune
if we could secure only one rascal and deliver him up
to justice; but we found no one—and, indeed, nothing
save a bag of meal and a cask of wine, which we let
run over the meal, as the only mode of revenge
left open to us.

'When all was ready to start, we went round the
house and examined under the window of our
bedroom, where we found a pool of blood, but did
not deem it prudent to follow the traces further than
the outskirts of the wood, up to which blood was
distinctly visible. This over, we set off at a gallop,
expecting every moment to receive a volley from our
foes. We had full two hours' ride through the forest,
and it was not until we were out of it that we found

the use of our tongues. By that time the sun was up; and when we had leisure to look into each other's faces, we agreed that we had more the savage look of murderers, than of men flying for their lives. From the first moment of attack, our attention had been so strained, our whole thoughts so exclusively occupied in guarding against the dangers that threatened us on all sides, that it was not until we were in the open country that we began fully to realise the horrors of the dreadful fate we had escaped from—an escape we owed to the prudence and coolness of my brother-in-law; for if the wretches had been able to obtain entrance into our bed-room, they would have cut us to pieces with their hatchets; and after obtaining possession of my brother's belt—the prize, it was evident, they most coveted, from their having left the horses and carriages untouched—they would have burned the carriages, killed the horses, taken off the booty to the woods, and nothing would ever have been known of us, or our fate.

'On reaching Bletteran, our first care was to make our report to the Procureur-Royal and the Gendarmerie, who told us that the house had long been *suspecte*, and more than once searched, on account of robberies and other crimes having been supposed to have been committed there; but nothing had ever

s

been discovered or proved against the people, and to
search the woods without a large armed force was
impossible, as horses could not penetrate far; and for
a few gendarmes to go on foot, was to cause death
without any good resulting from it. We left our
depositions in the hands of the authorities, and, after
travelling a few days longer with my brothers, I left
them to go farther south.

'About a year and a half after, on returning from
Paris, influenced probably by a strong desire I had
to know if anything more had ever come to light on
the matter, I again passed along the same road, but
this time in a diligence in the middle of the day,
and heard from the driver an exaggerated account of
our adventures there, with the additional information,
that, soon after, a troop of gendarmes had been despatched to the place, and, whilst making researches,
discovered the bodies of a young girl and a gendarme
buried in the cellar—that the house had been destroyed by order of the Government, and nothing had
ever been heard or seen of the old woman or servant-
girl, who were supposed to have gone off into the
woods, since the night of our extraordinary escape.
—And now, if the brandy is not all burned away, let
us have some punch.'

CHAPTER XIII.

In the intervals of smoking and sipping their punch, Mons. B—— begged that the children might be sent to bed, before he commenced his tale, as he assured us, it contained incidents of so startling and frightful a nature, that they might have a very alarming effect upon their nerves. Against this, the younger ones stoutly protested, assuring him that the more they were frightened, the more they liked it: but I saw that the little pupil was becoming nervous, until I whispered something in his ear that composed him, and enabled him to listen quietly to Mons. B——'s 'tale of horrors,' as he termed it.

'In the summer of 1840 my friend the Brigadier and I made a tour through the Upper Valais, and a portion of the neighbouring Canton de Berne; and, being both of us younger, more active, and sure of

s 2

foot than at present, when even the ascent of a few
insignificant rocks skirting a cascade is attended with
danger—(cries of " Order " from the Brigadier)— we
accomplished the difficult task of passing over the
Strahleck from Gründenwald to Grimsels, where we
slept at the Hospice, then tenanted by the celebrated
Zibbach, who gained his unenviable notoriety by
murdering a student a few years after our visit.

‘ Being dreadfully fatigued with our long and hard
day's journey of sixteen hours, we slept so late the
following morning, that it was afternoon before we
set out on our return to Meyringen, where we intended stopping two or three days.   Having lingered
on our way to sketch the lonely châlet of Roderichs-
boden, the only human dwelling between the Hospice
and the little hamlet of La Handek, we found that we
had consumed so much of the daylight, that we had
better stop and sleep at the latter place, where we
knew we could get both supper and a bed, and a
view of the Falls of the Aar in the morning, instead
of attempting to reach Meyringen that night.

‘ Before coming to Handek, the road passes, or did
pass, for some distance, through a forest of firs strewn
with shattered rocks—about as gloomy and murder-
suggesting a place as anyone can imagine—and we
began to wish we had retained the services of at least

one of the guides we had dismissed at the Hospice, when, below us, in the steep rough road, we saw several men hiding behind the largest rocks and trees, as if on the look-out to waylay unfortunate travellers like ourselves. So suspicious was their appearance, that the Brigadier whispered to me, "I believe those men have murdered some one;" and most assuredly neither of us relished the idea of going forward—but what were we to do? they must have caught sight of us, and to turn back was only exposing ourselves to still greater danger from having betrayed our alarm. A few moments' consultation decided us to proceed, although expecting that, if not killed, we should at least be robbed and beaten. We had no weapons but our alpenstocks, and our paint-boxes strapped to our backs: so, shoving the latter round on our side, so as to shield the region of the heart, and grasping more stoutly the former trusty friend, we marched with valiant strides to the spot where we had seen the men, and discovered—(look to the children!)—that these dreadful brigands were engaged in blasting rocks to make a better road!

'This alarming incident, as you may suppose, had so startling an effect upon our nerves, that we had not recovered from the shock by the time we reached the auberge at *La Handek*, where, finding seven or eight

desperate-looking men, each armed with a stout stick,
drinking in the kitchen, we were naturally led to
regard them with distrust, and began to have doubts
of the security of the place. The Brigadier, who
was always cooler and more philosophical than I,
quieted my apprehensions a little by remarking, that
murders were not often committed without some
motive, and he could see none in making away with
two poor fellows, with no more money in their purses
than was sufficient to pay for their night's lodging.
Though constitutionally a nervous man, arising from
my mother having been frightened by a spider, it is
a remarkable fact that my fears rarely affect my
appetite ; and on this particular night, I well remember, that I took my supper of coffee and boiled eggs,
as tranquilly as if I had been in my own rooms at
L——e, instead of being in the company of a lot
of villanous-looking peasants, and the recollection of
our afternoon's adventure fresh in my mind.

'When we reached our bed-room, I tried, like the
brother of our friend M——, to compensate for the
absence of any fastening on the door by rearing a long
bench against it, that I found in the room; so that,
in case of anyone entering, the noise of its fall would
awake me, and give me time to grasp my alpenstock
before I was attacked. The Brigadier was still so

fatigued with his exertions of the preceding day, that
he was asleep and snoring, long before I had completed
all the precautions I thought it advisable to take for
our safety, before getting into bed, where I lay,
thinking over the events of the day, unable to sleep,
until eleven o'clock, when I heard some one without
shoes ascend the stairs, that creaked as boards *will*
creak when anyone is endeavouring to walk stealth-
ily, and creep along the corridor to the door of our
room; and then the falling of my bench told me the
door had been pushed open! I was never a very
bold man; and when I found that the crash did not
awake the Brigadier, whose snoring was still regular
and distinct, I thought it better, before resorting to
so desperate an expedient as using my alpenstock, to
cover my head with the bed-clothes; but, after a
length of time that seemed interminable, during
which I could hear nothing but the beating of my
heart, I ventured to raise myself slowly in bed, and,
seizing my weapon, groped my way across the room
to the bedside of my friend, whom I asked in a
whisper, if he had not heard a noise. He answered
in the affirmative; but I must own that to this day I
am doubtful whether he spoke the truth, and, declining to rise and assist me in my search after the
intruder—who, I felt certain, must be concealed some-

where in the apartment—my courage rose in the presence of so much pusillanimity, and I began poking
under the beds, round the walls, and into every hole
and corner I could feel in the darkness, in the hope
of piercing the robber with the sharp point of my
stick.

'For full ten minutes I dodged backwards and
forwards, now and then hearing a breathing as of
some one close to me, but unable to discover anyone,
until all at once I felt my pole slip into some hollow
place: and only imagine my sensations when it struck
against something soft.   I pressed with all my force
against my victim, who struggled desperately; but I
pinned him fast while shouting for help, though
I cannot say I had any clear ideas respecting the
quarter from which it was to come; and the moment
I paused for breath, a voice from the gloom cried out,
"Please, monsieur, don't do me any harm—I sleep
in this recess; and, as I tried my best not to awake
you as I entered, I cannot think what made such a
great noise."   At the same moment, the door opened,
and in walked the master and mistress of the house
on their way to bed, our chamber, it appeared, being
the highway to all the rest, that were alcoves leading
from it; and, as the light of their candle revealed me
standing in my shirt, apparently in the act of killing

their poor man-servant, who was nearly dead with fright, I thought they would never have done laughing; and my shame and confusion were so great, that, ladies and gentlemen, I hope you will not oblige me to live over again these painful moments by relating them to you.'

The president pleading, that the duties of his office exempted him from tale-telling, our tall French artist was appealed to, for a contribution towards the amusement of the company, and, bowing profoundly, he said, very politely, that his own life had been so inadventurous that it possessed no incidents worth relating, but he would, if we pleased, read one that was told to him by a friend and fellow-student to whom it occurred, and which he had endeavoured to write out, since he heard that story-telling was to be the delightful entertainment of the evening; and, drawing a paper from his pocket, he read the narrative I shall relate, as faithfully as my memory will permit me.

'In the Département de la Nièvre there is a rocky woody district called Morven, inhabited by a half-savage race of people, who, in more than one respect, present a great resemblance to the Irish of twenty years ago. Like them, they live in wretched cabins, with their pigs, fowls, and any other animals they may be so fortunate as to possess, that are not too large to obtain entrance into the hovels. They are exceedingly ignorant, dirty, idle, and poor; their principal food consists of potatoes, varied occasionally with a little buckwheat or rye, made into a coarse kind of bread; and their clothes are of the coarsest and poorest materials. Numbers of these people have never tasted wine, spirits, or meat, save the small portion of the latter obtained from the carcasses of the wretched swine that share their meals while living, and, dead, help to prepare their porcine offspring, happy in their ignorance, for a similar fate.

'In spite of their meagre diet, these Morvendiaux possess amazing strength, as may be seen from their short, thick-set, muscular frames; but, truth compels me to add, even at the risk of being thought ungallant, the women as well as the men are unredeemably ugly. They are extremely quarrelsome amongst themselves; but should any stranger be so unfortunate as to give offence to any one of them, they immediately lay aside all private feuds, and, falling on the offender in a body to avenge the real or fancied insult, he is lucky if he escape with his life. On account of the bad character borne by these people, most travellers pass through the country they inhabit, in the daytime; but it occasionally happens, that an unforeseen circumstance compels an unlucky individual, like myself, to put up for the night at one of the few wretched inns to be seen here and there along the road.

'In the latter half of the year 1848—when the whole of France was still in a state of agitation and excitement from the convulsions into which it had been thrown by the events of the preceding spring, and the new police, appointed after the flight of Louis-Philippe, was not properly organised in the provinces,—these Morvendiaux had cunning enough to take advantage of the troubled times, and did actually, as was afterwards proved, waylay, rob, and kill several persons who happened at different periods to be passing through that part.

'It was during the course of that summer, that, being on a pedestrian tour I had been ordered to take for the benefit of my health, I was obliged, in order to avoid a long détour, to pass through Morven on my way from Autun to Moulin, the chief town of Nièvre, and finding, towards the close of a broiling hot day, that I had overrated my still enfeebled strength and walking powers, I was compelled, much against my inclination, to enter one of those miserable habitations that promise entertainment for man and beast, with the intention of remaining there till sunrise, and then getting on to Moulin before the great heat of the day came on. Not being ignorant of the habits of these people, it did not surprise me to find that the kitchen, which, as usual in these small auberges, served for dining-room as well—was in a state of filth little removed from beastliness; a fact easily accounted for by the presence of the half-starved pigs, who thrust their noses on to my plate, and grunted for a share of my supper of potatoes and bacon. If I had been in my usual robust state of health, I might have quarrelled with my quarters; but, as it was, I was too ill and tired to grumble at anything, if I could but have a bed to lie down on and rest.

'While the hostess was frying my potatoes, I had been absently scanning her appearance; and the more I looked, the more I was struck with her masculine figure, and hideous, repulsive features. She looked about fifty: but the peasant women in France, and in that district in particular, age so prematurely, that very possibly she might have been fifteen or twenty years younger:—but, young or old, she never could have been other than a fiend in looks. When she pointed out my bed-room to me, reached by a ladder-stair from the kitchen, she begged that, as soon as I had done with the lantern she gave me, I would put it outside on the little square landing, between the door of the bed-room and stair-head, as she wanted it to go outside and fetch some wood in for morning.

'No sooner was I left to myself, than one of those presentiments—those extraordinary intelligences of coming evil, that most of us have experienced at some period of our lives—shuddered through me, and for a few moments a fear, vague, mysterious, undefinable, but so intense and horrible that I felt as if I were in the presence of a malign power, completely unmanned me. To recover my composure, rather than from any idea of discovering anything, I searched more than once round the room, which presented nothing extraordinary, if I except its extreme bareness and dirtiness, there being no furniture save two chairs, a table, and bed, on which was a straw mattress and a few dirty rags. The door being without any fastening but a latch, did not excite my suspicion, because it is so common an occurrence; but certain it is that something—it might have been the state of my liver, that, oftener than we imagine, influences our tempers and thoughts, or my supper, or the forbidding appearance of the hostess—had so predisposed me to gloomy apprehensions, that, when I opened the window to admit a little fresh air into the close apartment, I caught myself speculating upon the possibility of effecting an escape that way. I lay down without

undressing, but not to sleep—for, independently of
the pain, fatigue, and depression from which I was
suffering, the fleas were enough to have roused the
enchanted princess.

' I heard the woman come and take away the lantern; after which there was a silence as of death for a
couple of hours, and I was beginning to feel more
assured and composed, and probably might have
gone off into a quiet sleep, when creak went the
stairs.   In a moment I was out of bed and at the
door, through the chinks of which I saw a sight that
froze the blood in my veins, and even at this distance
of time, makes me feel breathless to think of.   There
was that infernal old demon in her chemise, barefooted
and bareheaded, her grey locks hanging wildly about
her face, ascending the stairs, holding in her right
hand a knife such as is used for sticking pigs, and
in her left the lantern, the light falling on her hellish
features, leaving me not the shadow of a doubt as to
her murderous intentions.   The first idea that, quick
as lightning, flashed through me, was to take up the
chair and stun her on entering the room: but she
might have accomplices below; so, turning swiftly
round, I dropped noiselessly from the window, ran
across the little garden, jumped the fence, and was
at the other side of the field in less time than it

takes me to tell it you; and, turning round, *I saw the light was in the room I had left.* Fearing to be pursued if others were in the plot against me, I struck into the wood for some distance, now and then putting my ear to the ground to ascertain if I could distinguish any footsteps; and, after about half an hour of this Indian sort of flight, I ventured to take the road, along which I ran, I am sure, a couple of leagues. I walked all night, and, soon after sunrise, reached the little town of Château Chinon, where I stopped a few hours to rest, and state my case to the police: and I am glad to tell you that the woman was arrested, and sent to the galleys for ten years, having confessed that, seeing I was weak and ill, she had resolved to murder, and then rob me, having noticed, when I paid her before going to bed—as it was my custom when intending to start before break-fast the following morning—that my purse was pretty well filled.

'I must not forget to tell you, that the violent exercise I took that night in running and walking, or the excitement, or the distraction of my thoughts from my ailments—I am not doctor enough to say which—completely re-established my health: but I would not advise any one of my friends to seek for a remedy that was certainly worse than the disease.'

CHAPTER XIV.

No Hope for it—Adieux to Les Plans—Cascade Pissevache—
Gorge du Trient—Mountain-roads—Valaisan Hat—Goître
Crétins—Remarkable Cure of Goître—Clue to an Englishman
—Trident-fishing—A Patriarch—Trout.

As we let out our departing guests that night, the
snow lay so thick on the ground, that we wished
each other a merry Christmas, and the gentlemen
finished up with a game at snow-balling. The next
morning our friends came across, equipped for a
journey; they could stand the weather no longer, and,
having bribed David Bernard to take down their
traps in his cart, were following on foot. We told
them they were cowards—why would they not have a
little more patience? the weather was sure to clear
before long; even now there was an opening in the
sky, through which was actually peeping enough
blue to make a man a waistcoat: and one of the
children declared, they had seen a streak of sunshine
across the valley. Unconvinced, they shook their heads
and pointed to the west, where the clouds were still

gathered as thick as ever, and with many expressions of commiseration for our lonely fate, and promises to rejoin us for a couple of days, if we sent them tidings of a change for the better, they pulled their hats over their brows, and departed in the still pitilessly falling rain and sleet.

In less than an hour after we had said ' good-bye,' our sentiments about remaining had undergone a remarkable change; having no longer anyone to keep us company, and make merry over our mutual misfortunes, we began to feel it *assez triste*, and no longer talked in heroics about braving out the storm. Still it is not unlikely that if we had had only ourselves to consider, we might have starved on a few days more; but we had a visitor who had come all the way from England to enjoy the pastoral delights of living in a châlet, surrounded by the charms of Alpine scenery, in a warm and delicious climate; and with all the good-will possible we could not prevail upon ourselves to believe, that the best way to amuse him was to make him pass his holiday amid all the rigours of a Siberian winter, especially as we felt pretty sure that by descending to Bex we should find summer again; though I must do our friend the justice to remark, that he appeared perfectly happy and contented with his lot, and would, I am sure,

T

have been the last of the party to grumble, for he possessed a fund of wit, gaiety and good-humour, that was not only an antidote to all gloomy thoughts in his own brain, but quickly dispelled any that were beginning to gather in those around him.

It was not without a pang at being forced to forego many a cherished project, that we despatched a stout peasant down the mountains with a note to our host at the Union, desiring him to send up, the following morning, the necessary vehicles to take us and our luggage back to Bex; and then we had enough to do, with collecting our goods and chattels, to prevent our dwelling too much upon the pain of leaving a spot, that had become so cherished in our hearts. Our leave-taking of the kind peasants, among whom we had been so inexpressibly happy, was coupled with a promise to return for a few days before the real winter set in, and all being in readiness for departure, we paid a last visit to the little rooms in which we had known so much real contentment, and with a feeling in our hearts as if we were bidding adieu to a good and valued friend, we got into the carriages, where we were well packed with shawls, and shaking hands again with the black-eyed Louise, who cried at parting from her playfellows, we said ‘good-bye’ to the happiest period of our lives.

Long before reaching Bex we got into a different climate, and it was difficult to believe that not two hours before we had been shivering with cold. There the weather was splendid, though they told us, they had had two days' cold rain, and from the dense mists hovering over the mountains, they imagined we were getting much the worst of it. Our house smelt baked, brown, and dusty; but open windows, brooms and dusters soon made it sweet, and when we assembled on the balcony for dinner, with a curtain to keep off the sun, we agreed we had done well to come down. With the exception of the little fat old librarian, and his wee wife, who had a shop on the ground story, the house had been deserted some time; our proprietor was off for three months' soldiering, his wife with her parents, to whom she had fled after a domestic squabble, that ended in the way of which our police reports furnish so many examples. The summer had brought them no lodgers to occupy their smart rooms, and even the flies were dead, having perished from famine.

We had wasted so many days of our guest's precious vacation in doing nothing, that we set vigorously to work to make up for lost time, and spent the ensuing fortnight almost entirely out of doors, in fishing picnics to our old resort near the Rhone, where we were

within twenty minutes' walk of the Cascade Pisse
vache, that falls like soft clouds of floss silk, and is
so beautiful an object in itself, that one always regrets
nature has not been kinder in placing it where the
mountains are less bare, bleak, and ugly. The awful-
looking gorge through which the Trient rushes to
join the Rhone, was close to; and not seldom the tail
of the wind, that, no matter how calm and serene it
may be outside, roars and howls eternally in that extraordinary chasm, would reach us in the meadows,
upsetting the tent, and lead us a long chase before
we could get all together again.

We also visited many of the villages and hamlets
nestling so peacefully among the mountains, the
paths to some of them being a curiosity, even
in Switzerland, that can challenge all the world
for ingenuity in forming roads in places that appear unapproachable. One village, called Salvent,
was reached by a path wide enough for carts, carried backwards and forwards *sixty times* over a
steep ravine, down which tumbled a strong torrent.
The peasants were all busy collecting their last crops
of hay, or beating their hemp preparatory to storing
it for future labour during winter evenings. The
distance to which these poor people travel to collect a
scanty supply of grass—the whole produce of a day's

labour for two people being frequently carried home on their backs—shows the value of the article. The beating of the hemp, which here is never macerated as in France and Italy, sounds exactly like boys frightening birds in a field; and though pleasant and picturesque to look at from a distance, with the groups of peasants round the antiquated-looking machine in common use here for this purpose, it is a dirty and disagreeable occupation, from the quantity of fluff, dust, and dirt that fly out of the plant while being beaten.

Then there were afternoons at the Tour d'Huyn, a fine ruin perched on a rocky eminence that, rising abruptly from the centre of the valley, looks as if in unrecorded ages it had fallen from the giant mountains behind it; and one long day, from five in the morning till eight at night, was taken up in a journey to Champéry, the road to which, carried along the mountains on one side of the Valley *de l'Abondance*, takes you through one of the most smiling and luxuriant scenes in Switzerland. The inhabitants, too, as you get nearer Savoy, are decidedly less plain, and one might almost venture to call the women good-looking, if we were not afraid of being accused of gross falsehood, should any traveller, after reading our statement, see them before

he has visited the other parts of the Valais and the
Vaud, and discovered that, by comparison with an
ugliness that reaches deformity, a plainness set off
by cleanliness, fine teeth, and a more becoming
attire, may look handsome. For head-dress they wear
a bright red kerchief bordered with blue, the ends
tied in a knot under each ear, somewhat after
the fashion I have seen English haymakers make
caps of their pocket handkerchiefs—a far more becoming *coiffure* than the disfiguring hat common
throughout the rest of the Valais. It is the highest
ambition of a Valaisan woman to possess one of
these same hats, which are shaped much like those
worn by Welshwomen, but not quite so high in the
crown, that is always entirely covered with a fine
rich ribbon about nine inches wide, magnificently
embroidered and fringed with gold and silver. This
ribbon being sewn in *bouffantes* standing out far
beyond the rim, gives the hat a frightfully heavy
appearance, and is very unbecoming even when worn
by a pretty girl, as *once* it was my good fortune to
see it.

A woman without a *goître* is so rare a sight in
these cantons, that when you encounter one whose
neck is distended no wider than her face, it is impossible to avoid thinking her, if not beautiful, at
least particularly charming; and as those in the parts

I have been speaking of, are afflicted in a much less degree with this horrible malady, than any others I have seen in the Vaud or Valais, it is perhaps the reason why I retain an impression so favourable to their appearance. On the minds of all foreigners the sight of the victims to this disease leaves a most unpleasant impression; but this impression becomes far more painful when, after a residence in the country, your eyes are opened to the fact that in many extensive districts, not only very few families, but very few individuals, are exempt from it. In all Bex I do not know a female, young or old, that can be said to be entirely without it; if they have not the huge *goître* hanging to the waist, they have the lumpy, swollen neck; and though the dress of the men renders it less observable in them, it is rare to find one with a throat the size that nature gave him. Nor is the disease confined to man alone; animals frequently suffer from it; and from my own experience I can speak of two cases: one, our Spitz, that we had brought from Germany, had not been here above three months when she had a *goître* larger than her head, that was cured in a few weeks by rubbing with iodine ointment and applying bandages wetted with alcohol camphré; the other, a St. Bernard dog, was similarly attacked and also recovered. The *vétérinaire* who attended these pets told me, that such cases were by no means rare, and that he had just lost a favourite dog from the same complaint.

Among all the theories advanced as to the cause of *goître*, not one appears to be relied upon as the true one by medical men, who here appear to regard it with the same indifference and unconcern, exhibited by the people in general about it, and take little or no trouble, either in the way of cure, or of endeavouring to arrest its progress by spreading among the people a knowledge of the necessary precautions and remedies against the loathsome disease. The common belief among the people is, that it is produced by the glacier waters; and, unlike most widely-spread beliefs that, even amid a mass of errors, are almost certain to contain some germs of truth, this theory appears to be entirely without foundation; for if correct, how is it, it may be asked, that the malady is seen in its most aggravated form in the low swampy valleys where the air is filled with pestilential malaria, and not on the mountains nearest the source of the glacier torrents? As people all over the world

> Compound for sins they are inclined to,
> By damning those they have no mind to,

it may be said, *par plaisanterie*, that they have given this bad character to the pure element, in

order to afford to their consciences a plausible plea
for indulging in a vice, they love only too well.
Accustomed from their birth to the sight of this
deformity, the inhabitants scarcely regard it as an
evil, and the little children talk of ' getting a *goître*'
as of a thing inevitable, and as little to be dreaded
as cutting their teeth. If it were a disease that
more speedily affected the general health, it is to
be believed that more anxiety would be manifested
in procuring and applying those remedies that have
been proved efficacious; but, as its influence on the
system is usually almost imperceptible until the
tumour has attained a great size, when the breathing becomes painfully difficult, and the body, and
not unfrequently the brain, much enfeebled, very
few will ever take the trouble to give any attention
to it; and I am very far from jesting when I say,
that if not considered in the light of an ornament,
it is certainly not looked upon as a defect.

The true crétin, or beau crétin, as he is called,
has no *goître*, but is a stunted, deformed, loathsome
spectacle, without intelligence, will, or speech; with
a countenance in which it is difficult to trace the
least resemblance to the human face divine. Generally he is harmless, though there are occasional
exceptions to this rule; but the first sight of one

of these wretched creatures is enough to strike the beholder with terror and dismay, especially if it should be such a specimen as I have more than once seen in the miserable villages lying in the flat, damp valleys near the Rhone, where the people are about the most ugly, diseased, unhappy-looking race I have ever met with; for, in addition to *goître* and *crétinism*, they are dreadful sufferers from ague and other fevers. In one of our fishing ' outs,' I was sitting in the tent, and hearing a strange noise, unlike anything I ever listened to, looked out, and saw something creeping towards me among the long grass, that I took for an animal, but of what kind I was not able to determine. The children, who had been watching it some minutes, ran to me as it neared us; and when it reached the opposite side of the stream by which we were encamped, it raised itself upright, and, brandishing its long arms, uttered such awful, unearthly sounds, that we shuddered with horror. It was a crétin, and the worst I ever beheld; so like a wild beast in its movements, creeping on all-fours or leaping like a kangaroo; the noises it made in its frightful attempts at speech—its deformed head, so disproportionately large, covered with matted elfin hair—a creature so hideous, so revolting, and even terrifying, that pity for the misfortunes of the miserable being, was lost in a feeling of disgust.

A doctor, who has lived all his life in these parts, told me that, if the *goître* appeared in three successive generations in the same family, the fourth was invariably a crétin : and if this be true, it would be a curious matter of research for statistical heads, to discover *how many ages must elapse before Switzerland will be entirely a nation of crétins.*

Before I leave this melancholy subject, I must not omit to relate a remarkable case of cure of a *goître*. In the year 1847, some French soldiers passing through Martigny, met a poor woman afflicted with one of these tremendous swellings, and one of them, being drunk, passed his sword through it, saying, ' he would do her good service to rid her of her life.' Believing he had killed her, he got out of the place as soon as he could; but having, it appears, some stings of conscience for his wanton cruelty, he took the same route, on returning invalided from Italy the year following, for the purpose of making inquiries respecting her fate, and learnt, to his astonishment, and we may hope gratitude also, that not only was she alive, but well, and cured of her *goître* by the very stab he had so wantonly given her.

More than one *maître d'hôtel* in these parts has
told me, that if an Englishman gave no other clue to
his nationality, he would be sure to be known by
the first question addressed to the waiter, after
getting rid of the dust of travel: 'Garçon, I say,
is there good fishing hereabouts?' Ten years ago,
anyone asking that question in Bex would have
been certain to receive a reply in the affirmative,
with very likely the additional sentence, 'and
some of the finest trout in Europe.' But now,
through the want of proper laws and regulations for
their preservation, the fish have greatly decreased in
size and number, though there is still plenty for
good anglers, as the fishing-book of M——'s pedestrian friend, who was pronounced by the old gendarme near the Rhone to be the cleverest and
most successful angler he ever saw, would show.

The whole distance that the Rhone washes the
Vaud—that is, from a little beyond St. Maurice
to Lac Leman—it is bordered on the opposite
side by the Valais, in which canton there is no
restriction upon fishing, save the payment of the
small annual sum of five francs; and it follows, as a
matter of course, that anybody and everybody fishes
when and how he likes, to the great destruction of
the fish, especially during the months of October

and November, when the trout ascend the river for the purpose of depositing their spawn. In the Vaud, the fishing is let by the government to a company, for a certain annual sum, under certain restrictions, the most important of which are, that the company cannot re-let it, and that none of the members can give the gratification of even an hour's angling to a friend, unless he be present also. But there are no laws against fishing at those times and seasons, when, for the preservation of the fish, it is necessary to refrain from the sport. Latterly, however, public attention has been drawn to the alarming decrease of the fish, through their wholesale destruction during the breeding season, and the two cantons talk of passing a law, by which all fishing in the Rhone will be prohibited for six years to come.

Having heard a good deal of a way they have of catching trout with a trident by torchlight, I was anxious to witness the amusement, and on M——'s receiving an invitiation from a member of the Vaud Fishing Co. to accompany him on one of these nocturnal fishing excursions, I obtained permission to be one of the party; and one dark night in the beginning of November, when the river was pronounced sufficiently clear for our purpose, we set out, equipped for bad weather and rough roads, in com-

pany with Monsieur D——, and two men who carried
eatables, and, as our entertainer whispered, 'something else to keep the cold out.' On our way we
called for Rapaz, the fisherman, and his two sons, who
live in a large house he has built among his own
rich meadows, that stretch to the woods skirting the
river.   Down in the valley there he lives, after the
manner of a patriarch, with his sons, their wives and
children, and surrounded by 'possessions of land, and
flocks and herds.'   The old man is known to have
been a terrible fish-poacher in his time, and is still
believed to follow his darling sport, whenever an
opportunity offers of eluding the vigilance of the
gendarmes, against whom, as we wended our way
through the woods, his curses, not loud but deep,
through fear of the owl-like ears of Monsieur D——,
were vented in pretty strong language, mingled with
tales of fishing in the good old time, when the
gendarmes could be bought for a trout, and would
even help him to haul in his net; and trout that now
sells at two francs a pound could be bought for thirty
centimes, for there were more caught weighing
thirty, forty, and even fifty pounds, than there are
now of ten or twelve.

When we reached the Rhone, we walked nearly
a mile by its side before we arrived at the place

selected by the old man; as for this mode of fishing
it is necessary to choose those spots where the trout
have made large holes, and are observed to congregate
during the day. Our first care after our arrival was
to light a fire for the accommodation of those who
rested till their turn came, only one person being
able to fish at a time. The next thing to be done
was to erect a sort of landing stage; and for this
purpose a plank, about twenty feet long, was shoved
over the water, the nearest end resting on the shore,
while the farthest was propped above the water by
means of an upright piece of wood, and placed in
such a position that anyone standing on it could get
a good view of the hole below. About the middle of
this bridge a lantern, darkened at the back, threw a
brilliant light on the water, while it revealed nothing
of the figure of the fisherman standing behind. The
trident is a heavy iron instrument, from fifteen to
twenty feet long, weighing at least thirty pounds,
shaped exactly as you see Neptune's sceptre in Hort's
mythology, but with six teeth instead of three.
With this formidable-looking weapon in hand, old
Rapaz took his stand on the plank in the rear of the
lantern; and as I stood listening eagerly for the sound
of the trident falling in the water, I thought what a
strange scene it was. All around, save the two spots

illuminated by the fire and lantern, was wrapped in darkness, and glancing from the party encamped round the blazing fagots in the wood, to the motionless figure of the old man, who, grasping his long weapon, looked like a sentinel on duty by a watch-fire, Cooper's exciting description of Indian warfare rose up before me: the fisherman was La longue Carabine, and we were the party he was conducting through the wilderness.

Sitting on the bank, I kept my eye fixed on Rapaz, whose figure was clearly visible to me, though perhaps not to the fish. Several times he stooped a little, as if about to essay his skill, but as often drew himself erect as before; and after an hour's waiting and watching, I was on the point of thinking it rather a slow affair after all, when splash, dash went the iron in the water, and the cry of '*Il est harponné*' told me there was some chance of a supper. If the fish struck be a large one, it often requires the help of two or three people to assist the fisher; and Rapaz told me that more than once it has happened to him to lose his fish and trident together. But this time, unfortunately, no such assistance was needed, for in a few moments it lay struggling on the plank, and after unscrewing the teeth of the trident, which are formed like fish-hooks and cannot be drawn back, the old man politely presented me with the capture, that, after the small trout I had been accustomed to see in the English markets, looked to me quite a formidable fellow.

We remained out till midnight, when, the water becoming muddy and swollen from rain or avalanches higher up, we returned home, having caught in all seven trout, weighing from one and a half to four pounds, the first captured being the largest. M. went several times to these night-fishings; but though I was glad to have seen how the business was managed, I cannot say I enjoyed the fun so well as to make me brave the cold and damp the second time. I dare say I shall be accused of English prejudices if I say, that none of the trout I have eaten in Switzerland, not even at Basle, where at *Les Trois Rois* you may stand on the balcony and see hooked the very fish that a quarter of an hour after grace your table, has the same flavour as our island trout; the flesh is coarser, with a slightly muddy taste, very unlike the delicate sweetness for which ours is so much esteemed.

CHAPTER XV.

Winter—Fires and Fire-brigade—Sledging—Swiss Gallantry
— Balls — St. Sylvestre—Fairs — Christmas — New-Year's
Amusements—Burying the Carnival—False Shame—Mar-
riages—Christenings—St. Bernard Dogs—A Word of Advice.

A WINTER in Switzerland! Do not the words conjure
up in the imagination of my readers frightful snow-
storms, avalanches, houses destroyed, whole villages
buried beneath the snow, and all the miseries put so
prominently forth in the papers to excite the com-
passion of a feeling and liberal public? When we
first wrote to our friends in England announcing our
intention of spending the whole winter in the place,
their replies might have been in answer to an intimation that, before this reached them, we should
have put an end to our existence by means of a 'cup
of cold poison,' so full were they of commiseration
for our fate. One who lived in the North, where they
do know what severe cold is, said, 'I shudder when I
think of you shut up among those snow-clad mountains, for I am sure I never could survive it.' Know-

ing that formerly we had ourselves entertained the same idea regarding the climate, we were generously indulgent towards their errors, even when we found that they treated, as travellers' tales, our accounts of violets at Christmas, and the sun so scorching in the middle of the day towards the end of January, that a curtain was needed to shield us from its rays.

The next winter was said to be the most severe experienced since 1828, and then I confess we felt the want of those in-door comforts and luxuries that in England go far towards making amends for the defects of climate, and were more than once caught grumbling at the stupidity and ignorance of a people, who are too satisfied with themselves ever to desire other than they have, and have had for centuries; but when the cold was past, we felt rather ashamed of ourselves for having made so much fuss about a four weeks' frost, during which the supply of water in the fountains was never stopped, and could only excuse ourselves by supposing, that a portion of the common dread and dislike of the people to cold weather, must have communicated itself to us.

Imagine, my readers, that this Siberian winter did not commence till the second week in January, up to which time the weather was warm and bright as June, while primroses, violets, and cowslips, to

mention only those familiar to English ears, were
decking every hedgerow; that during the whole of
the frost we never had the least sign of a mist—the
sky was always blue, with a bright sun, whose setting
was even more lovely than during summer. Night
after night I have stood with M—— to watch those
sunsets, each quarter of the heavens a different colour;
in the south a pale green, the east a deep blue, in
the north the faintest yellow, while the west was a
blaze of crimson, that gradually spread round the
whole circle of the horizon, extinguishing the other
tints, till, having reached the west again, it softly died
away. It not unfrequently happened that so glow-
ing a red followed the setting of the sun as to cause
an alarm of fire being raised—people and engines
hurrying from all parts to some spot believed to be
the seat of the conflagration.

Quite the most amusing public diversions during
the winter are the fires—at least everyone here seems
so to regard them; for as everybody is insured, the
buildings generally tumbledown craggy structures
much better away, and nobody ever injured that I
heard of, one can enjoy the novelty and excitement,
without the dread usually accompanying such spectacles. All that I have seen since coming here—and
I really could not count the number—have occurred

in the night, when you are roused from your sleep by the tolling of the church bell; and after listening for a few seconds to ascertain if it is the ordinary one that rings all through the winter at four, and the summer at three, to wake up the inhabitants and tell them what o'clock it is, you hear the bells of Monthey, Massonger, Colombey, and indeed of every other place within seeing distance of the flames, beginning to peal, and, jumping out of bed, run into all the other rooms to call the children to look at the blaze, though at present, especially if it be behind the house, you have no idea in what direction it is, and then, opening your window, shout out to your landlord, who has just opened the entrance door, and, being captain of the fire-brigade—I never could ascertain of what or of whom it was composed—is obliged to turn out at the first sound of the tocsin, to know, where the fire is, upon which he gazes upwards and rubs his eyes for full five minutes, and at last says, in a very sleepy voice, 'that he really does not know;' and after receiving the same answer from half a dozen of the passing crowd, you descend to see for yourself, following the stream, composed of all the inhabitants of the village. Young and old, male and female, all are there, and on reaching the place of the fire—sometimes three or four miles off—

but you think nothing of the distance when you are running with the flames before you—a bucket is thrust into your hand, and you are somehow pressed into the ranks arranged for passing the water from the fountains to the fire-engines, that are positively as large as those used in England for watering gardens.

I really believe that on such occasions there is not a soul left in any village round, save the one where the fire is raging ; no weather keeps them from the fun, and everybody looks upon an extensive conflagration, as a very welcome *divertissement.* The houses, being generally of wood, burn very swiftly and throw up a tremendous blaze, which has a splendid effect in illuminating the mountains round ; and however one may laugh at the idea of leaving warm beds to take a long walk, or stand on a balcony for some hours, to look at a lot of old houses burning, I know that most people would catch the infection as we did.

My children, too, have caught another epidemic that usually rages in severe winters, but fortunately not a dangerous one—*au contraire,* it is very beneficial. They, the small fry, are the only portion of the community that really enjoy a frost, and to them it is a real godsend, especially if accompanied by a deep snow, as then they can indulge in their passion for sledging, which takes them out of their suffocating, unhealthy rooms, into the fresh and bracing air, and gives them, for once in their lives, a colour and expression more akin to those of children in other countries. It is so exhilarating and delightful an amusement, that I am surprised it has not long ago been adopted by the young people in England, where the severe winters afford so many opportunities of indulging in it. We have imported Christmas trees and other expensive games, while this, that can be enjoyed at a minimum cost, and is moreover the most healthful of sports, has been almost entirely disregarded. The sledges are the simplest and most inexpensive things: any boy can make one for himself, being composed of three pieces of wood, two at the sides seven inches high and a foot and a half or two feet long, rounded upwards at the front, with a third about fifteen inches wide laid on the top, the sides having iron on the edges resting on the ground, to prevent them from wearing away.

This machine is taken to the top of the hill, though it is not *necessary* to have more than a gentle slope to give it an impetus, and sitting on it, with their legs stretched out, and holding on before, they give themselves a shove, and off they go like lightning—guiding themselves by touching the ground with the foot corresponding to the side on which they wish to go, and never neglecting to shout ' Gare ! gare !' to keep others out of the way.   Sometimes three or more lads—I have seen as many as eight—get on each other's backs, knees, and shoulders, and go down together; but the most gallant mode is for each boy, as he seats himself, to hold out his hand to the nearest of the bevy of girls, each taking her turn, collected at the starting-place, and, seating her on his knees, with his arm encircling her waist, off they fly together.   If the descent be very steep—and for the sake of seeing what they can do, they will now and then choose places that are very little removed from the perpendicular—they are compelled to lie flat on the sledges, with their heads a little raised ; and when I saw the amazing velocity at which they flew, I wondered they were not killed; but before long I learned to look upon these *express* sledges with great composure, even when the exhibitors were my own boys and girls.

My first acquaintance with sledging was in S——, where, the winters being very severe, and fine roads ascending the hills from all parts of the city, one could enjoy the sport in perfection.   To be quite

comme il faut, there should be a number of little
bells fastened to the sides, and a bit of the skin of
some animal to sit upon; but this is for the well-to-do
classes only. For myself, I prefer going in a larger
sledge, lined with furs, drawn by a horse gaily
caparisoned, and reins covered with bells, making
pleasant music in the frosty air; but the children say,
it is nothing to the other way, that makes them as
warm as toasts; and there they are right. Sometimes when the nights are moonlight, the young men
and maidens extemporise a sledging party, enjoying
the diversion in pairs; but balls are their passion.
Winter and summer they dance away night after
night, spending all they save on their dresses and
other expenses attending these entertainments.

In this country, where the women have by far the
greater part of the laborious out-door work to do,
besides their domestic duties, it is not to be expected
that much chivalrous attention towards the weaker
sex (call them not fair) should be shown by the
young men; and for this reason I was agreeably
surprised to hear from our young tailleuse, when
talking of a coming ball, that the whole expenses of
it were to be defrayed by the gentlemen. I expressed
my satisfaction at hearing of this solitary instance of
gallantry, when she blushed and smiled, as if ashamed

to give utterance to the truth, and looking down said, ' But if they pay for one, *we*, that is, the girls, have to pay for the next; and they always expect us to give them a *hot* supper, which is much more expensive than the refreshment they provide for us.' I call this paying dear for their partners.

The two grand balls, *par excellence*, of the year take place, the one in November at the time of the great fair, the other on New-Year's Day, and on each of these occasions there is a grand procession of the dancers. The girls, dressed in white, with flowers in their hair, walk each with their partners, and preceded by men carrying lighted torches, flanked by little boys holding Chinese lanterns, and more torch-bearers bringing up the rear, they march to the Hôtel de Ville, where the balls are usually held. There are various societies of young men, quite distinct from each other, some composed of German, and others of French Swiss, who get up these balls, appoint the days on which they are to be held, and select a corresponding number of damsels as their partners; for here they have a fashion, which, if adopted in England, would save many a heart-ache to those partnerless young ladies denominated ' wall-flowers ' —namely, that every gentleman must take a lady. The ball in November lasts three successive nights—

we had almost said days too—being only interrupted
by a short interval of repose—an exploit that puts to
shame any dancing feat recorded of the most invete-
rate belle of a season.

Though citizens of a free republic, there is even in
this little village, where all the inhabitants are small
shopkeepers, artisans, or labourers, quite as much
division into classes as in the most aristocratic towns
in England, and it is laughable to hear talk of, *la
noblesse*, that is composed of hotel-keepers, iron-
mongers, and butchers.

On St. Sylvestre, or New-Year's Eve, all the lads
and lasses try to get a peep into futurity by essaying
a variety of experiments—such as pouring melted
lead into water or snow, the shape it assumes having
reference to their future trade or occupation; or
burning chestnuts in couples, in the same way as we
do apple pippins; or a lot of girls, each with a plate
and a thimble, visit three widows' houses, and presenting each her thimble with her back turned to
the door—for if they look the charm is broken—
receives it filled three successive times, first with
meal, next with salt, and lastly with water. These they
take home on the plates and form into a paste, which
they bake on a red-hot shovel and place under their
pillows, where it remains till they awake in the night,

when they eat it, and, going to sleep again, are sure
to have a vision of the one they are to take ' for better,
for worse.' They also go on foraging expeditions,
for the purpose of stealing fagots, the theft exer-
cising a magical influence on the wood, out of which
each person, blindfolded, pulls a stick; and woe to
the one who seizes a crooked one! for his or her
future partner in life will certainly be shaped as the
twig.

The fairs, that in some parts of the Continent are
so very entertaining and amusing, and even interesting from the vast numbers of people of all nations
you see collected together, and the splendid display
of wares of every description, here present no distinctive features from an ordinary country fair in
England. There is the same sale of cattle in the
morning; the same stalls filled with ribbons, cottons,
buttons, needles, pins, and laces—the same painted
wooden penny toys, and gingerbread kings and
queens with the gilt crowns, in the afternoon; and
the same shows, with ' the wonderful giantess,' and
' girl with hair as long and soft as silk,' and junket-
ing and dancing, at night.

Christmas passes over with very little or no notice
—a holiday, during which no one seems to know what
to do with himself, and a service in the church, that
no one attends, being the only recognition of the

day; but on New-Year's Day, and the day before and after, the whole population gives itself up to all sorts of frolics and mummery. Troups of boys, each lot driving a separate trade, parade the streets and neighbourhood, dressed in the most motley habits, as harlequins, hated Austrians (whose images one can see stuck outside most of the châlets, perforated with bullets), Punches (a popular character everywhere); while some carry pillows squeezed into the likeness of babies, which they kiss and hug with the most boisterous fondness, and others make the most desperate attempts to imitate military music by means of a little drum, tambourine, and whistle, and entering unbidden all the houses—for during those three days disorder is king—march upstairs, enter the rooms, and nearly deafen you with whistling and drumming, until you bribe them away for an hour or two, by giving them money or a sausage. At the end of the third day, the money and sausages collected go towards a feast, which the lesser boys share with an equal number of little girls, while the portion belonging to the elder ones is consumed the night of the grand ball. The wind-up of all this fun and rollicking is a procession, called the burying of the carnival; and as the first I witnessed had more humour and wit in the representation than the others, I will endeavour to describe it.

There is nothing the Vandois enjoy so much, as holding up to ridicule the priests of a sect, from whose domination they have formerly suffered, and whose debasing, degrading, and impoverishing influence is still so frightfully evident in the adjoining Canton du Valais, where the slovenly cultivated ground, that has not its equal in Switzerland for natural richness and fertility, the dilapidated cottages, and squalid, filthy inhabitants, contrast so powerfully even with the, only comparatively, well-to-do thriving look pervading the Canton de Vaud. The actors in the farce I saw could not have selected more appropriate weather for the exhibition—a very broad burlesque on a catholic funeral—it being wet, dark, and gloomy, with a drizzling rain falling, and, in spite of the cold and wet, was witnessed with delight by all the population of Bex and the neighbourhood, who actually left their hot rooms, and crowded after it with every manifestation of delight and approval.

A few feet in advance of the rest of the procession marched the cross-bearer, habited in a white petticoat tied round his neck, and carrying a long pole garnished with sausages ; and after him the Marguillier, or churchwarden, in a red petticoat, grey blouse, and white nightcap, stuffed at the end, and tied round to form a ball standing upright, an immense

pair of wooden spectacles on his nose, and one eye
blackened, chanting the responses; next walked *un
enfant de chœur*, singing, and habited in a white
shirt, ringing a bell, while the priest, who followed
arrayed in a black curtain with a hole to pass his
head through, a child's bib under his chin, and a
black worsted stocking for a skull-cap, kept turning
round while chanting the *De profundis*. After him
walked another chorister, dressed as the first, but
carrying a besom instead of a bell, representing the
Aspersorium, with which, after dipping it in the
pools of dirty water lying in the roads, he sprinkled
the body, borne on a ladder, a rather uncomfortable
bier for a live corpse, with his face hidden under a
mask, and two bottles tied together, in the form of a
cross, lying at his feet. After the body came the
relations of the deceased, shamefully drunk; the
father and mother, who walked nearest the bier,
howling like keeners at an Irish wake; and last of all
stalked a tall gaunt figure, arrayed entirely in black,
his dark hair hanging down each side of his face,
carrying a scythe, to represent Time.

At midnight, on New-Year's Eve, there is always
another procession of people dressed entirely in
white, to say farewell to the Old Year and welcome
the New; and certainly the actors do not follow the

precept we are in the habit of giving to our children,
namely, to turn over a new leaf with the commencement of another year, for they imbibe so many pota-
tions of strong drink, that, long before they have
perambulated half the village, most of them are left
lying in the streets.

That spirit of exclusiveness and pride, which forms
so prominent a feature in our national character, and
renders us so averse to having the secret of our
everyday occupations laid bare before the eyes of
any but our own household, does most assuredly
prevent our enjoying life so much as if we were more
simple, natural, and less ashamed of being seen engaged in those employments, that everybody knows it
is right should be done, or the order and comfort of
all homes would be at an end.   Who does not blush
at being detected in the act of dusting a room, or
tidying the fireplace? and what lady dare invite her
dearest friend, who shares the secrets of her heart,
into the kitchen while making her pastry or ironing
her lace? though if it were not for this false shame,
she might have the most charming confidential chats
while finishing her work, that otherwise will have to
be put aside for another morning.   The worst of
this is, that it makes us such terrible hypocrites; for
is it not impossible that while Angelina, who has left

her pastry spoiling, is embracing Clementina, and declaring, that she is enchanted to see her—is it not impossible, I say, that in her heart of hearts she should wish other, than that she had been a hundred miles away? The *stronger* sex, too, are not a jot stronger-minded in this respect: how many have I seen who have wished. themselves fathoms deep under-ground if caught grinding the coffee, greasing their boots, or nursing the baby to ease the aching arms of their patient hard-working wife, who with nine children has but one small maid-of-all-work, and the washing done at home!

I have been led to make these remarks by noticing the total absence of this sort of false shame among the Swiss, whose manners are just as easy and unembarrassed, whether they are found at the wash-tub, or arrayed in their best attire. I have never gone into society, here or in Germany, without wishing that the stiffness, mannerism, and disgusting affectation that positively prevent most English women, and many men, from speaking in their natural voices, and causes the tone of even our most friendly parties to be so disagreeably and fatiguingly ceremonious and constrained, could be exchanged for the naturalness and homeliness, everyone finds so agreeable in our intercourse with foreigners.

x

The Swiss, unlike us, have no idea of engaging
in any, save the most ordinary daily labours, without
the company and assistance of their friends and
neighbours; and this causes them to have a good
deal of fun and merriment during the winter evenings, for which times they lay aside a variety of
occupations in order that they may enjoy these
neighbourly gatherings, or, as the Americans would
call them, 'Bees.' There are the walnuts to be
cracked, picked, pounded and crushed, for the fine oil
they yield; the hemp, already dried and beaten in
the autumn, to be pulled, sorted, combed and spun;
sausages to be made, dried, and smoked—a job that
sometimes takes several days, as a family will make
enough at one time to last the whole year; grass to
be pulled, and mattresses to be filled; candles to be
manufactured, and a host of other things of the
making of which we know little or nothing, because,
fortunately, we can purchase them more cheaply, and
of a better quality.

Marriages are not generally supposed to belong to
one particular season more than another; but as I
have noticed that the Vaudois have a predilection
for solemnising them during the winter, it will not
be out of place to mention them here. The reason
of their preferring that time of the year above all

others, I have not been able to discover; possibly it
is that, during the rest, they are much too busily and
pleasantly occupied. In the Vaud there is no possibility of having a delightfully romantic runaway
marriage, under the age of twenty-three, as until
that time no man or woman can enter into the
holy bonds of matrimony, without the consent of
their parents, of which the curé of the parish must
be assured before he dare publish the banns. When
a marriage has been agreed upon, the parents of the
parties pay a visit to the curé, for the purpose of
telling him that, on a Sunday named, they authorise
him to announce the promise of marriage between
their children. These *annonces* are read three successive Sundays, as in England; and the names of
the parents are always read after those of the parties
to be married. A notice of the promise or engagement is always published in the papers, so that both
parties are held pretty fast, and neither could very
well defend a breach of promise of marriage case;
indeed, instances of unfulfilled marriage contracts are
almost unknown here. These laws are applicable to
all classes, there being no licences for the rich, as with
us; but in the private arrangements each class has a
fashion of its own—*the noblesse* imitating the English,
whilst among the peasants it is not considered *comme*

il faut to have the parents present at the ceremony, an old aunt and uncle of the bride, if possible, being always selected to accompany the cortége to church.

At midnight, before the bridal morning, they commence firing off cannon, which boom at intervals, varying according to the means of the parties, until the next night. The bride is always attired in black silk or woollen, a voluminous white veil, and a wreath of white flowers, the last being purchased by her three bridesmaids, who have also to provide a breakfast service as a present to the newly-married couple; the three groomsmen having, as far as I could learn, nothing to do but grace the procession, and assist in demolishing the hot dinner provided by the bride's mother. The ceremony takes place precisely at twelve at noon, and as the procession passes along, the by-standers throw corn in the way, in emblem of the abundance and plenty they desire may attend the future lot of the pair.

I never see a Swiss christening—with the portly *sage-femme* so proudly carrying the tiny babe, decked out in ribbons, laces, and robes that sweep the ground; the mother (we name her first on this occasion) and father, sisters, brothers, and other relations, following in their holiday dresses—without thinking of a picture representing such a scene in

Goldsmith's 'Geography,' a book that was my especial delight when a child. The clothes worn by the infant at the baptism, including a fine white ribbon sash, and lace veil, are all provided by the godmother, who, early on the morning of the day, sends them in great state on a large tray, covered with white paper, as a present to her god-child. The whole day is kept as a grand festival, the *sage-femme* being always, among all classes, the most honoured of the invited guests.

I am quite sure that the greatest amusement the villagers of Bex ever experienced, during their winter months, was in witnessing the breaking in of our two St. Bernard dogs, that M—— taught to run in a wooden carriage he had constructed to hold two children, as orderly, and almost as swiftly, as well-trained horses. It was extraordinary how soon, seeing that at the beginning they were just like two untameable lions, they became accustomed to the work, and obeyed the touch of the reins and voice of the boy-driver. These St. Bernard dogs, though docile, fine-tempered, and handsome, are not by any means the extraordinarily sagacious, magnificent-looking animals the popular accounts and engravings—the last generally to be found in seaside lodging-houses—would lead us to believe.

These pictures usually represent a dog of colossal proportions standing with one foot on the breast of a traveller, who lies insensible, and half-covered with snow, close to some tall pines, of which many more are to be seen higher up on the road leading to the Hospice, from which one sees issuing two or more portly monks, staff and crucifix in hand, to administer the last consolations of religion to the poor wretch, who appears already too far frozen, for any human aid to be able to restore him to consciousness.   The dog has always a bottle containing brandy tied round his neck, and a cloak strapped on his back; and this absurd picture is taken (I, for one, believed it most implicitly) as a true and faithful delineation of what actually occurs there.   Anyone who has been at the convent of Mont St. Bernard can see with his own eyes that not a tree grows within some miles, and that the dogs are not nearly so large as a well-grown Newfoundland; and as I have taken the pains to make very minute inquiries of the monks—who are the most polite, gentlemanly men I ever saw, quite *au fait* with all that is passing in the world outside, and the usages of polite society—I can venture to say one or two words on the matter.

In the first place, the dogs are never sent out

alone, nor with a cloak or any other garment
strapped on their backs, and a bottle of brandy
hanging round their necks ; and their sense of smell,
though good, is not of that wonderful, almost
miraculous, keenness attributed to them. Their
great usefulness, as one of the brethren told me,
consists in this—that as every day they accompany
the servants belonging to the monks to the *cantine,*
and the villages below the line of snow, for the
purpose of fetching fuel, hay, and provisions for the
use of the Hospice, they are so accustomed to the
road, that, when it is entirely lost under the deep
snows of winter, their instinct is a much surer
guide than human reason in helping to find it; and
as to the monks, whose hospitality and delightful
society I shall never forget, they are men of too much
humanity and practical good sense not to give their
first care to the revival of the body, and are far
more likely to gladden the awakening senses of a
frozen traveller with the grateful sight and smell of a
cup of hot tea or spiced wine, such as they provided
for one of our party who was exhausted with the
cold and fatigue, than a crucifix. The dogs at the
Hospice—which, I must not forget to mention, are
very liable to blindness, and are generally short-
lived—are not the *finest* specimens of the breed I

have seen; there are some scattered here and there in this and the neighbouring canton—for instance, one at the Abbey of St. Maurice, and another at the Hôtel Byron—that are larger and finer in every respect.

Before I leave this subject, I wish to give a word of advice to all English who may come to reside here, respecting dogs of all kinds, and that is, '*don't keep any*'—first, because of the madness, which is so common an occurrence that everybody talks of and dreads it; secondly, because of the obnoxious regulations respecting their muzzlement during the two hottest months in the year, which tends greatly to augment the evil it is meant to cure; and thirdly, because of the severe laws enacted against any dog that during that time shall be caught unmuzzled, or, worse still, shall bite anyone, even in defence of his master's house and property. The latter crime is punished with *instant death,* and the former with incarceration for forty-two days in the same dark den with other criminal dogs, some of whom are *sure* to go mad with grief and anger before the expiration of the time, and then your poor favourite has to be killed, for no other crime than having been thrust, and very unwillingly, into very bad company.

As it is well known—as any traveller may ascertain

by taking the trouble to inquire for himself—that the frequency of hydrophobia hereabouts is attributable to the wholesale destruction of female dogs, which no one likes to keep on account of the dirt and other annoyances they bring into a house, and as the prevention of this most awful and horrible of maladies is a grave duty, I think that the authorities ought to take some means for compelling the inhabitants to keep a more equal number of male and female dogs, or have none at all.

CHAPTER XVI.

Spring — Wild   Flowers — Fête   d'Ascension — Lessives —
Washerwomen—Anecdote.

O Spring, thou youthful beauty of the year,
Mother of flowers, bringer of warbling quires,
Of all sweet new green things and new desires,—
Thou, Spring, returnest.   *   *   *

HERE she is not the halting, shy, cool goddess of our
more northern clime; but, assured, warm, and rosy,
she comes with quick step that treads so soon on the
retreating footsteps of autumn, you can hardly say
you have had a glimpse of winter, before she decks
the trees with green, and changes the brown mossy
pastures into gardens of sweetest flowers.   As soon
as the first hepaticas open their lovely blue eyes to
the sun, the hills are all alive with peasants delving
their vineyards and pruning their vines; the songs of
innumerable birds mingle with the merry whistle of
the labourers, and the air blown to you from the west
is heavy with the perfume of violets that literally
cover the earth on hill and mountain side, in copse

and wood and valley, by dusty hedgerows and limpid streams; they are everywhere, and you wonder how all the hepaticas and primroses and cowslips and birds in a hedge, pink and white and yellow, and snowdrops and crocuses, ever find room to show their heads; but show them they do.

Here there is far more use made of the plants for medicinal purposes than with us, and amongst many others, the flowers of the sweet-scented violet are gathered in large quantities, and dried, to make an infusion that is considered an infallible remedy in low nervous fevers, from which the inhabitants suffer greatly at times, as well as for inflammatory colds, especially in children; but of the cowslip—smelling, too, like the sweet cow's breath—they make no use; and once, when I told some people about the sweet wine made from the pips, I positively could not make them believe that it was possible to manufacture anything drinkable from flowers and water.

In my winter walks I had noticed that the woods were full of a plant with a pretty leaf, green above, and under a reddish brown; and when February came, I found, to my delight, that the most splendid hepaticas were springing from every cluster of my pretty leaves. The first bunch I saw, I was almost beside myself with joy. I had been scrambling through a hill-side wood, looking at the gorgeous wood-peckers climbing the trees, and on coming to a spot where it was more open I saw a clump of flowers as blue as the heavens, and could scarcely credit my eyes when I found they were hepaticas. I carried them home, believing I had fallen on a treasure ; but before a week was over there was not a wood or field in which there were not countless millions ; and how different were the flowers to the miserable sickly-looking things that tried to smile in my borders in L——shire, after having been nursed and tended all winter through, as if they were of as much value as so many children ! I felt quite angry with myself for having taken so much care of such ungrateful little bantlings, when I saw the splendour of their relations here, who would be ashamed to call those I had reared their cousins-german. The prevailing colour was blue ; but there were plenty of white, rose, pink, and violet to be found also, and all with such lovely stamens as white as snow, looking like lace embroidery on the clear petals. With the cowslips come the nightin-gales that sing all night, and all day, for I have often distinguished their notes among those of other birds, warbling away in the large walnut trees fronting our balcony.

At the back of the house the meadow extends

some few hundred yards to the foot of the mountains,
that, facing the south, can always boast the first
flowers and leaves of spring, and the earliest and
finest vines; and it is there—among the trees growing
on the rocky uncultivated spots, where no vines can
be planted, but where the syringa and mezereon
bloom and scent the air—that the nightingales send
forth their first songs. Every night, for weeks, we
used to stand on the balcony listening to the en-
trancing melody, unable to tear ourselves away.
When the cowslips are faded, there come the lilies of
the valley, the beloved flowers that seem to be no
less prized here, where they are so common, than in
England, where they are comparatively so rare as a
wild flower. What thousands my children gathered
for garlands on May morning, taking knives to mow
them off, it being too much trouble to gather them
singly. Girls and boys, with baskets full of the same
tied in bouquets, that they offer you for five centimes
the half-dozen, besiege your doors; and though you
know your rooms are choke full, you cannot resist
the temptation of buying a lot more to deck your
window-sills, where every morning since the sun
shone warmly the old curé's pigeons come to be fed,
and remain cooing away nearly all day long. They have
become so familiar with us, that they visit us at the

breakfast-table; and yet even these innocent, pretty creatures have their enemies, for not long ago, as we were standing near the open window watching them pecking away at the crumbs we had placed on the outer sill for. them, down pounced an impudent wicked hawk, and flew away with one of the white ones before we could interfere.

The trees and plants here, as elsewhere, assume their summer dress early or late, according to the mildness or severity of the season; but not so the people, who one and all, no matter the temperature, throw off their winter garments for summer ones *le jour d'Ascension*, when the greatest fête of the year is held throughout the Vaud, and people come trooping down from the mountains to share in the amusements, as at *Mi-été* those from below ascend to enjoy the festivities at the pasturages. At seven in the morning, the whole military force of the district, dressed in full regimentals (my readers must come here to see what that is), assemble near the church, and, after going through a variety of manœuvres, very interesting from the display of individual character presented to the thoughtful spectator, parade the streets to the sound of a drum till nine, when there are various other processions of young men to the shooting-ground, the different

societies being distinguished by a different coloured
cord that rests on the right shoulder, and, passing
under the left arm, is tied with tassels of the same
hue. They carry their rifles across their chests, as
we hush off a little baby to sleep, and march so
closely upon each other's heels that they have only
room to take very short steps, and look far more
like an awkward lot of adults learning the *chassé*
in a dancing-school, than crack Swiss rifle-shots.

The last time I was at one of these fêtes, the
whole population of the village was assembled in
Monsieur Wagner's garden, facing the hotel, he
having lent it for the occasion, so that the visitors
might have a good view of the proceedings. An
orchestra had been erected in a large apple-tree,
and away they danced polkas and valses *à deux
temps*, with no other amusements, save skittles for
the elder men, and plenty of eating and drinking
for those who would pay for it, till six o'clock, when
down came the orchestra with a crash, several of
the musicians getting some scratches from the
boughs; and then, for the only time since coming
here, to their credit be it spoken, I saw a fight,
between a man, whose wife had been hurt by the
fall, and a young soldier, who was supposed to be
one of the authors of the mischief.

Any account of village life in Switzerland would be incomplete, without mention being made of the lessives, or large lye-washings, that each family has twice a year, in spring and autumn. From the infrequency of these washings, it may be supposed that the people must possess a large quantity of linen, mostly homespun, of all descriptions, and that, after lying dirty several months, it must take a more than ordinary amount of labour to make it clean again; so that the preparing for a lessive, the actual work itself, and the getting up of the linen, is in every household about the most important domestic business in each half-year. For a large one, six washerwomen are required, and they are such important and much desired personages that they must be engaged some time before wanted; you must also bespeak the fountain near which you reside, by nailing on to it a piece of paper, on which is written that, on a certain day named, Madame So-and-so requires the great stone trough into which the water runs, for her lessive, and then no one on that day dare put a finger in it without your leave.

The whole business of the wash lasts four days. On the first day the clothes are steeped in cold water only. On the second, they are all put together in an immense tub, over which is laid a strong linen sheet;

on this a great quantity of wood ashes is placed, and then boiling water is poured on to them till the linen is covered with the lye. They are then allowed to lie an hour, when the liquor is run off through a tap, more boiling water is allowed to filter through the ashes, and this process is repeated until evening. The third day the linen is taken out of the lye, and well washed with hot water and soap; and the fourth, they are removed to the fountains to be rubbed and beaten on boards, rinsed and blued. When the linen comes out of the lye, anyone unaccustomed to this mode of washing would be sure to think it was irretrievably ruined, so yellow is it; and it is not until it has been well thumped and rinsed in the fountain that it regains its colour, and becomes beautifully white.

These washerwomen are a peculiar and distinctive race. They are the greatest gossips, the loudest talkers, the biggest eaters, and sometimes drinkers, of any in the canton. They are all ugly, old, and bent, with lean hands, wizened faces, and thick legs. All wear immense hats, with a knob at the top; and their old petticoats and jackets might have been buried some hundreds of years and then dug up again. The three or four days that, twice a year, they are on a visit in your house, your servants have quite enough work in cooking a variety of dishes to suit their fastidious appetites, for they have a diet peculiar to their body; and if you don't oblige them in this respect, you are left in the lurch, and your linen must go unwashed.

After all is dried, there is ironing for several days, during which every female in the house is pressed into the service, as well as two or three laundresses; and then, when all is aired, mended, and put away, there is quiet in the house for five months and more; and I am not sure that, if we had but the same immense supply of linen, we should not find it a better plan, both as regards the bleaching of the clothes and the comfort of our households, than our everlasting, unsatisfactory, order-destroying weekly washes. All my life I shall think of those weird-looking women gabbling and bawling away at the fountains, and I am convinced that, if I could return to Switzerland two hundred years hence, the race would be unchanged, and that one of the first things my eyes rested on would be, to all appearance, the same crooked wizened hags standing in the mud round the fountains.

Before coming to reside here, I had believed the Swiss to be the most moral and sober people on the face of the earth; and as one is never alone in one's opinions, doubtless there are many of my readers who, after perusing this brief record of a long stay, will cavil at the statements I have made respecting the character of the people. To such I can only answer, that I have described them as I found them, and I am certainly not to blame if, discovering drunkenness and immorality, where I had looked for sobriety and chastity, I have given them to the world as they are: and saying this brings to my mind an anecdote not inapplicable to the subject, and with which I shall close my book.

In a Valaisan village among the mountains lives an old Catholic priest who not long ago closed his sermon in the following words:—'My dear brethren, when once I have departed from this world into Paradise, and St. Peter shall ask me, " Shepherd, what hast thou done with thy flock?" I shall bow my head and shall not reply; and when St. Peter shall ask me a second time, " Shepherd, what hast thou done with thy flock?" I shall still bow my head and shall not reply: but when for the third time he asks me, " Shepherd, what hast thou done with thy flock?" I shall reply, "St. Peter, thou hast given them to me thieves, and I have left them thieves." '

PRINTED BY SPOTTISWOODE AND CO., NEW-STREET SQUARE, LONDON